Fair Weather Ninjas

Fair Weather Ninjas

Michael Howarth

LITERARY PRESS
LAMAR UNIVERSITY

ISBN: 978-1-942956-30-3
Library of Congress Control Number: 2016947523

Manufactured in the United States of America

Lamar University Literary Press
Beaumont, Texas

For Jo-Ann Mapson
my good friend and writing sensei

Acknowledgments

As any true warrior knows, success happens when you have lots of support, which means people are fairly fond of you and are willing to put up with your antics.

Thankfully, my family members—Mom, Dad, my sister Liz, my brother-in-law Frank—are not known for putting the "fun" in dysfunctional, though they have put up with me for many years, and I want to thank them for never laughing when I rambled on about all those stories and characters that germinate in my head on a regular basis. Contrary to popular belief, I'm not always talking to myself; I'm simply brainstorming.

Matt Keating, always generous with his time, agreed to read an early draft of this novel. He offered me a list of detailed and insightful comments, many of which helped to smooth away the rougher edges of the narrative and to bring the story's conflicts and themes into a clearer focus.

I'm also grateful to Jerry Craven and Lamar University Literary Press for recognizing the humor and pathos in Tim's wacky life, and for welcoming this novel into such a great home in Beaumont, Texas.

Joey Brown—whom I often refer to as poet, carpenter, and wife—continues to stand as my voice of reason when I seem incapable of making choices. Her creativity and inventiveness, as well as her ability to shade in the finer details, never cease to amaze me and, despite what she often says, I really am listening when she talks.

Finally, a gargantuan thank you to author Jo-Ann Mapson for her wisdom, lectures, and sternness while I was her writing student at the University of Alaska in Anchorage; and for all her encouragement, time, and support once I returned to the lower forty-eight and continued to tinker and revise all those chapters that were scattered across my kitchen table. She met Tim when he was just a budding warrior and immediately saw the potential in this novel. Her edits and suggestions not only shaped this story, but offered me a master class in the art of fiction writing.

Contents

1.

Morph

I notice the smell of mothballs as soon as I enter the front doors of Marblehead High on the first day of school, a sharp, pungent smell laced with fresh paint and stale sweat, as if the school hasn't aired out all the teen angst from last year. A place of learning, the principal calls this rat-infested turdbox, a place to shape tomorrow's leaders. But in the past three years all I've really learned is that going to high school is like talking to a super hot chick. You become deluded by the glamour and ritzy showboating, entranced by the lure of parties and pals, until you finally realize she's as flimsy as a vague idea, just glued together with mood swings and trendy designer labels.

Tired and pissy, I shuffle up the stairs, sipping Evian water while everyone around me high-fives like a bunch of idiots, delirious with the beginning of a new school year. The girls giggle and blush, marinating in their makeup and sharing stacks of wrinkled love letters they've collected over the summer. They prance down the hallway like contestants in a Miss America pageant, swinging their imitation Gucci handbags and wobbling on clear platform high heels.

The guys smack each other on the back and dip snuff in the bathroom, bragging about how much ass they've each gotten over the summer. They all sport a deconstructed look, showing off clothes that look lived in and worn down, wearing their pants so low that they're constantly yanking them up by the belt loops like mumbling, inner-city gangsters. Why the hell would anyone spend good money to buy a new pair of jeans with painted spots and gaping holes and frayed cuffs? I can do that for free with a bottle of white-out and a pair of Mom's scissors.

I get to homeroom one minute late. Mr. Hussey hasn't taken attendance yet, so I sit in the back of the room and stare out the window. In front of me, three hulking seniors are discussing the upcoming football season, but I don't bother joining the conversation because I already know our team is gonna suck real bad.

Dan Browning, asshole extraordinaire, leans over his desk and says to me, "Tim, can I have your autograph? I've never met a real ninja before."

I turn in my chair so I'm facing the wall. I usually don't like being rude, but stupid people rarely notice, so it's probably not a big deal.

Undeterred, Dan bounces an eraser off of my forehead. "I heard a story once about a ninja who was eating dinner at Long John Silver's and when some infant dropped his pacifier the ninja went berserk and killed everyone in the restaurant with cyanide chopsticks. Is that true?"

I take in a deep breath, and exhale through my nose, wanting to punch him in the stomach, but also remembering the top three rules of being an elite ninja:

1. A ninja's first priority is to avoid danger and escape with his life.

2. A ninja favors deception over violence.

3. A ninja only engages in combat as a last resort.

I realize this might sound strange coming from some gangly, upper-class white kid living in Marblehead, Massachusetts, but I'm not crazy, and I'm not on drugs. Not unless you consider being addicted to awesomeness a serious problem.

And yes, being a ninja is totally frigging awesome.

I'm pretty sure I'm the only ninja in Massachusetts, probably the whole East Coast. And it's all thanks to my father. He was a soldier, and he met some ninjas in Iraq during the first Gulf War. The ninjas confided in him, told him they were setting up a base camp somewhere in the desert to help U.S. forces. They asked him for tactical advice and GPS coordinates, and eventually, after he gained their trust, they made Dad an honorary ninja. Before he died he taught me everything he knew about their inner circle.

He passed me the nunchuck, so to speak.

And ever since then, I've been following the path to enlightenment.

Freshman year, I broke a board in half with my bare hand. Sure, it was a piece of driftwood I found at Devereaux beach, but it still counts.

Sophomore year, I learned how to sneak up on people and startle them. At first I practiced at the food court in the mall, but then the security guard kicked me out because the customers were screaming and freaking out. There I'd be, lurking in the corner next to a trash can, and suddenly I'd yell, "Hiyah" and everyone would drop their egg rolls and French fries and greasy slices of pepperoni pizza.

Junior year, I purchased a set of instructional DVDs off of Amazon and learned how to maintain my balance and control my breathing. I managed to hold my breath for almost two minutes and even posted a clip on YouTube so everyone wouldn't think I was a liar. Then, to celebrate, I went on eBay and bought my top five favorite ninja weapons:

1. Nunchucks (for splitting head open like ripe melon)
2. Fighting fans (for assbeatings on hot summer days)
3. Zatoichi sword (for slicing body into sushi)
4. Chain whip (for sneak attack when enemy asleep)
5. Shuriken throwing stars (for torture and maiming only)

I've spent the past three years honing my craft and now here I am, poised for action, ready to begin my senior year of high school, which already seems anticlimactic. All the guidance counselors swear we're moving on to bigger and better things, and, looking around the school, that seems like a pretty safe bet. I guess I'm supposed to have certain expectations, like filling out college applications, landing a girlfriend, and receiving my diploma. I'm supposed to get laid in the backseat of a really cool car and punch someone in the arm when the football team scores a touchdown.

My guidance counselor told me that high school would be the best four years of my life. Right. I'm living at home, I don't own a car, and I'm not getting laid. If these are the best years of my life, then I might as well pack it in right now.

Normally I'd be super depressed to begin what will undoubtedly be another shitty year of waking up early, getting shoved into lockers, and being ignored by girls, but I'm feeling confident that great things lie in store for me. That might sound pompous and conceited, but lots of teenagers are famous for their accomplishments. If you don't believe me, then consider for a moment that Mary Shelley published *Frankenstein* when she was nineteen; Alexander the Great founded his first colony when he was sixteen; Louis Braille created his own writing system when he was fifteen; Chester Greenwood invented the earmuff when he was fifteen; and King Tut, with his club foot and cleft palate, ruled Egypt the whole time he was a defiant, pimply teenager.

If I work really hard, then I can add my name to that impressive list. I've been feeding my mind with patience and proverbs. I've been mastering self-control and learning how to meditate. And I've become absolutely fearless, mostly through a daily regimen of sit-ups, jumping-jacks, and Power Smoothies.

So trust me, I'm a ninja.

Granted, I've never met an actual living, breathing ninja, but it's number one on my bucket list. Do you want to know my top five?

1. Shake a ninja's hand (warning: if a ninja hugs you, he's about to kill you).
2. Visit Japan with a ninja as my tour guide (added bonus: a photo

of us chillin' in front of Mount Fuji).

3. Eat Ramen noodles with a ninja (oriental flavor, so he won't feel homesick).

4. Watch *Enter the Dragon* with a ninja (while eating a huge bag of Skittles because they're a ninja's favorite candy).

5. Get punched in the face by a ninja (he'll respect my tolerance for pain and hand me an ice pack).

The idea of meeting a ninja makes me feel giddy and lightheaded, like I'm five-years-old and jumping up and down on a king-size bed. Seriously, if I was walking down the street and saw Jesus Christ, Albert Einstein, and a ninja, I'd say:

"Hey, what's up?"

"Hey, what's up?"

"Holy shit, you're a real ninja!"

So I have big dreams, way too big to wrap my arms around, and because of them people kind of make fun of me all the time.

Like Dan Browning.

None of these dickheads have any frigging clue of what a ninja actually is. Their idea of a ninja comes from watching badly-dubbed Asian flicks on late-night cable. They think ninjas are agile men who run around in black pajamas and recycle their own bath water. They think ninjas run up the sides of walls and fly through the air with fists of fury, screaming "Hiyah!" as they slaughter fifty bad guys without blinking an eye.

I pick up Dan's eraser and throw it across the room. "Ninjas don't take too kindly to insults. They'll gut you, sashimi-style, and then dip your ass in wasabi. They're silent, but deadly."

He laughs. "Like a fart?"

"Actually," I say, squinting my eyes into a steely gaze, "I was thinking more like carbon monoxide."

***

Fifth period, study hall. I'm sitting in the back of the classroom, wondering who the hell's in charge of regulating the temperature in here. The humidity isn't stifling, but it's certainly uncomfortable. I can feel drops of sweat running down my back and soaking into my boxer shorts. My shirt sticks to my skin and my bangs cling to my forehead. I fan myself with a rolled up copy of my Advanced Biology syllabus and stare out the window, wanting nothing more than to be outside in the Massachusetts sun, sipping the salty air. I want to be at Lynn Heritage State Park, sitting on the cool grass and watching the girls in shorts and halter tops play Frisbee.

I'm doodling in my notebook when who should poke her head through the door but my guidance counselor, Miss Connelly. The woman is held together with wrinkles and skin cream, and her face has more lines than a Rand McNally road map. I try to slink down in my seat, but she spots me in mid-slouch, glaring at me with those giant bug eyes that might be less freakish if they came with a pair of antennae and a set of mandibles. She points to where I sit and makes a motion toward her office.

I follow her upstairs, keeping a few paces behind so as to avoid the overpowering stench of Ben-Gay that wafts from her clothes. When we finally get to her office she sits down at her desk, kicks off her shoes, and starts rubbing her feet together like she's trying to start a fire.

I sit on the edge of a crummy metal chair. "How are you, Miss Connelly?"

"Fine, Timothy." She doesn't even look at me. She just flips through a large stack of papers, licking her index finger every time she turns another page.

Two minutes later the smell hits me. It travels across the room in a thick fog of mold, dust, and flaky calluses. I don't want to gag or throw up, so I put my hand over my nose and try breathing through my mouth.

"Timothy!"

I glance up. "What?"

Miss Connelly frowns. "It's only the first day of school, Mister, and you're already checked out."

"I'm a straight-A student," I tell her.

"Yes, I know you're in the top five percent of your class, yada, yada, yada, but it's my job to make sure you're considering all your options."

"Then mission accomplished. Congratulations."

"I meant the rational ones based on common sense. Not the ones that require a black belt in stupidity." She opens her desk drawer and takes out a piece of paper and a pen. "Regardless of your animosity, you need to start acting more like a grown up and less like a cartoon. Which colleges are you considering?"

"U-Mass will be my safety school," I tell her. "As far as other schools, I was thinking about Cornell or NYU. Maybe Holy Cross."

"Top-notch schools," she says. "What's their appeal?"

"Good business programs. I need to become an entrepreneur so I can mass market my skills. Kind of like a one-man UNICEF."

"Drop the ninja routine," she says. "It was cute at first, but you've milked enough attention from this silly charade. It's time to crawl out of the playpen and grow up."

I wonder if Mary Shelley ever got teased in her writing circle. Or if Alexander the Great got ridiculed for his battle plans. Or if jokers ever tripped Louis Braille because they thought it was funny. Or if his subjects ever yelled "Gimp!" whenever King Tut rode by in his chariot. It's hard to imagine, but I guess there was a time when no one believed in any of them either.

Still, I shouldn't be surprised. Everyone around here pretty much treats me like an amusing afterthought, including my sister and mother. The two of them are worse than a nest of Chinese scorpions. Liz tells me I should learn to write secret messages in invisible ink, and that I should buy a bonsai tree for a sidekick. She says the best part of being a ninja is that I get to wear the same outfit every day.

My mother says, "If you want to be a ninja, then why aren't you learning how to kick someone in the pelvis or meditate in the lotus position? Shouldn't you be trying to reach your moment of Zen instead of watching stupid kung fu movies?"

More and more, I'm having to remember that ninjutsu is a challenge, that the trail to glory will surely be littered with expensive booby traps and multilingual assassins. My father once told me that a ninja should have a heart as kind and pure as a flower, which means I can't afford to be bullied by a nagging past. I have to master the art of self-control, and the longer I put up with my unenlightened family, and stupid school administrators, the closer I get to fulfilling my destiny.

"You want me to be like everyone else?" I ask Miss Connelly. "A bunch of losers who don't know anything, so they wind up doing nothing. A bunch of losers who sit on their asses and stare off into space, gabbing on their cell phones and watching reality TV. Who hate themselves so other people will love them."

She looks down at my file. "Last year you tried coercing the cafeteria staff into serving sushi, which violates about a dozen school health codes. Then, last spring you put an ad in the school newspaper looking for a concubine. Really," she says, laughing, "are those productive ways to enrich your life, Timothy?"

"Well, I think they are. So there."

She frowns, and the little hairs on her mustache twitch. Gross. I want to hold her down so I can tweeze them all. "It's great that you want to go to college and do something industrious with your life," she says, "but that shouldn't include jabbing someone in the eye, or lopping off their head with a Samurai sword."

"Ninjas and samurai don't hang out together. Besides, ninjutsu isn't a martial art, Miss Connelly. It's a way of life. A ninja only engages in combat as a last resort." I take a long sip of Evian. "In fact, the ninja philosophy is not to kill."

She takes off her glasses and rubs the dark circles under her eyes. "Please tell me why you're always bringing bottled water to school. There are plenty of drinking fountains, at least five on this floor alone. Plastic is bad for the environment, Timothy. Aren't ninjas supposed to be eco-friendly?"

I turn the bottle so she can see the label. "Miss Connelly, this is the most patient water you will ever drink. It spends fifteen years filtering through a huge aquifer in the mountains. Think about all the different events that happened while that itty bitty stream was just meandering its way through a bunch of rocks and minerals."

"You're kidding, right?"

"How many people do you think died?" I ask her. "How many husbands and wives divorced? How many students had a bad day at school and cried wah-wah-wah all the way home? Do you realize this water has bits of history floating around in it?"

"I'm pretty sure that bottled water is just tap water that's been purified. You might as well save yourself some money and buy a Brita filter."

I grab a Kleenex off her desk and blow my nose, really loud because I feel like being an asshole. "Sorry to be a fun wrecker, but I have to get back to study hall."

"Do you want to talk about your father?" she asks me.

I look down at the beige frieze carpet, clenching my jaw as I fight hard to swallow the growing lump in my throat. I close my eyes, hoping this heat flash will subside, but instead I see his body crumpled in a heap on the bathroom floor, his eyes open but not moving, pieces of brain stuck to the shower curtain...

"Timothy." She snaps her fingers. "Pay attention."

I throw my Kleenex toward the trashcan, but it bounces off the rim and lands on the floor. "If this is your idea of counseling, then you might want to consider a career change," I shout at her. "Because if this is how you help students, then the world's more screwed up than I thought."

She rubs the wrinkles on her face in clockwise circles, and for a second I think I see a lump in her throat, as if she's fighting down the urge to abandon the Wicked Witch routine and suddenly become caring and compassionate.

17

But Miss Connelly doesn't apologize. She just stares at me for another minute before finally saying, "You're the angriest high school student I've ever known, Timothy Dimmick." She signs a hall pass and holds it out to me. "And that also makes you the saddest."

***

After study hall I head down to the cafeteria. As I maneuver my way through a throng of tables, I almost vomit for the second time today. The food smells awful. The pizza: put a napkin on top and it's like dropping a paper towel into a toilet bowl. The hash browns: soggy as cornflakes. The vegetables: explode with pus when you stab them with your fork. The salad buffet seems like a safe choice, but the lettuce is brown and flaccid.

Cafeteria food can kill a ninja faster than a samurai sword. Just to survive, I need a daily arsenal of organic fruits and fresh vegetables, which is why I've been brown-bagging my lunch since freshman year.

My sister sits at a crowded table in the center of the cafeteria. She's a sophomore. And a complete bitch. Plus, she's the most popular girl at school, always prancing around in glittery designer clothes. I probably wouldn't hate her that much if she wasn't so smug all the time, putting on airs just because she's Mom's favorite child. It's totally unfair. If Liz comes home an hour past her curfew, nothing is said, whereas I get crucified if I leave the toilet seat up. If Liz breaks a nail, the first-aid kit is suddenly wide open on the kitchen table, but when I tripped and fell down the stairs last spring, my mother just told me to walk it off.

And don't even get me started on all the taunting and name-calling. Apparently, my sister can make fun of ninjas all she wants, but I can't poke fun at her dyslexia because it's not cool to be insensitive. I make one little joke about ten out of two people having numerical dyslexia and suddenly my mother suggests I watch *Rain Man* and prioritize my life.

My mother thinks Liz can do no wrong. She buys her whatever she wants. She takes her wherever she wants. And she pretty much does it 24/7. Every Saturday the two of them go shopping at the Marblehead Mall, traipsing through Spiegel and Brooks Brothers before venturing into Victoria's Secret for perfume and unmentionables. They invade dressing rooms and antagonize sales clerks, and by the end of the day the backseat of Mom's BMW is loaded with purple and pink bags, and piles of ornate boxes wrapped with ribbon and lace.

Even though I keep to myself, I really wouldn't mind a little nagging attention every once in a while. But Liz holds a special place in my mother's heart. Right in the middle where she can command the most attention.

Me? I'm just renting a tiny corner that Mom never bothers to check because she thinks it's condemned.

But wait, it gets worse. This past June my sister started dating Emil, a foreign exchange student from Romania. Now she acts like a worldly sophisticate, just because she knows how to say "Hello" and "Thank you" in a garbled language that sounds like someone is trying to talk with a mouth full of rotten sauerkraut. She can't even pronounce the words correctly. She just scrunches up her nose, eyes half-closed, and spits out each roughened syllable like she's trying to seduce all of Eastern Europe. She thinks it's so chic to date a guy who's half gypsy, smokes unfiltered cigarettes, has a receding hairline, and eats blood sausage like it's going out of style.

Right now, Emil is leaning into Liz's shoulder and nibbling the side of her neck, rubbing against her ear with his slicked-back Transylvanian hairdo. He's wearing white jeans, a blue T-shirt, and a tan sports coat, and his English sounds as broken as shattered glass.

Liz is waving her right hand in the air, showing off the new Zoppini bracelet that Mom bought her as a back-to-school gift. (I got a new pair of chinos, which I immediately threw in the back of my closet.) Raising her arm higher, she shows off the bracelet's three charms: an angel fish, a ladybug, and a butterfly. The animal motif is the newest rave, as all the girls are sporting necklaces with turtles, ankle bracelets with bumblebees, and linen skirts decorated with assorted jungle fauna.

Why does every high school student need a theme?

As I walk past the table, Liz shouts, "Hey, Tim. What do you think of my new present?" Smirking, she holds up her wrist, turning it from side to side so I can hear the bracelet jingle.

"I think imitation platinum looks good on you, Medusa."

"Leave," she says, "or I'll have Emil kick your ass."

"If he does, I'll have to drive a stake through his heart."

She flips me off. "I would so slap the shit out of you right now, but that would be animal abuse."

"You're just jealous," I say. "Because *I'm* destined for greatness, and *you're* destined for mediocrity."

She laughs. "Ninjas aren't even real, dumbass. They're just mythical creatures, like wood sprites or the tooth fairy."

"Finish eating your salad," I tell her, "so you can run along and play with the rest of the herd." I use my arm as a makeshift trunk, pretend I'm an elephant, and stomp over to an empty table in a corner.

I sit down, thankful to be away from the madding crowd. I've just removed my lunch from a tatty paper bag (dried apricots, edamame, and a thermos of green tea) when a dorky group of freshman bombard my table, spread their lunches across the entire area, and then have the audacity to ask if they can join me.

I curse the idiots under my breath, watching as they drop dime-size crumbs onto the floor and spill chocolate milk all over the table. They ogle all the upper-class girls, anticipating bliss and popularity, yearbooks filled with unreadable signatures, and bulky class rings whose fake stones shimmer in the bright lights of a Friday night football game. While they whisper about all the cool parties they'll never attend, I mentally will them to spontaneously combust.

One of them taps me on the shoulder. He's chewing a tuna fish sandwich, and when he speaks his breath screams, "The Sea!"

"Are you a senior?" he asks me.

"That's right," I tell him. "I'm logging in my fourth year at this shithouse."

They put down their sandwiches and stare at me. One of them says, "Is it true that you can smoke cigarettes in certain classrooms?"

I laugh, almost choking on a piece of edamame. Technically, these kids aren't hopeless, but I'm pretty sure that stupid is leading them on a high-speed chase.

"Let me offer you guys some advice," I say. "Freshman year, memorize every player's name on the male and female sports teams, even cross-country. Then, make sure you know all the positions they play. The athletes will think you're king shit. They really want to believe that you actually care about them breaking the school record for most touchdowns, or setting a state record for the fastest mile run.

"Sophomore year, go to Sam's Club and buy a large supply of Kleenex. Learn how to masturbate. Build up some endurance so you can actually last longer than a minute when some girl decides to rock your world while she's piss drunk at some really lame party."

The freshmen look at each other and smile, practically drooling at the opportunity to brag about their first lay in an Internet chat room.

"And watch lots of porn," I tell them. "I recommend *Night of the Giving Head*, *The Sperminator*, or *Romancing the Bone*. It'll increase your stock if you know some sexy thrusting techniques ahead of time. And make sure you pick some awesome mood music, too. You can't go wrong with Marvin Gaye or Barry White, maybe even some Teddy Pendergrass. My suggestion would be blues or jazz. It has an erotic charge that sparks the ladies into submission."

I sound damn convincing, especially when you consider that I've never even had a girlfriend. All my love affairs involve Jergens hand lotion and a box of tissues. For me, a relationship ends when I wad up the Kleenex and make a three-pointer into the trashcan.

"Now we come to junior year," I say, "and this is typically the year of the license. As soon as you pass your driver's test, and I'm talking that very same night, you need to borrow your parents' car and cruise the mall. Speed through the parking lot while old people flip you off, but make sure you slow down when you pass a group of girls so they'll know it's you inside. And brake hard. You want your tires to squeal on the pavement. If you do it right, you should smell burnt rubber and feel yourself being thrown into the steering column.

"And have music blasting from the stereo. Something popular and catchy, but lacking artistic value. Something so loud it dry-humps your eardrums and you can't understand the lyrics. Any rap song will usually suffice."

I drink the rest of my green tea. "I can't talk about senior year because it just started, but the biggest challenge will be college applications. Load them up with all sorts of clubs and activities, even if you don't actually belong to any of them. And don't let your guidance counselor push you around. Chances are she's old and bitter, and smells like a nursing home."

I stand up and grab my books. "I have to go now, gentlemen. But I wish you the best of luck." I offer them a naval salute and walk away from the table. I can feel their starry eyes burning into my back. I can hear their pens scribbling furiously on white-lined paper. And as I toss my garbage into the trashcan, as I head toward the double doors at the far end of the cafeteria, I can hear a loud metallic screech as they all stand up and slide their chairs closer together, eager to anticipate the future in hushed and excited whispers.

***

The last class of the day is gym, but I'm in no mood for physical activity. I'm tired and I have a splitting headache from listening to everyone rant on and on about their endless summer: beach trips to the Vineyard, clubbing in Boston, and shopping sprees to Kittery. Every conversation is weighed down with insecurities. If John got laid five times, then Matt got laid six. If John bought a used car, then Matt bought a new one with tinted windows. If Jane bought three pairs of shoes, then Susie bought four. If Susie's are made of leather, then Jane's are made of cashmere. On and on they'll bicker until every possible animal has been slaughtered for the comfort of their feet.

When I walk into the gym, the students are already sitting in a circle on the floor. Mr. Holcomb walks the perimeter with his mustard-yellow clipboard, taking attendance. "Now listen up, you animals! Today we'll be playing a game called Morph. It's a team-building exercise. Everyone starts out as an egg, so you can either kneel or squat. The eggs have to move around on the floor and crawl over to another egg. When you find a partner, you'll play rock, paper, scissors. If you win, you become a chicken, but if you lose, you stay an egg. After a chicken, you become a dinosaur, then a ninja, then a superhero."

Ninja! I lean forward, my interest suddenly piqued by this creative fusion of ninjutsu and calisthenics.

"If you lose," Mr. Holcomb says, "then you regress to the previous level. You'll never stay what you are. Each time you meet a partner, you'll either move up or down. And you'll always battle someone who's at the same level. Understand? The game ends when there's only one egg left, or when someone becomes a superhero."

I jump up. "Hell, yeah! Let's do this."

The entire class stares at me, as if I'm some freaky sideshow attraction at the local carnival. What do they know? They're all eggs.

Mr. Holcomb blows his whistle. "The chickens need to strut around, so stretch your head into the air and make some clucking noises. Dinosaurs need to stomp on the floor and lumber around like they're thirsty for blood. And ninjas," he glances at me with a worried look, "need to show some karate moves. I don't mind some fancy leg work, but I don't want any physical contact.

"Superheroes fly around," he continues, "so remember to make that 'whoosh' sound when you fly. And before you play rock, paper, scissors, you need to introduce yourself and tell your partner the highlight of your summer. Is everyone ready?" He blows his whistle again and walks over to the Exit door. Then he props it open, lights up a cigarette, and watches while we hop around like a bunch of fools.

I crawl around on the floor, stalking my first victim. No one wants me for a partner, so I choose an easy target: Crystal Bowen, the shyest girl in school. Rumor has it she once called her therapist in the middle of a job interview because she didn't know how to answer a question. In the past three years I've heard her say only nine words: "Please don't talk to me. I don't like people." Now she's off in the corner of the gym, facing the wall like a toddler in time-out. She isn't moving, though. She's just squatting on the floor, swaying back and forth. She's a terrible egg.

I crawl over to her. "What's shakin', bacon?"

She covers her face with her hands. "Go away, Tim. Large crowds make me sick."

"Maybe you should move to Greenland."

She bends her head even lower, brushing waves of blonde hair over her face until it looks like she's hiding behind a curtain.

"What did you do this summer?" I ask her.

"I stayed home and wrote poetry. Go away."

"Does it rhyme?"

"No, it's free verse. Go away."

"Have you published any?"

"I'm afraid to send them out. I can't handle rejection." She peeks out from behind her curtain of hair. "You can be the chicken."

I jump up and begin flapping my arms, cluck-clucking as I rear back with a vengeance, and then I bring my head forward with a loud shriek. I take long strides and spin around in circles. The other students try looking away, which is difficult because I keep running over to squawk in their faces. Clucking and flapping, I keep my eyes fixed on the newly-waxed floor, staring at my reflection as if I'm searching the ground for extra feed.

The first chicken I meet is Tina Cherino, captain of the cheerleading team. For a cheerleader, she has no spirit. Her head isn't moving, and both arms flap limply at her side.

"How was your summer?" I ask her.

"I sat by my pool and read *Vogue*. Then I went to cheerleader camp. Happy, loser?" She sticks out her hand. I throw out rock; she throws out scissors.

"This game is a lot like cheerleading," I tell her. "Except no one's staring at your ass, and you probably won't get laid behind the bleachers."

"You're a fucking joke," she hisses. "Don't be surprised if at the end of the year you're voted most likely to suck."

"It's better than being voted most likely to have three children and enormous calves by the time you're twenty-one."

She leaps forward to gouge my face with her fake nails, but I back away and deliver a brilliant T-Rex roar.

Feeling bold, I stomp across the floor in search of my next prey, but the only other person who's acting remotely like a dinosaur is Nathan Tinsleberry, who brings new meaning to the word "Gothic." Black pants.

23

Black shirt. Black beret. Black earrings. Black shoes. Black socks. Even his nails are painted black. He looks like a French serial killer.

He's trying to raise his chubby legs in the air, but his feet keep sliding every which way on the newly-waxed floor. He's panting and wheezing, his face sweaty and red, and for a second I wonder if I should call a doctor. "Are you supposed to be a dinosaur?" I ask him. "Or are you having some sort of seizure?"

"I'm a Spinosaurus," he says. "They're faster and stronger than a T-Rex."

Nathan throws out paper. I throw out rock. Damn.

He laughs. "Have fun being a chicken again, dimwit."

"Wait! What did you do this summer?"

"I got a girlfriend. And I had wild sex all summer long. Because that's what real men do."

"Is she a succubus?" I ask him. "When you sacrifice small animals, does she get to hold the knife?"

"Why don't you strut home and channel your father's ghost." He turns away from me and swings his hands through the air like he's batting away a hornet. Then he tries executing a few quick jabs, but instead of being threatening he just looks like he's drunk. He's a disgrace to the name of ninja.

I trudge across the gym, humiliated. I feel like I'm headed for the chopping block. I cluck around in my own private circle, trying to control my breathing. I need to concentrate on becoming a ninja, so I flap over to Craig Armstrong, two hundred pounds of raw muscle and star blocker for the varsity football team.

"How was your summer?" I ask him.

"I visited my grandparents in Pittsburgh. They're practically deaf, so I spent the entire month of June screaming. Then my psycho girlfriend broke up with me, and if that isn't a big enough shit sandwich to swallow, she also gave me a little present before she dumped me. My dick looked like it ate a chili cheese dog and then threw up."

He throws out paper, I throw out scissors.

"I got some lemon juice in my eye once, and it burned really bad," I tell him. "So I definitely know how you feel."

He glances past me, watching the rest of our classmates flop around on the floor like dead fish. "Scram, Dimmick. It's the first day of school, I'm sweating my balls off, and I'm rolling around on the floor as a fucking egg. And I don't even like eggs."

I run away as fast as my little dinosaur legs can carry me.

For the next ten minutes I move back and forth between a chicken and a dinosaur. I'm just about to pounce on my next target when Mr. Holcomb blows his whistle and shouts, "Alright, eggheads. Everyone take a seat. Game over."

"What!" I shout. "I haven't been a ninja yet."

"Life's full of disappointments, Dimmick."

The class forms a circle, and I sit down, fuming.

Mr. Holcomb pulls some note cards out of his pocket and begins to lecture us on sportsmanship and honor, about the importance of team players. I sit Indian-style, my head in my hands, watching him finger his red Olympia whistle. Nobody pays him any attention. The girls play with their split ends and pick lint off their clothes. The boys scratch their mosquito bites and pick at volcano-size zits. They wipe the pus on their jeans and smile at the girls, the tater tots from lunch still mashed between their teeth.

Finally, just when I think my head will explode, Mr. Holcomb says, "So that's my spiel, ladies and germs. And don't you forget it." He looks at his watch, and then turns to me. "We still have a few minutes left, Dimmick. You want to tackle another round of Morph?"

Only moments before, I thought my shot at glory had vanished, and it had left me feeling uncomfortable, like when you tear open a fortune cookie and there's no fortune inside. Eager for a second chance to prove myself, I'm about to jump up when I glance over at my classmates, their eyes half closed, paralyzed by boredom, dejection, and indifference. They sit on the floor in puddles of sweat like eggs sizzling in a frying pan.

Dad taught me that a true ninja demonstrates patience and self-discipline, and if I'm meant to be a ferocious warrior, if I'm supposed to veer away from the tangle of high school underbrush and announce myself as a force to be reckoned with, then perhaps I should hang tight and wait for the stars to align, anticipating that transcendental moment when fate knocks on my door like an old friend.

Because if I'm not patient, then I might not hear that knock.

Mr. Holcomb fingers his whistle. "Well, Dimmick? Shall we play another round?"

I look over at him, and as I do, my eyes fall on a thin shaft of light streaming in from the exit door that's still propped open. A yellow sliver, it lies on the gym floor, wavering slightly in the Massachusetts heat. I sit transfixed, watching the light twist and bend like a tormented ghost. Its golden hue is seductive, luring me outside into a world I desperately want to conquer. A world I hope to change and control. A world that will someday respect me for who I am, instead of putting me down for what I'm not.

I stand up and step outside the circle, shaking my head with a definite firmness. "No, thanks, coach. I'm done playing."

2.
Fetus Dreams

When I die I hope it's during a shift at Blockbuster Video; the difference between life and death will be so slight that I won't even notice it. For the past year I've been a corporate slave to new releases. I block videos, vacuum carpets, and deal with angry customers who scream at me because *they've* racked up twenty dollar's worth of late fees. I'm required to wear khaki pants and white shoes, no doubt to accentuate the navy blue golf shirt I'm forced to wear like the scarlet letter. Printed across my chest, in urine-colored cloth, are the words "Blockbuster Video." My manager tells me it's professional attire. I tell him its second cousin to a prison uniform. I had to pay for the shirt, by the way.

It's a Saturday night and Wynn and I are the only two working in the store. He's a twenty-one-year-old high school dropout who believes education is overrated. He's tall and round-faced, and his goatee looks like someone glued a clump of steel wool to his chin. Originally from Culpepper, Virginia, his family moved to Gloucester a few years back when his father decided to pursue his dream of becoming a commercial fisherman. Wynn is also my personal chauffeur. He drives me to work because Mom won't let me use her BMW.

We've only been working for fifteen minutes when he turns to me and says, "Sometimes I feel like everyone quit drinking except me. You ever feel that way, Tim?"

"Not really," I tell him. "But sometimes I feel more enlightened than everyone else. The ninjas call it sakki, the ability to detect danger, kind of like a sixth sense."

"Maybe I'm in a funk." He says this in a thick southern accent, a drawl that drips from his mouth. "Right now I could use a nap, a blowjob, and a bottle of Mountain Dew. Not necessarily in that order."

Like me, Wynn has big dreams. He wants to move out to Hollywood, California and become a famous filmmaker. He wants to sit in a green director's chair with his name etched in yellow silk across the back, shouting orders through a bullhorn and taking an hour-long lunch break with A-list actresses in his double-wide trailer. He's writing a screenplay

27

that he claims will revolutionize the motion picture industry. It's titled *Fetus Dreams*, but he refuses to divulge any plot points because he's superstitious.

He stares off into the comedy section, his shaved head shining in the overhead glare. "We need to find you a sweetie, Tim. Someone you can spark with."

"I've been with women before."

"Internet don't count, dude. You should probably infiltrate some coffee shops. The gym works alright, and parties are good, too, but not clubs. You need someplace where you can dazzle the honeys, and you don't want any of that Eurotrash influence to fuck things up for you."

He talks like one of those toothless fishermen who cast their nets into Gloucester Bay, but in spite of all his cussing and spitting Wynn is actually a certified member of MENSA. His vocabulary and intellect spar with each other on a daily basis, yet he scored at or above the ninety-eighth percentile after he decided to take the test as a joke.

"If you want to hook a marlin," he says, "then you need to drop a chum line and get your hands dirty. You can't sit on your ass and catch minnows in the tide pool." He puts his hand on my shoulder. "Remember, if you're not getting rejected by at least seventy percent of the girls you ask out, you're not setting your standards high enough."

Even though I sometimes get seasick, I understand his point, although I prefer to troll the South China Sea. Because I know, as sure as a nunchuck can shatter a man's skull, that someday I will merge my soul with an attractive Asian woman who loves sashimi and abhors the Samurai. We'll get married in early April at the base of Mount Fuji, and after the ceremony we'll make love on a kake futon. We'll eat Peking duck and sip hot sake until the sun drops behind the surrounding temples. Then, in the flickering light of countless Japanese lanterns, I'll pull her close and whisper, "Aishite imasu." I love you.

It's about this time that the Tae-Bo girl walks into the store. As usual, she must have come from the gym because she's wearing a pair of hot pink sweat pants, and a lime green T-shirt that sticks to her body like a mouse on a glue board. Her brunette hair is still wet from the shower, pulled into a bun with a brown tortoise-shell clip. She smiles at me as she walks past the counter. I blush and look down at my shoes.

I don't even know her name, but almost every Saturday night she comes into the store and rents a Tae-Bo video. It's the high point of my week. She's not even Asian, but any woman who pays inflated prices for fifty-minute's worth of grainy calisthenics is a gold medal winner in my book.

I leave Wynn behind the counter and head out onto the floor. The Tae-Bo girl walks over to the exercise section and grabs a DVD off the bottom shelf. I linger in Drama, peeking around the side of the rack so I can watch her bend down. I'm enjoying the outline of her thong, and trying to get up the nerve to walk over and talk to her, when a girl my age suddenly steps right in front of me and says, "Excuse me, do you have *The Big Lebowski*?"

"Um...I don't know." I look over her shoulder. "Is that the bowling movie with Jeff Bridges?"

"You've never seen *The Big Lebowski*?"

"Sorry, no." I put my hand on her shoulder and gently push her to the side. I'm not trying to be rude, but she's blocking my view.

"Are you kidding me? It's absolutely hilarious. It's one of my favorite movies. I've seen it at least twenty times."

"That's fantastic." I couldn't care less about her taste in movies, but I don't want to seem completely boorish and disinterested. The last thing I need is for Brian, our manager, to drag me into his office and lecture me for an hour on my crappy customer service skills.

"I have a theory," she says, "that every man secretly wants to be the Dude. Probably because every guy wants a really cool nickname?"

Though I'm barely listening, I do realize that a nickname would make me more enticing to the opposite sex. Maybe the Tae-Bo girl would find me completely irresistible if I introduced myself as "Mr. Iron Fist" or "Karate Chop Dimmick."

"It's so popular it even has a yearly festival devoted to it," she tells me. "In Chicago, I think. Actually, there might be one in Kentucky, too."

I crane my neck to watch the Tae-Bo girl disappear down another aisle. "I'll have to rent it sometime."

Pushing past her, I return to the front of the store where Wynn is building a huge rubber ball out of elastic bands. I lean my elbows on the counter and watch the Tae-Bo girl pop back into view. She wears red flip flops, which cluck along the carpet as she walks. My eyes are drawn to her feet as they shuffle down the aisle. I notice her nails are painted red, and I feel a sudden craving to run over, drop to my knees, and feel her arches in the palm of my hand. I want to caress the underside of each foot, embracing her moans as my fingers trace Chinese letters down that softest part of her body.

Wynn slaps me on the back. "What are you dreaming about, Casanova?"

"The Tae-Bo girl. I'd love to give her a sensual foot massage."

"Don't they bind women's feet in Asia?"

"They used to," I tell him, "but they stopped in the early nineteen hundreds."

A line forms at the checkout counter. I log onto the computer and start scanning videos.

Wynn lingers beside me. "It doesn't seem natural, though. A foot isn't a piece of silly putty. You can't mold it and shape it any way you want."

I'm busy talking to customers and scanning their membership cards, but in between the cash transactions and computer checks, I educate my southern friend on the art of foot binding.

"Typically, they start between the ages of four and six," I say. "First, the girl's feet are soaked in warm water, sometimes animal blood, sometimes herbs. This causes any dead flesh to fall off. They want the foot as soft as possible before they mummify it. Then her toe nails are cut as short as possible so they don't grow into the foot. Then she receives a foot massage to get the blood flowing. And then, check this out, the four smallest toes on each foot are broken."

I feel a collective shudder ripple through the line at my register. I hear someone mutter, "Disgusting!" Another whispers, "What movie is he talking about?"

"Then the mother soaks silk or cotton bandages in the same liquid that the girl's feet were soaked in. Then the bandages are wrapped around the smallest toes and pulled as tight as possible to the heel. And then, about every two days, the mother removes the binding and rebinds the girl's feet."

A customer gives me a twenty-dollar bill. I return his change and hand him three DVDs.

"Anyway, this process goes on for about two years," I say. "At which point the girl's feet are maybe three to four inches long."

Wynn steps back and looks at the line of horrified customers. He points at me with a dramatic gesture. "Timothy Dimmick, ladies and gentlemen. He'll be here 'til Thursday." Then he turns to the other cash register and yells, "I can help somebody over here."

Everybody in my line gravitates five feet to the right, and the only person left standing in front of me is the Tae-Bo girl. She walks up to the counter and says. "Do you have *Billy Blanks Tae-Bo Believer's Workout*?"

She's never spoken to me before, and I practically catapult toward the ceiling, balancing on my tip-toes as the butterflies in my stomach soar upwards. I swallow a mouthful of saliva and stammer, "Uh, I'm not really sure. Let me check." I type in the title and press enter. Looking up, I notice a strand of hair has fallen across her cheek. I want to reach out and sweep it behind her ear. Instead, I grip the underside of the counter and hope she won't notice my erection.

The computer finishes its lap around the cyber track and delivers a "Not Found" response. "Sorry, but it looks like we don't carry it. We do have *Tae-Bo II- Get Ripped*."

"Okay, thanks," she says.

I can see her breasts resting quietly inside a low-cut Mardi Gras T-shirt. They look so soft and white, like two scoops of vanilla ice cream. My erection throbs, so I reach below the counter and dig around in my pants, trying to secure some breathing room. I try to think of something cool and esoteric to say like, "What I love about Tae-Bo is that it's not just a self-defense course. It's a nice combination of boxing, Tae Kwon Do, and aerobics. It exercises your body from the inside out, and it gives you confidence."

Instead, I knock over a coffee cup full of pens, and when I bend down to pick them up I smack my head on the edge of the counter.

"Ouch," she says. "Are you okay?"

I stand up, massaging the large dent in my forehead. "I'm fine. I have a high tolerance for pain."

She laughs. "Well, thanks for your help," She leans forward to read my name tag. "Tim." Then she tucks the lonely strand behind her ear and moseys back to the exercise section.

I've never been smooth with women. I get flustered in their presence, and I spend way too much time choosing the perfect words. I want to be the guy that girls wave to in the high school parking lot at the end of the day. I want a girl to call me late at night because she wants my voice to tuck her into bed.

My father once told me that relationships are like 7-10 splits. "You feel like you're being asked to do the impossible," he said, "and somehow you have to bring it all together. But if you concentrate really hard, if you're slow and steady and don't wind up in the gutter, then you might just come out a winner. Remember, Tim, you are the only person in this family who can carry the ancestral torch. You are the Semen Prince of the Dimmick dynasty."

I thought he meant seaman, as in sailor.

So I've been trying hard to find that special woman, and I really feel like I have a connection with the Tae-Bo girl. Call it spiritual, call it hormonal, but we're definitely sharing charged particles in this breezy summer air. The first time she walked into the store, on a snowy day in November, I felt that electrifying jolt my father once spoke of. I actually had to step outside for some fresh air. Later, she bent down to tie her shoe in the foreign section. It was a sign.

Now she's in the store again, and those same heat flashes are igniting my skin in a flash fire of goose bumps. I consider following her into the exercise section, but there are a dozen customers in the store, and I don't want to start a romantic conversation only to have to run back to the register. Besides, I still have a massive erection.

Wynn comes up behind me. "Talk to her, man. She's primed for you."

I grab the pens off the floor and set the coffee cup back on the counter. "Don't rush me. I need to let the moment simmer. Besides, she's in here constantly. I'll just catch her on the rebound."

Wynn laughs. "First you have to catch her name. Besides, what if there isn't a next time? How do you know there isn't an asteroid the size of Alaska hurtling through space right now to wipe out mankind?" He rolls up his shirt sleeve. "See this tattoo? This is the only incentive you need, my man."

I've seen his tattoo a million times since he had it done in May. It's a tattoo of the world, the size of a mandarin orange, and for him it symbolizes the frailty of life, the understanding that nothing is definite. It must be a MENSA thing. The tattoo is on his bicep, and whenever Wynn is bored, he'll walk up to people, flex like Popeye, and say, "Welcome to my world, folks."

I first noticed my father's tattoo while visiting my grandparents one summer on Cape Cod. We were building a sand castle at Old Silver Beach. As he knelt down, scooping out sand for the moat, I noticed it at the base of his neck, a sequence of symbols that hung like half a wreath. I touched it with my hand and asked him what it meant.

"They're Chinese words," he said. "Instead of letters they use characters." He smiled as I ran my hand over the strange designs. "It's an old proverb. It says, 'dream different dreams on the same bed.'"

I must have looked confused because he sat me on his lap and said, "We all have our own desires and fears, our own separate fantasies. You can never truly know someone." He stared off toward the ocean, his voice trailing away with the wind. "Each family has its own kind of hell."

"Wynn," I say. "If you're so convinced that the world will end tomorrow, then why are you working at Blockbuster Video? Is this how you want your life to end? Putting movies back on a shelf?"

"Listen, ass jockey. I never said the world would end tomorrow. I just said you have to pull some carpe diem shit, and not sit around with your thumb up your ass. Besides, I need money, and I don't play lotto, so I'm working here until my screenplay is finished."

Just then Brian comes out of his office. He walks over to the counter and stares at the two of us. "Tim, I need you to block all the new releases starting with the letter 'S'. That whole right wall is looking pretty shabby."

Blocking videos is the most boring job in the entire world. It's worse than shucking corn. All you do is make sure the videos are evenly spaced on the shelf with the cover box positioned directly in front of the rental case. It's supposed to make the environment look professional.

But I don't mind blocking videos tonight. Mostly because the Tae-Bo girl is one row over from me, perusing the exercise section. I tell myself I'm going to walk over and talk to her. I promise myself that when I reach the letter "U" I'll take a break and initiate conversation. But then "U" becomes "V" and "V" becomes "W" and before I know it I've finished blocking the whole right wall.

I stand there in the middle of the aisle, my palms sweaty and my heart pounding like fists of fury. I cross my fingers and whisper, "You're a ninja. You're a ninja. You're the Bruce Lee of New England."

A few minutes later, I walk over to the Tae-Bo girl. She's bent over again, examining the bottom shelf. She's wearing a red thong, and the thought of peeling it off her tight body raises my erection to another standing ovation.

"Do you need any assistance?" I ask her.

"I'm just browsing," she says. "But I'll probably just end up getting the one you suggested." She holds up a copy of *Tae-Bo II- Get Ripped*. "Thanks for the recommendation."

She turns to walk away, and I lurch forward. I can't let her walk right out the door and desert me for another week. I can't handle seven more nights with just my right hand and a bottle of Astroglide. Social activity? Yes. Spiritual enlightenment? No. I'm a ninja. I deserve more.

"Hey," I shout, "if you're interested in watching any Asian films, just let me know. I'm kind of a connoisseur on the subject. In fact, I'd recommend anything with Sho Kosugi in it. He was in all the popular ninja movies during the 1980s. *Enter the Ninja. Revenge of the Ninja. Ninja 3: Domination. Pray for Death.* And *Aloha Summer*, which is a great flick if you like Hawaii."

"Okay, thanks for the tip." She turns around, tucks the DVD under her arm, and walks over to the comedy section.

I hurry back to the counter where Wynn is playing Yahtzee on his iPhone. "So?" he asks. "How did you make out with the Tae-Bo girl?"

"Same as always."

"That bad, huh?"

"I'm a ninja," I tell him. "I'm supposed to be smooth with women. Look at me out there. I'm the anti-pimp."

"Tim, you're trying too hard. Maybe this whole ninja thing just isn't for you. Have you ever thought about being a pirate? You might actually look good with an eye-patch."

As good a friend as he is, Wynn will never understand the void that ninjutsu fills in my life. "Don't be so cavalier," I tell him. "I don't make fun of your obsession."

He starts bouncing the rubber band ball against the computer screen.

"Come on," I say, "tell me what your movie is about. I swear I won't put it on the Internet. Please."

He chews on his upper lip for a few seconds. "All right, hoss. But this shit stays between you and me. I don't want any greedy little bitches trying to milk a gold mine from my kick-ass idea. Got it?"

I make the sign of the cross.

He glances around the store to make sure no one is listening. "Okay, it's about this woman, her name's Brandy, and she starts having these really fucked up dreams. We're talking Excedrin migraine dreams with the sweaty sheets and the 'holy shit I can't breathe' feeling. After seeing all these doctors, she goes to a psychic and realizes that she's sharing the same dreams as the fetus of the twin sister she never knew she had. See, Brandy lives in Boston, and her twin sister, Sandy, lives in Los Angeles. The fetus dreams are leading her on a cross-country journey to California."

"Damn," I say. "That sounds pretty sweet."

"I know, right. That shit took me months to outline. But, wait, it gets better. Because on her way to Los Angeles, Brandy learns she has healing powers. The closer she gets to L.A., the stronger her powers become. I've got this scene where a little boy chokes to death on a piece of ham in a diner and Brandy brings him back to life by holding him in her arms, you know she's got her eyes closed and she's chanting, and she presses her hand against his heart while all the waitresses gather around. Then she sucks the ham out through the kid's nostrils. It'll be in slow motion, though, to accentuate the suspense."

34

"So she's like that guy in *The Green Mile*?"

"Sort of. Except she's a woman. And she's not black. And she's never been to prison. Anyway, it turns out Brandy is a disciple of God and Sandy is a disciple of Satan. See how I'm playing with the idea of duality? The fetus is the antichrist, and it's leading her to L.A. so it can kill her. Can you believe that? It's all a trap, see. The fetus wants to take over the world and establish its rule over mankind."

"That's exactly the kind of movie that Hollywood would kill for," I tell him. "Just throw in a love story and you're set."

Wynn smiles. "You're reading my mind, bro, because on her way to L.A., somewhere in Kansas or Nebraska, Brandy shacks up with this ex-priest, Michael, who's now an alcoholic traveling salesman selling ceramic pigs. There are a few steamy sex scenes, shades of *Basic Instinct*, and eventually she rekindles his faith and gets him to quit drinking. Together they travel to L.A. where they have to fight for their lives against the forces of evil, basically Sandy and the fetus. I've got this awesome scene where Sandy's water breaks in a supermarket and the fetus drops from between her legs and kills everyone in the frozen foods section. The climactic battle takes place at a huge abortion rally. Lots of explosions and fake blood. It's really cool."

I'm totally stunned. "So, it's basically *Road Trip* meets *Rosemary's Baby*, right?"

"Sort of. It's scary, but it's also funny. It's an apocalyptic comedy thriller with a heart."

A voice behind me says, "Excuse me? Is this line open?"

I turn around and there stands the Tae-Bo girl, her head cocked to one side, strands of wet hair still clinging to her face. She places her DVD on the counter and hands me her membership card for the very first time. I freeze. Usually, whenever she approaches the checkout counter, I run onto the floor so I can block new releases or pick lint off the carpet.

I look at her card: Kimberly Reed. A voice speaks in my head. *Talk to her. Don't be such a dumbass.*

"So...I...uh...um."

The voice speaks again. *Ask her to dinner. See if she likes Italian.*

I scan the movie and hand back her card. She pays for the rental. I try to say something romantic, but my tongue is a lump of clay. I finally will it to move, and all I can stammer is, "This is due back Thursday. Have a great night." I want to call her by name, but it doesn't feel right. She still hasn't properly introduced herself.

She takes the DVD from my outstretched hand. Our fingers brush.

35

Another erection. When I blink, she's gone.

Wynn comes up behind me. "Catch her before she leaves, Tim!"

Without even thinking, I hurry through the doors and step outside. The night is hot. I can still feel the day's heat radiating off the pavement. The Tae-Bo girl pulls her keys out of her purse. She unlocks the door and gets into her Corolla. I watch her toss the DVD onto the passenger seat and fix her hair in the rearview mirror. She starts the ignition and turns on the radio. Bob Marley's voice seeps into the night, and his rasta beats remind me of an old reggae song my father used to play in the car during those Sunday family drives that no one seems to take anymore.

I step off the curb, wanting to profess centuries of undying love. I want to fit whatever image she desires. I want so much for her to want me. But who am I kidding? I don't have the nerve.

She pulls out of the parking lot and drives out of my life for another week.

I turn over my hands and study my palms. The lines are thin and shallow. Some true warrior, I think, and then I clench my fists and sigh. I gaze up into the night sky, and I imagine Sandy and Brandy locked in a game of cosmic bowling, the planets lined up like ninepins, the stars roaring through the galaxies down an endless lane of constellations. The full moon hangs low in the sky like a fat, heavy blister, and I wonder if right at this moment an asteroid is barreling its way toward Earth, leaving in its wake light years of death and destruction.

3.
The Mean Man

Last night I had another nightmare. The same one I've been having since Dad died nine years ago. It was about the Mean Man, that tall, dark shadow that stalks suburban neighborhoods to collect misbehaving kids. Whenever I was snotty or threw a tantrum, my mother would pick up the phone and threaten to call him, announcing that she'd seen his rusted brown van creeping down the street, complete with tinted windows and a silver skull for a hood ornament. "He steals them," she told me once after I punched my sister in the nose. "In the middle of the night. Because they don't listen to their parents. They refuse to follow the rules. So they live with the Mean Man for the rest of their lives, all alone in a rundown house, in the middle of the deepest woods, and they never see their families again."

I always assumed the Mean Man got hundreds of calls a day. Maybe he had a 1-800 number. I pictured him in his dark, shabby house, answering a rusty telephone that lay on the floor, plugged into a blood-spattered wall and resting in an inch of dust. He would have a notebook caked with spider webs, a chunk of granite for a makeshift pencil, and in my mind I saw him etching children's addresses onto mildewed paper.

I know everyone has childhood fears, like the boogeyman hiding in the closet or the slimy monster that lives in the basement, but for years the Mean Man has been breathing down the back of my neck, creeping through my life with slow, deliberate footsteps. I see him hiding behind every door and lurking at the bottom of the stairs, moving through bedrooms and hallways as if searching for something important that he dropped along the way.

In my nightmare I see him tiptoeing across the carpet at the top of the stairs, inching his way toward the bathroom. The door is half open, and a thin shaft of light trickles into the hallway. I hear my father washing his hands in the sink. I run toward Dad as fast as I can, but every step is like sprinting through wet cement. I try to shout a warning, but when I open my mouth I can't speak. The Mean Man turns to me and smiles. He seems to float above the floor. Greasy hair falls across his forehead in thin strips, shining like razor blades. He puts a blackened finger to his cracked lips. "Shhh," he says. "You're not in trouble, son. It's your father who's been bad." I watch the Mean Man shut the bathroom door. I hear him laugh when he bolts the lock. Then I'm bathed in darkness, all silent save for the lone gun shot.

I woke up this morning feeling sick to my stomach, like that time in first grade when I ate the scabs on my knees. I've spent all day holed up in my bedroom eating Top Ramen, drinking green tea, and watching a Chuck Norris marathon on TNT. My laptop sits beside me, and during commercials I've been searching online dating sites for Asian women, not the skanky mannish ones with too much makeup, but the exotic, cream-colored beauties with straight black hair and tea-brown nipples.

I'm scoping out some Japanese sex bombs, wondering if they really prefer men with hairy chests, and Chuck Norris is just about to kill the Latino mob boss, when Liz barges into my room.

"Hey, dipshit. That's the third time this week you've left the toilet seat up."

I flip her off. "Why don't you run outside and play hide-and-go-fuck-yourself."

She leans against the doorframe. "Boy, it's no wonder women scatter like leaves when they see you."

"I have high standards, that's all."

She shakes her head. "People with high standards are compensating for low self-esteem."

"Quit making fun of me, Liz!"

"I'm not making fun of you. I'm profiling." She glances over at my computer and starts laughing. "Do you really think one of these jail-bait, sushi-eating sluts would hop on a boat and come to America for a dumbass like you? No one is that hopeless."

"Worry about yourself," I tell her.

She shrugs. "Fine, but Mom is going to be super pissed when she finds out you've been wooing the entire Shang Dynasty."

"Mom doesn't have any idea what I'm doing. She's too busy filling the house with random shit from Saks and Neiman-Marcus."

"Mom deals with things in her own way, Tim. You have Asia and she has interior decorating."

"Whatever," I say, "she'd probably do a friggin' back flip if I moved to another country and got married."

"Speaking of which, do you know what ninjas use for birth control?"

I ignore her.

"Their personalities," she says, laughing.

I want to tell Liz that she's really ugly and has bad breath, but we both know it's just not true. With dirty-blonde hair, high cheekbones, and bee-stung lips that accentuate her China doll complexion, my sister is easily the most attractive member of the family.

So I say, "Did you hear about the dyslexic devil worshipper? He sold his soul to Santa."

She punches me on the arm and hurries out of the room before I can throw a pillow at her. I get out of bed and walk over to the mirror to study my reflection. Dark brown hair curls around my ears, tapered at the neckline and dotted with random cowlicks that I never bother to comb. And I'm sporting a few freckles on my chin, but I think they qualify me as cute because they're not huge or cherry-colored. Normally, I might worry about my pasty complexion, but most Asian women are pale-skinned, which means we'll have something in common. Actually, I think I'm a decent-looking guy. I'm a smaller version of my father, but no less a warrior.

Emboldened by this self-validation, I decide to create my own profile on Match.com. I post a grainy black and white picture, the only one I can find, that shows me smiling in a suit and tie. I want to look professional, not desperate. Then I type up a few lines about my interest in ninjutsu and the fact that I'm a straight-A student who loves sashimi and can count from one to ten in perfect Japanese.

I spend the next few minutes describing Marblehead. I try to make it seem obnoxiously attractive, like one of those cheesy postcards they sell in the gift shop down by the pier. I tout it as a vacation paradise, a seaside town eighteen miles north of Boston with historic buildings, weathered antique shops, and a picturesque main street pulled directly from a Thornton Wilder play. I hype up Devereux Beach and Hawthorn Pond, and Crocker Park's gorgeous views of Marblehead Harbor. I even slide in a remark about the population being only twenty-one thousand, as if there's extra room for busloads of tourists and Internet girlfriends.

As an extra selling point, I describe a typical summer day: Stingrays and Boston Whalers slicing through the crests of waves, their hulls barely skimming the ocean's surface; the smell of fresh seafood drifting out of family restaurants, the air heavy with steamed lobster and deep fried cod; bare-chested men hurrying along the splintered docks, hauling coils of rope and scraping barnacles off tugboats; and deckhands marching up and down the pier with thick, black hoses, washing blood and fish guts into the ocean, and momentarily staining the water crimson.

I type up this portrait of small town New England life, making sure to highlight some of our more popular draws, like the Fireworks Committee or the Council on Aging, or the quaint starter homes that cost four-hundred-thousand dollars. I neglect to mention the sailboat snobs who play bridge at the marina, sipping ten-dollar margaritas in their Tommy Bahama golf shirts, or the retirees who congregate at Riverhead Beach for a Friday night clambake, tossing their empty wine bottles into a smoldering pit of burnt seaweed and broken quahog shells.

In closing out my profile, I stress a simple desire to share myself with a woman who truly seems to care about me, a woman who shows compassion and understanding, not because she's obligated to, but because she's taken a genuine interest in my topsy-turvy life.

Two days later I receive an e-mail from Sadako Takano:

> I was very glad to get your greetings. Thank you for writing to me. You are very handsome guy. I'm 19 years old and I'm student at Kyoto Institute of Technology. I want to be engineer. I'm very sociable and emotional girl. I like traveling too and I am interested in places where I was not yet. I have been to China, Thailand, Hawaii, and Mongolia. Now I am interested in Japan. Here there is a lot of beautiful places, where I was not yet. For example, I am going to visit in next summer in town of Sapporo (can be you something heard about it?). I adore live music and I often go to different concerts. I like dancing too, but unfortunately it's not often. I have light blue eyes, therefore this color pursues me in life. Even my room is made out in this color. By the way, I has found on a map your city. It is unreal far. It is terrible to present how many between us km. It something is. The night deep behind my window. It is time to sleep. You likely have sun touching the gold beams, so Good Morning. I'm sorry Tim! My English is bad. I'm studying it.

I print out Sadako's e-mail. Then I tape a piece of fishing line to each end of my bedroom so I can immortalize our first official date using a brand new pack of colored clothespins. Lying in bed, I stare up at that gorgeous font and dream of sailing across the Pacific Ocean on an antique junk.

Three days later I receive another e-mail:

My Dearest Tim.

Hello there. I missed you. Maybe sometime you come visit me and bear away in the sky in the great iron horse. What do you like more? Sunset or sunrise? What do you think is more beautiful? I like sunset more. They are more warm and romantic and make you dream on something good. Sunrises are rather optimistic and besides they are too early. Are you an early bird or late bird? I like to sleep long but some days I like to get up early and do a lot of things. Do you like coffee to bed in the morning Tim? Would you bring me sometimes???? I like dogs over cats because they smile at you and catch Frisbee in mouth. You know what I am thinking about when I think about you, Tim? I am thinking "Have I really found a man of my dreams?" I hope I have. One of my friends asked me when I would get married! Can you believe it! I said I have a boyfriend Tim but he lives far away from here, but we will meet and get married. I wanted to ask about children. If we get married (or better when we get married) when do you think we should have the first kid? I think we should wait for about a year this would give us time to know each other very well. What do you think about it? Hot Kisses to you Tim!!! Till next time!!!

Sadako.

A week into my new relationship, and I've almost forgotten about the Mean Man. His image is nothing more than a hazy outline, like smoke breaking apart when you wave your hands in the air. I'm practically tap dancing my way through the house, giddy with the thought that a real Asian woman is interested in my regular morning routine, and that she's actually considering me as a potential life partner. Not to mention the fact that she thinks I'm devilishly handsome.

Of course my mother has to ruin the moment. Wednesday morning she charges into my bedroom, her brown hair flying in all directions, cursing and shouting at me because I've transformed her scalloped-edge, lace doilies into origami cranes.

She holds them up so I can admire my handiwork. "Do you know how expensive these are? Am I made of money?"

"I'll buy you some more, Mom."

"Do you have any idea how hard it is for me to make this house look presentable and still work forty hours a week at the firm? Forty hours of back-wrenching labor so I can put food on the table. If you weren't so..."

She stops midsentence, finally noticing all my love letters hanging above the bed. She drops the doilies into the trashcan and walks over to the sagging clothesline.

"Hey," I shout. "Those are personal."

She looks at me, confused, as if she doesn't recognize me, and then she turns to read each letter. She snatches one off the clothesline and waves it in front of my face. "What the hell is this?"

"A letter," I tell her. "From a pen pal. Her English is rusty."

"Rusty? How about nonexistent? Are you sure she's even legal?"

"Yeah, sure."

"How do you know?" She asks me. "How do you know she's not trying to milk some money out of you? Wise up or you'll find yourself in jail."

"You don't even know her, Mom."

She sits down on my bed. "Okay, tell me about her, then. Where does she go to school? Where do her parents work? Did you tell her what a kick-ass ninja you are? Or were you going to surprise her when you got off the plane, maybe throw a few jabs at the airport?" She crumples up the letter and throws it at my feet. "Come on, Tim. You can barely hold a job at the video store, and now you want to wine and dine some Asian honey because she swore that she'd love you until the end of time?"

"I need to get love somewhere," I say, staring down at the hardwood floor.

My mother stands up, and for a few seconds neither of us speak. The silence is maddening. Finally she takes a deep breath and says, "I don't want you corresponding with this girl any more. Do you understand?"

Then, as if I don't already know how much of a disappointment I am to her, she says, "Get this Asian shit out of your system, Tim. You've already wasted enough time on a bunch of silly stories your father told you."

"You can't make me forget about Dad."

"His mind was broken," she says, putting her hand on my shoulder. "Can't you understand that? He told you what *he* needed to hear."

I sit down at my desk and stare out the window. Across the street some of the neighborhood kids are selling homemade lemonade for twenty-five cents. "I feel sorry for you, Mom. I really do."

"Well, I'm not surprised," she says. "There seems to be a lot of that going on around here."

My mother thinks she's an expert on everything, but what she doesn't know about life could fill a monastery. She's just upset because I'm the only one who cares enough to remember Dad. No one else wants to talk about him. To her, all his lessons are nothing more than silly fairy tales, and all his advice is just a jumble of warped phrases, splattered across the household by a disgruntled veteran whose mind was slightly out of order.

So what if Dad wasn't completely normal? Don't we all have weird quirks, like counting cracks in the sidewalk, or not eating mushy foods? Probably, but no one ever knows because we don't drag them out in public for everyone else to see. It's healthy for someone to have deep dark secrets, to tuck away an aspect of his life that exists for nobody else.

Like the ninjas.

I'll never forget the stories he used to tell me, whispered at night while he tucked me into bed, one hand drawing the sheet to my chin, the other clutching a glass of Jameson held between his trembling fingers. He told me a ninja visited him in the military hospital after he was hit by shrapnel, and that the ninja nursed him back to health with sacred chants and shitake mushrooms.

I know Dad wasn't perfect, but unlike the rest of the family I'm willing to forgive all those obstacles he faced on his crooked path to enlightenment. Like that time he brought a gun to Sunday dinner. How he just walked into the kitchen and placed a Glock 22 in the center of the table, real calm like he was laying down an extra fork. "In case they show up," was all he said as he began to pick at his Caesar salad. And before I could ask who else had been invited to eat with us, my mother grabbed the gun and steered Liz and me into the living room to watch cartoons.

Soon he started hiding in the basement and shouting at himself in the bathroom mirror. He left empty beer bottles around the house like a trail of breadcrumbs, and at night I heard him pacing the front porch, the smoke from his cigarettes crawling through my open window. Oftentimes, we'd sprawl out on the front lawn and look up at the stars. We'd talk about the Shinobi clan and Eastern philosophy, and why self-control is a ninja's greatest asset. One night he put his hand on my shoulder and said, "Don't let your emotions speed through red lights. If it's a green light, go, but always look both ways before screaming obscenities."

I was the only one who tried to understand my father's pain, and now I'm being punished for it.

One week later, I receive my third e-mail from Sadako:

Tim!

I told my parents that I was corresponding with a man from another country and maybe we would meet and marry one day and I would go live to you. They did not show much surprise. As I said I am not too close to them. Especially my Mom and I cannot say they were very upset. Or maybe they did not take it seriously. Anyway, I informed them. ☺☺☺ The thing is that I would be the one making the decision about my future because this would be my future. Well, now they know my intentions at least. I dream for you!

Sadako.

Now I'm ready to steal my sister's Tiffany catalogue and shop for an engagement ring. I'm ready to swipe my mother's charge card and book a first class ticket to Tokyo. I want to bow down before Sadako's parents and ask them for her hand in marriage. I want to propose to her at the Isoshimizu Spring in Kyoto, where virgins dance and cherry blossoms sing.

Everything is so perfect that the last thing I expect is to be dumped over the Internet. But that's exactly what happens. At first I'm not worried, figuring that maybe she's just busy tending to her Zen garden, but after sending her twelve e-mails, and not receiving a single response, I start to get nervous. So I send simple one-liners asking her if she's in the hospital, or if she's been kidnapped by the Yakuza. But then, a few days later, while I'm wondering if she died from eating a pufferfish, I discover that all my e-mails from the past week have been sent back unopened with a subject line reading "Returned Mail: Host Unknown."

"No!" I scream, hammering at the keyboard. "Sadako, where are you?"

I get up and pull down the clothesline. Then I throw it into the trashcan and hawk a loogie on it. Then I dig the clothesline out of the trash and hang it back up. Then I re-check my e-mail. Finally, on the verge of tears, I rip down the clothesline again so I can shred all her letters into itty bitty pieces and sprinkle them into the trashcan. I consider lighting them on fire, but I don't want the smoke detector to start beeping because then my mother will charge upstairs and celebrate my misery.

I walk over to the window. Outside, a cardinal teeters on a telephone wire. The branches of an oak tree scrape against the side of the house. The sun shines high in the sky, muscling its way through a depressing blanket of thick gray clouds. I bang my fists against the glass, angry at being trapped inside this two-story house where so much has gone wrong during the past few years.

I really thought I had it all figured out this time. I thought Asian women might be different from all those bottom feeders that wander around my high school like a bunch of texting zombies. I'm not trying to be an expatriate, but I just can't ignore the fact that American girls don't share any of my interests. They don't want to talk about ninjas or feng shui or the secrets of yin and yang. They want to share local gossip and count their calories. They want to invade the mall and be seen at football games. How can you have an intelligent conversation with someone who loves to read Facebook, but has never read an actual book?

And now, besides striking out on American soil, I'm also quite the failure in Asia, having squandered a golden opportunity to woo a bona fide mail order bride who, up until the moment she dumped me, I honestly believed was ready to pack up all her kimonos so we could be together forever.

Looking out into the backyard, I glance over at a small patch of dry, crusted grass. It's an eyesore among the flower beds and the herb garden, a dull yellow scab on a lush green lawn, but it's also a constant reminder that if I want to succeed as a ninja, then I have to knuckle down and claw my way through a never-ending tangle of thickets and thieves.

That dead patch of grass is where my father and I shared one of our last conversations, only a few nights before he died. It was raining outside, and I awoke to a strong wind banging against my bedroom window. Sitting up, I saw a shadowy figure standing in the middle of the backyard, and I thought it was the Mean Man come to collect me. I pictured his van parked in the driveway with the engine idling. I imagined him bursting through my bedroom window to snatch me up.

The figure lit up a cigarette. A cloud of smoke drifted across the lawn, and the tip of his cigarette glowed bright red. Moving closer to the window, I peered through the trees and recognized my father's silhouette. He walked around in a tight circle and flicked his cigarette into the grass. He picked something up and held it in his hands. Then he sank into the ground.

I crept downstairs in my pajamas and hurried outside. I heard my father grunting, the sharp sounds of metal striking earth. He stood knee-deep in an enormous hole, his bathrobe covered in mud.

"Dad," I whispered, "what are you doing?"

He looked up at me and smiled. "I'm digging, Tim."

I stared down into the hole, watching his hands tremble and shake. The darkness pooled around him like dirty water. "What are you looking for?"

He stared at me, confused, and then he shook his head. "I don't know," he said, "but I'll know when I find it."

I backed away and wiped the raindrops from my face, shivering as my bare feet sank into the soggy ground. My father kept on digging, growing smaller and smaller as he slung shovelfuls of mud into the cold night air.

Over the years, that spot has grown thin and sparse, hard and dusty like an arid desert. My mother reseeds it every spring, nurturing the soil with fertilizer and expensive minerals, even planting hydrangeas and chrysanthemums. But she usually gives up by mid-July, and the only moisture that patch will ever get is from a small amount of summer rain. It's forgotten among a clutter of fancy lawn chairs, victimized by an overbearing sun.

All I want are some answers, and I don't care anymore how they're presented. And since my mother is closed for business, I have to be innovative in my approach. Which means it's time to consult my Ouija board. The board itself is faded and stained, and the planchette is cracked down the middle like a broken heart, but it was my father's, so I'm hoping to obtain some practical advice through spiritual osmosis.

A couple nights after the Sadako disaster, I turn off my bedroom light, switch on a flashlight, and walk into the closet. I close the door and sit down, my back pressed against the wall. I smell mothballs, and it reminds me of the night my father died. How I huddled in the corner of my closet after the paramedics arrived, listening to sirens wail, watching the red and blue lights twirl through my bedroom window. How my mother went into shock and the ambulance brought her to the hospital.

Huddled atop a pile of dirty laundry, my knees touching my chin, I close my eyes and take a deep breath. I push that night as far away from me as I can. Then I open my eyes and stare down at the Ouija board, running my fingers over the smooth wood surface, whispering softly as I carve a path through all those letters and numbers. I'm about to ask my first question when there's a knock from the hallway, three quick raps followed by a moment of silence and one long bang. I lean forward and crack open my closet door, watching as my mother switches on the

46

overhead light. She pulls my sister into the room and points toward the ceiling.

"He had it hanging up," she says. "Like a parade banner. Do you think I should be concerned?"

Liz leans against my desk. "It's impossible to keep track of all his obsessions."

"I know. But I'm still worried. He's been very moody these past few weeks."

"He's always moody."

"True," my mother says, "but he usually revels in it. Lately, his sulkiness has lacked purpose. It's depressing instead of entertaining."

"So why don't you send him to a shrink?"

"Are you kidding me? There's no way in hell he'd agree to see a therapist. He burned that self-help book I bought him for Christmas last year."

"Mom, does Tim honestly believe that he's some super, covert ninja? Because the kids at school say he's just acting like this because he has no friends."

"Your friends are such brilliant detectives, aren't they? Pointing out the same flaws in everyone else that they never seem to notice in themselves." She picks lint off her blouse and watches it flutter to the floor. "I'm very aware that your brother is a bit confused, and I'd love to put him right-side up, but every time I try talking to him he gets mad and storms off."

Liz laughs. "He's always been a freak, hasn't he?"

My mother slaps her across the face with the back of her hand. "If you'd woken up that night, then maybe things would be different, but it was your brother who came downstairs. Not you." She's breathing heavy now, her face flushed. "Don't presume to know how he's felt all these years because, sister, you haven't got the faintest idea."

Stunned, her face sporting a large red handprint, Liz stares down at the floor. "He needs guidance, Mom, and not from some stupid Buddhist temple buried deep in the Himalayas."

My mother gives her a hug. "Guidance, honey, is the last thing that every teenager thinks they need."

The two of them look outside, watching storm clouds gather as claps of thunder rumble in from the east and raindrops hit the side of the house. Peering out of my closet, I can see leaves petal down from the oak tree in our backyard, its branches shaking in the stiffening wind as they knock against my bedroom window. I can see lightning bolts zigzag across the darkening sky, looping and crisscrossing each other in massive cursive scribbles as though God is some moron who can't master the Palmer method.

I push away the Ouija board and listen to the rainstorm. I'm angry at my mother, shaken by her flippant attitude that I'm not the man of the house, but, instead, some bumbling idiot who can't even find the pieces, let alone put them back together. I feel tired and sluggish, like a bottle of soda that's going flat in the back of the refrigerator. I'm sick of being jettisoned by everyone around me, especially people who are supposed to love me, so now I'm finally prepared to seek some expert help, no matter what the cost.

After they go back downstairs, I sneak into Mom's bedroom and lift her credit card from her wallet. Then, once I'm lying on my queen-size bed, a new bottle of Evian on the nightstand beside me, I pick up the phone and dial the psychic hotline.

"Hello, my dear," a Cajun voice answers. "This is Miss Flossie. How may I help you?"

"Miss Flossie, my name is Tim Dimmick. I need answers. Badly."

"Of course, Tim. I sense your urgency. But first I must have your credit card number."

I read off the numbers one at a time. "Please, Miss Flossie, can you help me?"

"I sense you are frustrated and desperate," she says. "I perceive great sadness and confusion."

"Yes!" I shout again. "My father's death."

"Your family is unstable," she tells me. "But you are not alone. Tell me about your girlfriend."

"I don't have a girlfriend."

"Are you sure?"

"Umm...I think so. Unless she reactivated her e-mail account."

"I see a girlfriend in your future. A pretty girl with nice cheekbones and long eyelashes. An athletic girl who practices yoga and believes in unconditional love. Is this the type of girl you like, Tim?"

"I guess."

"You will meet her. I have seen it in the stars."

"When?"

"Later, when you have accepted your true calling. When you are ready to become whatever it is you want to become."

"I don't want to be ordinary," I scream into the phone. "Tell me, please. Am I destined to become a ninja?"

"The first card is the Three of Wands," she says. "I see you traveling

48

the world as a visionary to spread peace and goodwill, like an Asian Robin Hood."

"Awesome!"

"Let me consult another card. Aha. Here is Death."

"Shit! I can't die. I'm only seventeen."

"Do not worry," she tells me. "You will prevail. I see you riding an inescapable fate into an Eastern sunset."

I look outside. "Doesn't the sun set in the West?"

"It's a metaphor," she says. "You know, the East, Asia, ninjas live in Asia?"

"Be honest with me, Miss Flossie. Can I become an American ninja?"

"Of course, Tim. You are an American, and Americans are the best at everything they do. That's why everyone fears us. Because we have automatic weapons and big cars." She pauses for a moment, and I hear her light up a cigarette.

"Ah," she says, "I see rivers and lakes, mountains and plains. I see you beginning an adventure, both spiritual and physical. Ah, suddenly it is all so clear. You must train, Tim. You must join with a master and learn the ways of the ninja. You must build your own dojo."

"My own dojo?"

"Yes," she says. "Only in the field of construction will you find the answers you seek. Only there will you find peace from your father's death. The circle is open, Tim. You must close it. Become a ninja. Build your own dojo."

My heart is racing and my legs are shaking. This is better than anything on *Crossing Over*. "Miss Flossie, thank you so much for sharing your incredible powers with me."

"Do not go, Tim. There is still so much to be said, so much to be revealed."

"I'm sorry, Miss Flossie, but I must begin my quest for a dojo."

"Wait, I see financial gain!"

I hang up and walk over to my desk. Already, I can picture my own dojo somewhere in the White Mountains. I can see myself meditating in a lush green valley and grilling trout next to a gurgling stream, sipping hot sake while squirrels crawl into my lap and drop acorns as a sign of friendship. I see myself living the simple life. Kind of like Thoreau.

I'm wondering if I should start watching reruns of *This Old House*, or if I should quit my job at Blockbuster Video and land a summer job cutting drywall and hanging sheetrock. Either way, I realize that my construction of the perfect dojo begins with admittance into a first-rate business program, maybe at Stanford or Northwestern. And I know there's only one way to locate my future alma mater: the Internet.

I boot up my computer. I hear the screen crackle with static, and I smile at the sound of a new beginning, like the quiet hush of a thousand tiny voices cheering me on. I can almost feel my father's presence as he walks up beside me, beaming with pride. He puts his arm around me and whispers, "Don't be afraid, son. Charge onto that battlefield, stand tall, and seize your own destiny."

4.
Scream Three Times

By the time Wynn arrives I've already taken the head out of the refrigerator. I've carried it upstairs to my bedroom and placed it in the middle of the floor, positioning it atop one of my mother's red satin pillows. Around the head, in a fiery ring, I place the five feng shui candles I bought at SpaceScapes, one each for metal, wood, fire, earth, and water.

For the séance to succeed, my room has to be in harmony with these elements. For example, wood feeds fire, which, in turn, burns to create earth. The earth contains metal, which, when melted, flows like water. And water, as any idiot knows, helps wood to grow. On the flip side, wood feeds off the earth, and the earth soaks up water. Water extinguishes fire, fire melts metal, and metal cuts into wood. I'm not sure how many candles I need to burn, but I'm prepared to torch the entire house if it means channeling my father's spirit.

I also place incense around the room: cinnamon, frankincense, and sandalwood. Cinnamon provides warmth and energy, frankincense expands the consciousness, and sandalwood helps focus the participants' attention on the supernatural task at hand. Even though there will only be three of us, I still bought name tags. Finally, to create a soft and relaxing mood, I bought a CD entitled *Season of Séance, Science of Silence.*

My bedroom is completely dark, save for the flickering candles that cast long and jagged shadows into every corner. The flames writhe and twist like a nest of snakes, their silhouettes shadowboxing on the walls. The only two visible objects are my father's Ouija board and the head of lettuce that, decorated with black magic marker, actually resembles some of Dad's more prominent features, at least in profile.

Looking outside, I can't believe that autumn is officially over. Halloween was only a few weeks ago, and by then the leaves had fallen and turned brown. Already we've had two winter storms. The grass is frozen and stiff, and the driveway is slick with black ice. Plus, large snowdrifts have built up around the mailboxes and stop signs, and icicles have formed under the eaves. Usually, I'd be a bit depressed to see winter barreling down on me, but according to the Discovery Channel, ghosts are more active when it's cold, so this is the perfect time to connect with the spirit world.

The doorbell rings just as I finish the preparations. I run downstairs before my mother has a chance to put down her glass of Chardonnay and get off the couch. I'm trying to be secretive, but I think she's getting suspicious. She gave me a strange look when I pulled the lettuce out of the refrigerator, and when she asked why the entire house smells like stale potpourri I told her I was trying to mellow out and thought it was a better option than pot.

When I open the front door Wynn saunters inside, shivering and blowing into his hands. "I can't believe I'm missing CSI so I can sit in the dark and sing Kumbaya."

"We've already gone over this a thousand times," I tell him. "For a séance to be official there needs to be at least three people."

He takes off his jacket and hangs it up in the hall closet. "Can we get this show on the road? I have shit to do tonight. And it's already ten-thirty."

"Don't blame me. Right before midnight is supposed to be the best time. Something to do with the spirits being more laidback. Besides, we can't start until Akasma gets here."

"Akasma? You asked a Turkish foreign exchange student to come to your house and participate in a séance? On a school night?"

I punch him on the arm. "Can't you support me like a real friend?"

"Hey, I'm here, aren't I?"

"If this is going to work," I tell him, "then you need to drop the shitty attitude and put on your game face."

Wynn yawns and leans against the wall. "Dude, I know you're having some serious family issues, but this stir of echoes vibe is pretty creepy."

"Awesome. Way to be positive."

He looks down at the burgundy carpet. "Honestly, Tim, what do you expect to get out of this? Your dad is dead. Let the poor guy rest in peace."

"Do you have any chronic diseases?"

"What? No."

"Good. We don't want any negative energy clouding up the room."

He pokes his finger in my chest. "Listen up, because I'm about to drop some truth all over this room. What you need to do is stop feeling sorry for yourself. Okay? You need to quit obsessing over the past and start thinking about the future."

"Thanks. I'll file that away for future use. Now come on." I put a finger to my lips, point to the living room, and hurry up the stairs.

Wynn follows me, his steel-toed construction boots banging on the treads with each step, shaking the entire house.

Once we're in my room, I close the door and motion for him to be quiet. "If my mother knew we were holding a séance up here, she'd go postal. You know how mad she gets when I mention my father. If she walked in and found candles burning and the Ouija board spinning out of control, she'd call an exorcist."

"I'd pay to see that. It might actually do you some good."

I grab a sheet of paper off my desk. "I need to ask you some questions. Sort of like a ninja quiz."

"A fucking quiz? Tim, I dropped out of high school to get away from shit like this. Besides, I'm not a ninja."

"I'm sorry, but it's part of the process. I can't afford any weak links in the spiritual chain."

"What about Akasma? Does she have to take your stupid quiz?"

"She's half gypsy," I tell him. "I'm not worried about her aura."

Grumbling, he walks over to the window. "What happens if I don't want to answer your silly little questions? Is a ninja gonna climb through my bedroom window and fillet me with a Ginsu knife?"

"Number one. Who is a ninja's sworn enemy?"

"Oh, wait, this was on double jeopardy last night. It's either the religious right, or Wal-Mart employees."

"Can you please be serious? This isn't a joke. And for your information, the answer is a samurai warrior."

"Fine." He walks over to my bed and sits down. "Ask me another one."

I look down at my list of questions. "Number two. What is the best way to assassinate someone?"

He shrugs. "Either staple his face to a billboard, or back over him with a monster truck."

I think he's being a jerk, but I can't tell because his arms are folded and he's not smiling. "Well, technically they're both correct," I tell him, "although *I* would have said poison or nunchucks."

Wynn looks over at the Ouija board, at all the candles set up around the room. "I'll be your wingman for the séance, alright, but I am not taking some stupid ass quiz."

"Do you believe in ghosts?" I ask him.

"I've never seen one," he says, "but once I finish writing *Fetus Dreams* I'd like to write a screenplay with some ghosts in it. It's only a matter of time before the horror trend comes back around. I've been thinking about a story where the ghost isn't a person, but a chicken that haunts a farm and tries to get revenge on the farmer who cut off his head and ate him."

"But do you believe people can communicate from beyond the grave?"

"Not really. I mean...well...I guess there's always a presence, but it's more of a residual effect from when that person was still alive." He stares down at the head of lettuce. "Besides, do you really want a dead person offering you advice on how to live?"

Just then my mother hollers up at me from downstairs. "Timothy, there's someone at the door for you."

I race downstairs to find Akasma standing in the foyer. She's wearing a moonbeam skirt with a corsair belt and a brown ganza jacket, her long black hair braided with red beads. As she reaches out to shake my hand, I notice all the jewelry weighing her down: five gold bangles on one wrist and three on the other, a ruby ring, a gold-coin necklace, five Georgian earrings in each ear, and a diamond nose ring that actually looks cute.

Akasma plans to attend Princeton next fall. Her dream is to open a high-end Turkish restaurant in Boston, entrancing the city with mussel pilaki, chard mousakka, and zucchini carrot bread. Emil introduced us at one of the football games, and I think she was impressed that I'd heard of Istanbul and know what a mosque is. She agreed to monitor the séance, for safety reasons she later said, and although she demanded payment in cash, she did explain how her ancestral ties to the Sky-God will aid us in conjuring up my father's spirit.

"Hello, Timothy," she says, curtseying like we're in a restoration drama.

"Hi, Akasma. Thanks for coming." I turn to my mother. "We'll be upstairs reviewing for a test."

My mother lays her hand on my arm. "Can I speak with you for a moment?"

I look at Akasma, who clearly doesn't know whether she should linger in the foyer or proceed up the stairs. "Go on up," I tell her. "My room is the first door on the left."

She smiles, lifts the bottom of her skirt, and walks up the stairs as if tiptoeing across a puddle.

As soon as she's out of sight, I turn to my mother. "What?"

"You didn't tell me anyone was coming over. It's ten o'clock at night and I'm standing around in my nightgown."

"Which looks great on you, by the way. It really brings out your eyes."

"Tim, are you high?"

"Akasma is a stranger in this land, Mom. I'm just being a decent, good-hearted American."

A faint smile curls the edges of her mouth. "You've never mentioned this girl before. Are you two dating?"

"No, Mom, we're just studying. And Wynn is up there, too, so relax. We're not having a threesome."

"I thought you were writing your college application essays?"

"I'm doing that, too," I tell her. "I'm multi-tasking."

She looks at me as though I'm a shady car salesman who can't entirely be trusted. "So why is Wynn here? I thought he dropped out of school to work on that screenplay. What's it called? *Placenta Visions*?"

"His IQ is one-fifty-six. He's practically a genius."

"Who works at Blockbuster Video?"

I edge closer and drop my voice. "He's here because of Akasma, okay? He has a gypsy fetish, so I thought I'd invite her over, maybe see if the sparks fly."

"So now you're a matchmaker? Like some character out of a Jane Austen novel?"

"I'm not fate, Mom. I merely nudge it in the right direction." I give her a hug, which shocks her. My mother and I rarely hug, and when we do it's usually about as long as a handshake or a pat on the back. "Can I go now?"

She stares at me for a minute, and then shrugs. "Fine, but I don't want them here past midnight. You and Akasma have school tomorrow, and Wynn has to work on his movie. Tell him his title sucks."

"I will. Thanks, Mom. I really appreciate it."

As I'm halfway up the stairs she shouts, "There are snacks in the kitchen if you guys get hungry."

In my room I find Akasma sitting cross-legged on the floor, staring at the head of lettuce. The edges of its leaves are beginning to brown and wilt.

"Creative," she says, touching the crude Picasso nose I drew on with a black sharpie.

"It's iceberg," I tell her.

Wynn is still sitting on my bed, biting his nails. "Let's get this freak show started. If we wait much longer, the light of the moon might seal off the gateway to another dimension."

I turn off my bedroom light. Then I take the black sharpie and scribble our names on the blue and white sticker labels. "Here, put these on."

Wynn walks over and snatches the label from my hand. He slaps it across his flannel shirt. "What's this for? In case we develop Alzheimer's before the spirit festival begins?"

"Try to act professional, okay?"

I watch as Akasma peels off her label and places it over her left breast. She rubs it on with the palm of her hand, pressing it into her linen blouse with slow circles.

Wynn says, "Come on, Tim. It's just a head of lettuce. The only thing you'll channel is a rabbit, or maybe a bottle of vinaigrette."

I turn to Akasma. "What happens if we make contact?"

"Sometimes there's a decrease in the room temperature. Sometimes you'll feel intense pain in certain parts of your body. So if the deceased died of a heart attack, then you might experience some chest pains."

"How often have you communicated with the dead?" I ask her.

"Many times. I've been participating in séances since I was a little girl. It's part of my culture. Sometimes you're lucky enough to communicate, but not always. Even if your father doesn't respond, though, I'm sure he'll be aware that you initiated contact."

"Well, today is Veteran's Day," I tell her, "and my dad was a veteran, so I think we might get lucky."

She motions toward the Ouija board. "If the planchette moves on its own, then that's usually a pretty good sign the spirits are trying to communicate." She taps the rug with one of her long silver fingernails. "Why don't you both take a seat so we can get started?"

Wynn and I sit down. Akasma takes the Ouija board and places it in front of me. The three of us join hands. The planchette, which looks like a plastic croissant, rests in the middle of the board between the "yes" and "no" signs. Suddenly I feel weird. After all, we're sitting on my bedroom floor, surrounded by tiny candles, and staring intently at last week's produce.

My stomach rumbles. I'm thinking Caesar with croutons.

Akasma scoots closer to the Ouija board, her bracelets clanging together like an operatic hymn. I notice she's taken off her sandals. I can see her toes poking out from underneath her waxy legs. The nails are painted gold, and her index toe is longer than the others, which signifies intelligence. I picture her naked in a Turkish bath, smoking an Egyptian hookah, her tawny breasts ensconced in pungent clouds of hash. Suddenly I have a massive erection.

"I want you both to take some deep breaths," she tells us. "In through the nose, slowly, and then out through the mouth, slowly. Clear your mind. I want you calm and comfortable. Just let your mind wander into nothingness."

Wynn laughs. "Is this yoga or a séance? I've seen exercise videos better than this."

I close my eyes and smell the wood and fire candles. I hear Akasma breathing beside me. I hear the television downstairs, and I imagine my mother pouring herself another wobbly glass of wine. I concentrate on my breathing like Akasma instructed. I establish a steady rhythm, my shoulders heaving with each breath, my chest muscles stretched taut with each long-drawn-out intake.

I become sleepy, and it seems that the world is spinning around me. I'm alone now, exploring the labyrinth of my mind, and immersed in total darkness. Far away, I hear cries and pleas, a familiar voice that alternates between anger and grief. I hear glass breaking, a woman screaming, and then I see a Glock 22 lying in a pool of blood. I see shards of broken glass and a blonde-haired angel drowning in dirty water, her enormous white wings stretching into a gray sky.

Then the scene shifts. I watch the Mean Man walk up the stairs, his bony fingers gripping the banister. He glances toward my bedroom, winks, and then opens the bathroom door. He steps inside and disappears. I hear a gunshot. I try to run, but I'm sinking into a pile of wrinkled clothes. The smell of mothballs suffocates me, and I reach for a hanger to protect myself. I hear sirens and scattered voices.

Actually, I hear Akasma's voice, soft but tempestuous, her Turkish accent slicing into me like a knife into a shish kebab. "Now that we've relaxed our minds," she says, "I want all of us to repeat the following words: 'Our beloved James Dimmick, we ask that you commune with us. Please move among us and acknowledge your presence.'"

The three of us tighten our grips on each other and softly begin to chant. "Our beloved James Dimmick, we ask that you commune with us. Please move among us and acknowledge your presence. Our beloved James Dimmick, we ask that you commune with us. Please move among us and acknowledge your presence. Our beloved James Dimmick, we ask that you commune with us. Please move among us and acknowledge your presence. Our beloved James Dimmick, we ask that you commune with us. Please move among us and acknowledge your presence. Our beloved James

Dimmick, we ask that you commune with us. Please move among us and acknowledge your presence. Our beloved James Dimmick, we ask that you commune with us. Please move among us and acknowledge your presence. Our beloved James Dimmick, we ask that you commune with us. Please move among us and acknowledge your presence."

I'm repeating the words, but they sound like someone else's, as if they're hundreds of miles away, a bunch of distant voices vibrating underwater. I'm trying to concentrate, but I keep catching slivered moments from my own chaotic life. They tiptoe behind me, sneaking into my peripheral vision, every recollection just another crumbled tombstone, dozens of them laid end to end until I'm trapped in a graveyard of painful memories, wandering in confused circles as I try to read each faded epitaph.

And while my eyes are searching through so much blackness, as I'm waiting to hear my father's gruff voice call out to me from another dimension, I'm suddenly transported back to April 25th, 2004, the day I lost my innocence.

***

It was a crisp Sunday afternoon. My father and I were at Castle Rock Park, eating hot fudge sundaes we'd bought at Mrs. O's of Marblehead. He had asked me to take a ride with him so the two of us could have a man-to-man conversation. This was momentous, and I felt on the verge of a great discovery. So when I'd scraped the last remnants of hot fudge from the bottom of my cup, I folded my hands and waited.

My father stood over me, a toothpick dangling from the corner of his mouth. "When you're young, people like to say you can be anything you want, and that you can do anything you want, but that's a bunch of whimsical nonsense. The cold, hard truth is that we don't live in a world where anything is possible. To succeed in life, to find your calling and embrace it, a man has to be chosen and committed. He has to be selfless and honest. He has to possess a great desire to learn. And in doing so, he becomes fearless and self-reliant."

I nodded, completely lost.

He scooted closer, dropping his voice in case anyone overheard. "I'm talking about becoming a shadow warrior, Tim. I'm talking about the power of Ninjutsu, that ancient art developed by Japanese mountain clans in the eleventh and twelfth centuries. I'm talking about deception and invisibility, espionage and attack, defense and tactics of escape. That's the palette a ninja uses to paint his life story."

"Where do ninjas come from?" I asked him.

My father shrugged. "Some say mountain creatures called tengu first taught ninjas their art. That later they taught them kuji, which is a form of sorcery. But what's important is that they're out there, roaming the world. I've seen them. I've talked with them."

"Were you scared, Dad?"

My father tsked. "Hell, I nearly shit my pants when they snuck into the hospital. They have a command of stealth like you wouldn't believe. One minute I was writing a letter to your mom, and the next thing I knew they were standing over me with a bottle of hot sake and three mochi rice cakes wrapped in nori seaweed."

"Wow!"

He nodded. "They taught me the secrets of ninjutsu."

"What secrets?"

He sat down next to me, his arthritic knees creaking like rusted locks. "It's a privilege to be invited into the world of ninjutsu. I was chosen to preserve its history and knowledge, and to pass it on to the next generation for nurturing and safekeeping. And that's what I'm going to do with you, Tim. But the path is rocky, and we must walk it slowly."

"Why did they recruit you, Dad?"

"To help fight the enemy."

"What enemy?"

He looked toward the west. "There are two kinds of people in this world, Tim. There are fair weather ninjas, those who prefer clear skies and long sunny days, and there are foul weather ninjas, who prefer pounding rain and big, black storm clouds. Fair weather ninjas jive on world peace. They love mankind, they're friendly and optimistic. They'll walk right over and shake your hand, strike up a pleasant conversation. But foul weather ninjas are cautious and guarded. They know that man can never be trusted, and they understand that violence is an unfortunate, but often necessary, part of life."

"How can you tell if someone is a fair weather ninja or a foul weather ninja?" I asked him. "Do you need a special thermometer?"

He smiled. "You have to be patient, my young grasshopper. The weather is completely unpredictable, and about the only thing you can count on is that it's always changing."

"Do you think I could be a warrior? Just like you?"

"Of course," he said. "It's your destiny. That's why I'm sharing all these stories with you. So you'll become more cultured and aware, so you can protect yourself when the world gets pissy and turns its back on you."

He put his arm around me. "I won't always be here for you, so you'll need something else to hold on to."

I was giddy and lightheaded. I lay down on the blanket and stared up at the sky, watching the clouds soar past on their way to a thunderstorm. Around me, people were throwing footballs and chasing after Frisbees. I heard dogs barking and birds chirping. I heard moms yelling a long list of do's and don'ts to a mob of screaming kids who kept rolling down the hill in their grass-stained shorts, and climbing across the monkey bars with exaggerated grunts. All of these sounds melded together in a crashing crescendo, like an enormous waterfall spilling over me. The air crackled with energy, a light breeze blew through the pine trees, and I hugged myself, thinking, "Move over, James Bond. Timothy Dimmick has a license to jab."

***

Back in my bedroom, the three of us are still chanting: "Our beloved James Dimmick, we ask that you commune with us. Please move among us and acknowledge your presence. Our beloved James Dimmick, we ask that you commune with us. Please move among us and acknowledge your presence. Our beloved James Dimmick, we ask that you commune with us. Please move among us and acknowledge your presence. Our beloved James Dimmick, we ask that you commune with us. Please move among us and acknowledge your presence. Our beloved James Dimmick, we ask that you commune with us. Please move among us and acknowledge your presence. Our beloved James Dimmick, we ask that you commune with us. Please move among us and acknowledge your presence."

My mouth is getting dry, and I can feel my jaw cramping up. I should have set out a few bottles of Evian, or at least bought some lozenges. I'm starting to jumble my words and trip over sentences. Worse, the three of us aren't even in sync anymore. Akasma is singing the words like some washed-up country singer; I'm shouting them like a televangelist; and Wynn is delivering them in iambic pentameter.

Listening to our off-key screeching, my stomach still rumbling like a volcano, I remember a Chinese recipe my father told me about called Scream Three Times. Supposedly, newborn mice are taken from their mother (the first scream), dropped into a hot frying pan (the second scream), and then eaten (the third scream). I'm not sure what the health merits are in devouring small, feeble critters, but most Chinese people live well into their eighties, so they must be doing something right. Anyway, I wonder if that's what we sound like right now, three helpless mice just kicking and clawing and squeaking.

Akasma continues to watch the Ouija board, but the planchette still hasn't moved. Now she raises her hands. "If you are with us, James Dimmick, then please acknowledge your presence. Are you with us tonight?"

The planchette doesn't budge.

She repeats the incantation. "I say again. If you are with us, James Dimmick, then please acknowledge your presence. Are you with us tonight?"

Silence. Not even the heater kicking on, or a rattling floorboard. She continues the incantation for ten more minutes. It's obvious she's speaking to nothing but empty air. What more does my father want? A welcome banner with balloons and party favors? It's bad enough to be mocked and ridiculed by the living, but to receive similar treatment from the dead is downright degrading.

Finally, Akasma stands up. "Tim, I don't think the spirits are with us tonight. Let's try again some other time? Maybe when it's not so cloudy, or when there's a full moon?"

Wynn looks up. "I didn't know the lunar cycle was important in necromancy."

"It's really not," she says, blushing. "I was just trying to sound optimistic."

"You're sweet," I tell her. "Thanks for all your help. I really appreciate it."

She slips into her sandals and gives me a hug. "I'll find my own way out. I think you need to compose yourself. Disappointment is often difficult to grasp."

"Don't worry," I tell her. "I'm used to it."

She squeezes my arm. "Maybe that's why we failed."

I stand up and kick the Ouija board across the room. My father always swore that ninjutsu would lead to greater rewards and self-fulfillment, but I really need him to point me in the right direction, to show me a map that might bring the surrounding landscape into a sharper focus. Instead, he's refused to show up for his own party, and now I'm sitting here in the dark, looking like king dork.

Lately, it seems like I can't depend on anyone to come through for me. I'm even afraid of letting myself down.

Akasma turns on my bedroom light and blows out the candles. Tiny wisps of smoke climb into the air, and the lettuce sags into the satin pillow, wrinkled like a deflated balloon. She waves goodbye. I hear her creep down the stairs and close the front door, her feet crunching into the snow as she moves across the front lawn.

Wynn says, "You know what scares me? The whole time we were meditating I kept thinking about all the people who are dying at this exact moment, whether they're geezers jacked up on morphine in some hospital, or little kids suffering from some incurable disease. All those people who will never speak again, or eat again, or kiss someone again, or take a dump, even. Doesn't that depress the hell out of you? The brevity of it all."

"Sure. Why not."

"Sometimes it keeps me awake at night," he says. "Knowing that eventually the day will come when I flatline, and there's nothing I can do to prevent it. Sure I can floss and eat my vegetables and get a yearly checkup, but it's still unavoidable. It might be years from now, or days, or even a matter of hours, but the certainty is always there, like some crazy itch you can't quite reach. I crack jokes about it, but only because it terrifies the holy piss out of me." He glances down at the Ouija board. "When you think about it, Tim, the unknown is some pretty persuasive shit."

"Come on," I say, steering him toward the door. "If you're lucky, you might be able to catch the last half of Letterman."

He pats me on the back and hurries down the stairs. I hear him grab his coat from the hall closet and then lock the front door behind him as he pulls it shut. I walk over to the window and watch as he shuffles toward his car, whistling that god-awful theme song to *The Greatest American Hero*. His breath spirals into the air, thin and wispy like foggy lattice. Stopping in the middle of the driveway, he lights a cigarette and pulls a pair of white cloth gloves from his jacket pocket. Curled into tiny balls, they remind me of newborn mice. I rest my head against the cold windowpane and close my eyes. I picture a dozen hairless rodents, so innocent and weak, flailing about in the slippery depths of a nonstick-coated Wok, their high-pitched screams merging together in a cacophony of sizzling oil and searing flesh.

5

Children Shouldn't Play With Dead Things

NEW YORK UNIVERSITY

Personal Statement/Essay

This essay offers an opportunity for you to help us become acquainted with you in ways different from grades, test scores, and other objective data. It allows you to demonstrate your ability to organize your thoughts and express yourself. With this in mind, please write an essay, approximately 2000 words in length, on the following topic:

Select a creative work—a novel, a film, a poem, a musical piece, a painting, or other work of art—that has influenced the way you view the world and the way you view yourself. Discuss the work and its effect on you.

I, Timothy Dimmick, am applying to New York University's Leonard N. Stern School of Business because I hope to gain entrepreneurial skills that will help me finance and construct my own personal dojo. In addition to a fully functioning cafeteria, an indoor sauna, and a sandstone garden complete with Tiki torch fountains, my dojo (which I plan to christen the House of Whirling Zen) will achieve international acclaim as New England's largest and most prestigious ninja camp.

My interest in ninjutsu first began with my father, James Dimmick. He befriended ninjas while fighting in Operation Desert Storm, and later, after returning home, he joined forces with them to run reconnaissance in and around our neighborhood. When I was six-years-old, my father took me under his martial wing. He disclosed centuries-old information that the ninjas revealed to him while he was recuperating in the V.A. hospital. He explained mind control tactics and pressure points, the secrets of invisibility, and even the real reason why ninjas never sweat.

To me, the ninjas seemed superhuman, as if cast from the hand of God himself, a combination of power and restraint and intelligence, all packed together within layers of tight black cloth. In a way, ninjas are covert exorcists, cutting away the fat of society so people can feel safer. They also possess heightened intelligence, which explains how every ninja knows that it's just as effective to poison an enemy as it is to strangle him with rusty piano wire.

I treasured my father's ninja stories, held them close to my chest like a magic talisman, and every night I looked forward to hearing a new adventure. Those were the times when we were closest, when he would sit me on his lap and smile, tousling my hair as he tucked me into my Spider Man bed sheets, acting the role of a typical suburban dad. In my father's stories I was the dashing hero, needed and loved by peasants and maidens, a pint-sized ninja scaling the Great Wall of China and fighting for justice in shady roadside taverns.

My father promised me fame and glory, and I was eager to wrap my arms around a future that was jam-packed with hard-fought victories and fearless determination. Afternoons, I'd dart through the house shooting rubber bands at the television set or the microwave oven. I pretended they were sheaf arrows, and that I was a highly trained ninja infiltrating the jungles of South America. Or my sister and I would duel with the morning newspaper, twisting each section into two-handed swords. Leaping over the furniture, we'd stab each other with the obituaries, inflicting paper cuts on our arms and legs, my sister yelling for Mom whenever I tried to run her through with the sports page. Those weekly scuffles proved to be crucial training exercises for a budding warrior, and every day I felt privileged and special, an ordinary boy who'd been handed an extraordinary mission.

But all that changed when my father pulled the trigger.

And when that shot echoed through the house so many years ago, it was me who reached the bathroom first, wrestling with the blocked door until my bare feet began to squish in the forming pool of blood. While my mother screamed into the phone, while neighbors rushed over to investigate the gunshot, I slammed into the door as hard as I could, bruising my shoulder over and over until I was able to squeeze my head inside and look down at his body. At the blood that encircled his head like a halo. At pieces of brain stuck to the shower curtain.

For the first month after his death I didn't know how to feel. I wandered through the house, staring at his wrinkled clothes and baseball caps, and sitting in his chair at the kitchen table. I wasn't sure if being dead meant the same as having died, but when I asked my mother to explain the difference she just choked back a sob, uncorked a bottle of Merlot, and sent me to my room. Since my father's death, she did nothing but mope around the house. She called the accounting firm and used up all her vacation time. She ordered Chinese food, took one bite, and left it on the coffee table where it grew moldy and attracted flies. Whenever I walked by the living room I'd see her sitting cross-legged in her blue nightgown, staring out the bay window while heaps of Kleenex piled up around her like a snowdrift.

She was so distraught she couldn't even arrange the funeral, so her brother, Jack, drove up from Boston to stay the week. He called Murphy Funeral Home to schedule a wake, and he visited the church to set up the burial. He bought Liz and me ice cream cones and board games, and he cooked gourmet dinners sprinkled with garlic cloves and chopped parsley. He even vacuumed the house and washed all the dishes. Night after night, he sat by my mother's side, holding her hand while she crawled away into bottles of Valium and cheap red wine.

One afternoon, about three months after the funeral, I was rummaging through the hall closet when I stumbled across a flimsy card-board box filled with dusty videotapes. It was my father's horror collection, a who's who of werewolves and mad scientists and psychos wielding hacksaws. Holding that box was like hugging an old friend, and since I had no one else to talk to, I carried it upstairs when my mother wasn't looking. Hiding inside my bedroom closet, I pulled out each videotape one at a time. I spent the entire night staring at grisly box covers and reading gory plot descriptions.

After that day, I spent part of each morning in the living room, a blanket drawn to my chin while I watched *Frankenstein* and *Psycho*, or *Rosemary's Baby* and *Halloween*. I became friends with Boris Karloff and Bela Lugosi, with Peter Cushing and Christopher Lee. Instead of riding my bike around the neighborhood, I visited abandoned graveyards and the Bates Motel. I trembled through moonlit forests and musty cellars. I yearned to be Dr. Frankenstein, and one afternoon, after my mother refused to talk about my father's suicide, I ran into the garage and tried to build my own monster.

I drew sketches and diagrams, and I hoped to construct it from severed limbs I was bound to find somewhere in my neighborhood. I planned to piece it together with duct tape and wads of chewed bubble gum, and then straighten out paper clips and stick them into the body as though performing remedial acupuncture. In my moment of triumph, I would jam a fork into the creature's hand, shove the hand into an electrical socket, and re-animate my patchwork creation. It might have worked, too, but I just couldn't find anyone who was willing to donate his brain in the name of science. Plus, the woods behind my house were short on human limbs.

For the rest of the summer I ignored my mother and sister, choosing instead to hide away behind eerie music and bloodcurdling screams. Roaming that horrific landscape, I took pleasure in other people's pain and torment, satiated by fancy props and special effects. My mother, still trudging upstairs and downstairs in an alcoholic trance, simply shrugged off my viewing choices as just "another childish phase."

Channel nine used to broadcast horror films on Sunday afternoons, and so I snuck downstairs one rainy day for a three o'clock showing of Bob Clark's cult classic, *Children Shouldn't Play with Dead Things*. Low budget, it rates about a two on the shock-meter, but it scared the living hell out of me. I watched zombies crawl out of the muddy ground and rip people's heads open. They stared into the camera lifelessly, stared directly at *me*, while blood dripped from their mouths and they gorged on intestines. They scooped out brains the same way my mother eats a grapefruit.

Up until that point, I'd been amused by psychos and demons and nature run amok, and I never suffered a single nightmare, but after watching *Children Shouldn't Play with Dead Things* I became convinced that my backyard was a haven for hundreds of flesh-eating ghouls just waiting for the chance to clamber up the back porch and use our house as a rallying point for world domination. Six months passed before I was brave enough to walk downstairs in the middle of the night for a glass of water. Every thump, creak, and groan had me whirling around in dread, certain that clammy, decomposing hands would suddenly grab me by the neck and choke me to death.

Before seeing the film, my father's stories were simply an added comfort in my unsettled life, like an extra pillow or a spare blanket. But every time a zombie popped out of the ground, I realized that evil could tackle me at any moment. To prepare for these frenzied assaults, I needed to bench press Dad's stories. So I began reading books on Asian history. I tried to learn Japanese with Rosetta Stone, and I watched Jackie Chan's entire filmography. I practiced Yoga and new age meditation, and I even went tanning because my sister told me that pale ninjas make easy targets. As sure as a throwing star can rip out someone's eye, I know I am destined to become a ninja and roam the earth, much like David Carradine in the television series *Kung Fu*. Only for real.

Because of this newborn resolve to announce myself as a bona fide

East Coast ninja, my mother tried to make me see a therapist. Offended, I told her I had no need for a shrink. What's the point? Dad's stories are the only protection I need against an uncaring mom, a Mean Man roaming suburbia, and flesh-craving zombies. Yes, I'm annoyed that nobody bothers to take me seriously, but their constant ignorance only bolsters my belief that, like all great leaders, my father and I are fated to be misunderstood.

In preparation for my world-class dojo, I also plan on mastering the art of feng shui. I'm convinced that harmonizing the natural energy force of my room will aid in my ninjutsu studies. Feng shui means wind and water, two of earth's natural elements, and I honestly believe the world would be a better place if people simply moved their bed five feet to the left or pushed their dresser in front of the window. Dorm rooms are small, I know, but with proper attention and detailed maps, I believe I can shape a room that will best harness my full intellectual capabilities. I do realize that next year I'll probably have to share a room with another student, and while I hope this does not disrupt my study of feng shui, I also hope my roommate is comfortable with the fact that I am not just a student.

I am also a ninja.

6.
Rasputin of New England

Tonight is Christmas Eve, and I'm standing outside at Our Lady Star of the Sea, waiting for midnight mass to begin. Marblehead is practically deserted. There are only a few cars parked against the sidewalk, and in historic Old Town the evergreen trees are strung with extra large Christmas bulbs, their colored lights shimmering through the haze as their gnarled branches bow under the weight of winter. Weather reports predict a late-night storm, and already the flakes are as big as half dollars, blanketing the ground in glittery whiteness.

I stomp my feet to keep warm, shivering into a fleece coat as I wait for Uncle Jack to finish his fifth cigarette. We've been standing on the steps for fifteen minutes, nodding politely as people file past us into the church. The organ music drifts outside through the propped entryway, and the ground is littered with cigarette butts. My coat smells like unfiltered Camel Lites. My fingers are numb.

I blow into my gloved hands. "Come on, Uncle Jack. I'm freezing."

He takes another drag off his cigarette. "Quit whining. Mass doesn't start for seven minutes. Besides, Father Milaney always keeps us the full hour."

"You're filling my body with secondhand smoke," I say. "I'll probably lose a lung, just like Dad did."

He taps ash into the air. "No one's forcing you to stand here, champ."

"I can handle myself," I tell him, suddenly feeling like a whiny wuss. "I'm a survivor."

He laughs. "Don't talk about being a survivor until you've been divorced, fired from your job, or ridiculed for your sexual stamina. And I've endured all three, so consider me the Rasputin of New England."

"Whatever." I look up into the sky and open my mouth, tasting metallic water as snowflakes melt on the tip of my tongue. The sky looks emerald and turquoise, washed out by city lights reflected off the falling snow, and a thin sliver of moon peeks out from behind a ribbon of streaky clouds. Dozens of flakes are dissolving on my nose and cheeks, and drops of water are trickling down my chin. I'm tired and hungry, and I can't feel my toes. Right now, I'm wishing I was anyplace else but here.

Uncle Jack flicks the rest of his cigarette into the bushes. "Why don't you get into the Christmas spirit," he says, "and quit sulking like you're two-years-old."

I kick slush off the top step with the tip of my oxfords. "I hate going to church," I tell him. "I always feel like my soul is being strip searched."

"What do you have to complain about? Do you have to pay car insurance? Or health insurance?" He coughs, and pulls a crushed pack of cigarettes out of his jacket pocket. "Tell me, how many times a week do you have to buy groceries and balance your checking account?"

"Do you ever have to write essays and study for tests?" I ask him. "Do other kids ever make fun of you in the hallway and knock books out of your hand? Tell me, how many times a week do you worry about not having a girlfriend, or being alone for the rest of your life?"

"Easy there, champ. I paid my dues in high school. Just like every other guy my age who had to put up with the same exact bullshit you're dealing with now. It's called growing up." He lights another cigarette, just to piss me off. "You think Bruce Lee never worried about women? You think Chuck Norris never argued with his parents? Hell, Jesus was the Messiah and even he had to go through puberty."

I hang my head and stare off down the street. I'm really not in the mood for some moronic lecture that strings together a bunch of random thoughts on Jesus and hormones and high school, and then mashes them all together into some hodgepodge lesson that I'm supposed to apply to my own life.

Uncle Jack blows a smoke ring into the chilly air. "You need to start seeing past the end of your nose, Tim. Trust me, you won't learn the secrets of life wandering through your dumpy little high school. Or making out with some big-tittied girl at the movies." He pokes me in the chest. "You want to be the guy who educates himself in the real world, the guy who says 'What the hell am I doing, and how can I do it better?'"

"Why?"

"Because that's what Jesus did. And that's what committed, motivated men do. They persevere. They get down on their hands and knees and they carve their own niche." He drops the rest of his cigarette onto the top step. "So get off your ass, grab some common sense, and start chipping away, okay?"

And without another word he places his hand on my shoulder and steers me into the church.

69

My mother and sister are already seated in one of the back pews, scoping out the rest of the congregation and making snide remarks about fashion and etiquette. People take off their scarves and shake out their wet coats. They squeeze into the pews with elaborate twists and turns, blocking the aisles so they can wish each other a Merry Christmas. The altar boys are lighting candles, and the organist is playing *O Come All Ye Faithful*.

I glance around as people push past, dropping clumps of snow onto my shoes and wetting the bottom of my pants. Uncle Jack sits next to my mother, and I take an aisle seat next to Liz. The wooden pew is hard and uncomfortable.

My mother looks at me and mouths the word "Behave."

I nod, already bored, trying to feign interest in watching people genuflect and pull wrinkled dollar bills from their purses and wallets. Luckily, I only come to church once a year, usually on Christmas Eve when I'm feeling generous enough to let my mother drag me. I can't fault her for trying, though. Every couple of months she feels guilty and suggests we all go to church. She tries really hard to make it sound oh so exciting, like we're all going bungee jumping. But not even the threat of eternal damnation can make Sunday mass sound worthwhile. What's fun about standing in line for Christ Crispies, or shaking hands with a bunch of germy strangers who only pay me attention because they're worried about getting into heaven?

When I was six-years-old my mother made me memorize the "Our Father," "Hail Mary," and "Act of Contrition," that sonant hat trick of religious servitude. Then she bought me *The Children's Illustrated Bible*, hoping it would act as a liaison between me and the Almighty. The pages were large and shiny, but the illustrations looked like they were drawn in a kindergarten art class (a stick-figure Moses wandering through a water-color landscape).

I found the stories entertaining, kind of like sword and sandal comics, but even at six-years-old I had trouble accepting the idea that a burning bush could talk, or that a really bad thunderstorm could destroy the entire planet. It baffled me as to how Jesus could feed five thousand people with only a few loaves of bread and two measly fish, or why he would curse a fig tree just because he was hungry and cranky.

I'm not trying to slam God, but if he really is all-powerful and all-forgiving, then why didn't he save my father? If Christians pride themselves on an endless supply of guardian angels, then where the hell were my father's protectors when he put that bullet into his head? I've experienced way too much pain to believe in guardian angels. If they do exist, then mine are the laziest bastards in the universe.

While I'm fuming over God's warped sense of natural selection, Liz flips through a shabby looking hymnal, tapping her shoes against the kneeler. She won't even acknowledge me. I guess she's still pissed about her Christmas present. I bought her a FetaPet, an animal fetus preserved in a glass jar filled with formaldehyde. The choices were limitless, but in the end I selected a FetaKitten, which arrived with a red collar and a name tag that identified it as Mooshie.

There had been a lot of shouting and arguing when the UPS man delivered it to the house earlier today. I tried telling my mother it was a great pet for someone who didn't want a lot of responsibility, but obviously she wasn't in the Christmas spirit because she sent me to my room and made the UPS man take Mooshie away. I could almost hear her non-existent meows as she disappeared down the street.

I lean over toward Liz. "Are you still mad about my gift?"

"It was disgusting," she says. "Not to mention cruel and unethical."

"Chill out."

"It's a fetus, Tim. In a glass jar." She turns the hymnal upside down and drapes it over her knee. "I just redecorated my bedroom and now you want me to stick that floating blob on my bureau? Our house is not Dr. Frankenstein's laboratory."

"You don't have to walk it," I say, trying to rile her. "You don't have to feed it. It won't even shit on the carpet. If you get sick of it, you can just stick it under your bed for a few weeks, or hide it in your closet with all those expensive clothes you never wear. Seriously, Liz, how can you possibly give back a cute little kitten?"

Before she can answer, the lights dim and the entire congregation begins to sing "Hosannah in the Highest," crooning and swaying like a bunch of drunken sailors. Father Milaney proceeds down the aisle, flanked by two pimply altar boys as he lip-synchs to the music and gives everyone the sign of the cross. After wishing us a Merry Christmas, he starts going through the holy motions, some of which I remember, but none of which are interesting. The reading passages are all about shepherds and camels and starving peasants, and they're filled with quirky dialogue that makes Yoda sound like a tenured English professor. I guess they're supposed to scare people into being good, though it's hard to understand how reading about Elijah and his male pattern baldness can cause someone to praise God, light a few votive candles, and make some radical life change that typically involves a low-carb diet.

I close my eyes for a quick second while Father Milaney reads from the gospel according to someone. The entire room is hushed, and the winter wind slams against the stained-glass windows, rattling the wooden panes and whistling through cracks in the door. I'm about to take a power nap when Uncle Jack smacks me in the back of the head and almost knocks the hymnal out of my hand.

Yawning, I pick up one of the psalm books, flipping through the pages as if I'm sitting in a doctor's office and perusing the latest issue of *GQ*. When I glance up, Father Milaney has finished his reading and is now standing at the lectern, his bony hands gripping the worn sides.

"Let me be the first to wish all of you a Merry Christmas," he says, smiling. "And let me also be the first to remind you that Christmas is not just a time when families gather together to celebrate the birth of Jesus. Christmas, my friends, is a time when we also celebrate the birth of a brand new year. It is a time when God gives us the opportunity to reexamine our past mistakes. When he provides us with a new beginning."

He looks out over the entire congregation, his eyes roving from left to right. "Every year the Good Lord presents us with new friends and new moments. He hands us tough moral choices, and he challenges us with difficult decisions. But how will you respond to those challenges? Will you find the strength to persevere, or will you hide in the shadows?

"The Good Lord is testing you, my friends. He wants you to exercise patience and praise. He wants you to lean on your friends and family for moral support. And yet, how often do we cast aside these simple obligations because of our need for acknowledgement and material possessions? How often does our need to fill replace our need to give?"

Father Milaney gives us his most winning smile, and then he doesn't say anything for at least fifteen seconds, probably to ramp up the drama. "We must always remember to appreciate that which we already have. A simple message, yes, but one that we often forget. Our memory is our muscle, and we must use it to beat down fear and hesitancy. It's true that we are all guilty of neglecting the present, not because we obsess over the future, but because we agonize over the past."

I lean back and close my eyes. If Father Milaney had a main point, then I might be somewhat entertained, but right now he's just tossing random ideas into a sleepy crowd, hoping that some of us will leap up, grab a few doozies, and bring them home so we can participate in his "Heaven or Bust" program.

"...and in the book of Luke, chapter one, verse twenty-six," he continues, "God sends the angel Gabriel to Nazareth, to the Blessed Virgin Mary whereupon he tells her, 'Greetings, you who are highly favored. The

Lord is with you.' And we know that Mary was troubled, but the angel told her not to be afraid, told her she had found favor with God and would be with child. And the angel told her that the Holy Spirit would come upon her, and that the power of the Most High would overshadow her. And this is how she endured, my friends. She let the power of God embrace her. She let the power of God steer her toward love and understanding, toward the responsibility of raising a savior" He scratches the stubble on his chin. "We would do well to remember this lesson, my friends, especially on the eve of a brand new year. And we would do very well, every single day of our lives, to imitate the Virgin Mary."

Trying not to blush, I press the psalm book into my face. I can't help it, but whenever I hear the word "virgin" I have to laugh. It's childish, I know, but so is the assumption that faith-based abstinence programs actually work. If I had a healthy sex life, then I might find his comments amusing, maybe even downright hilarious, but all his ranting does is remind me that I don't have a girlfriend, and that any intimacy I might actually enjoy is strictly provided by yours truly with considerable help from my laptop and a box of tissues.

I think about the Tae-Bo girl, how she puts one hand on her hip when she's browsing through the horror section, or how she plays with her split ends whenever she walks past action and adventure. Every week I swear I'll ask her out, but whenever she walks up to the counter I just scan her membership card and stutter something about the rewards program. I've considered the possibility that one day she might stop renting exercise videos, but even that scenario can't shock my body into asking for her phone number. Like the snow outside, I know she isn't guaranteed forever, and it's only a matter of time before she melts away.

My mother leans over and taps me on the shoulder. "You might want to pay attention to this, Tim. At some point you need to pull your head out of the clouds and quit acting like player one in some schizophrenic video game full of nunchucks and ninjas."

"Whatever," I say. "This is a bunch of shit."

She leans closer. "Excuse me?"

"I said, 'I have a hunch that's it.'"

She bites her lower lip, her cheeks turning red. She looks like she's about to slap me across the face, but then she takes a deep breath and crosses her arms. "If you're not going to act civilized in church, then maybe you should wait outside."

"Sure, why not," I tell her. "It's just as cold in here as it is out there." I shove the psalm book into the rack, trying to make as much noise as possible. Then I zip up my jacket, slide out of the pew, and walk down the aisle. I don't bother to genuflect or dip my fingers into the holy water. I just charge down the aisle, push open the front door, and stumble outside into the fresh air.

By this time there are a few inches of snow on the ground, and the flakes are coming down hard. Shivering, I hide my face in a Lands' End scarf that Mom bought me last Christmas. This year she bought me a pair of wool socks, some Polo shirts, and a book entitled *The Art of Manliness: Classic Skills and Manners for the Modern Man*, which offers such helpful advice as how to deliver a kick-ass speech and start a fire without matches. Obviously, talking about guy stuff is something I should be doing with Dad, but I guess I should give her props for at least trying to look like a concerned parent, even if she thinks it's fair game to resuscitate my "Y" chromosome with discount literature purchased off Amazon. Which she tends to do during major holidays. Every Christmas we try to talk like a real family, but it's so much easier to open boxes of homemade fudge and eat slices of chocolate cream pie. I guess it hurts less to watch the Hollywood Christmas Parade, or to make detailed lists of every gift we want to return. Every opened bottle of wine is just another conversation that dies in the kitchen, slain by the corkscrew my mother carries around in her back pocket.

I've been standing outside for fifteen minutes when the front door flies open and a young woman staggers out of the church. She sits down on the top step and moans. Then she puts one hand over her forehead and the other over her abdomen.

"Are you okay?" I ask her.

"I'm cramping," she says. "I need some fresh air."

I nod as if I'm generally made aware of such issues. I try to glimpse her face, but it's dark and she's wearing a Red Sox cap pulled down to her eyebrows. A flannel scarf covers her mouth, and when she speaks her words are soft and muffled.

"How's the third act?" I ask, motioning inside.

She smiles. "No idea. I was playing Transylvania on my iPhone. I was just about to shoot the werewolf when I doubled over in the pew. Felt like someone punched me in the gut."

Her voice sounds familiar. "Do you go to Marblehead High?"

She peers at me from under her cap. "You're Tim Dimmick. The judo guy, right?"

"Ninjutsu, actually."

"Oh, so you're like a ninja?"

"Technically, yeah. I mean..." I'd like to say more, but I'm not sure if this complete stranger is ready to share my worldview. I've started to realize that everyone's sense of reality is not as finely shaded as my own. "Well, you know, it's kind of like...umm..."

Should I toss out some juicy facts about the art of stealth and the power of concealment, or should I just keep things civil and make some cheesy comment about the weather?

"It's not that big a deal," I finally tell her. "My dad just happened to meet some ninjas when he was fighting in Iraq. And he ended up...well...he became a sort of consultant."

"I didn't know there were ninjas in Iraq."

"They're branching out. Like Starbucks."

"Are you a black-belt?"

"I don't really believe in labels," I say. "But I do have a ton of different skill sets. I'm like a human Swiss army knife."

"You're quite sure of yourself, aren't you?"

"It's not ego," I tell her. "It's knowledge based on experience."

She slaps my leg. "You're funny."

That wasn't the response I had hoped for. I was shooting for admiration and awe, but I guess I should be happy that it wasn't the usual comeback: ridicule mixed with disbelief and then topped off with a splash of pity.

"I'm Mellisa," she says. "Mellisa Wright." She shakes my hand and stares at me for a couple of seconds. "So what are you doing out here? Besides freezing your ass off."

"Escaping."

She laughs. "You didn't get very far, did you?"

"It's a work in progress."

"I know how you feel," she says, both hands now pressed against her abdomen. "It's all so painfully boring. It just sounds more profound because we're sitting inside a beautiful church, jacked up on sugar cookies and singing cheesy Christmas carols."

I nod, surprised that a total stranger is interested in having an intelligent conversation with me. Lately, I can't seem to command an audience, not even with family members who are obligated to pay me some attention. It seems like whenever I start talking about myself I just end up pissing someone off. Either that or I wind up defending my father. But Mellisa isn't here to berate me or tell me that I'm wrong. She just wants to forget about her menstrual cramps.

"It's kind of exhausting, isn't it?" she says. "Being judged all the time."

I catch a snowflake on the tip of my tongue. "Sure is. That's why I'm into a more eastern spirituality."

"Meaning?"

"I'm more into Buddhist thought?"

She stretches out her legs. "How come?"

"Cause it's a way of living. It's not based on dying."

"And you think Christianity is?"

"Sure, it is."

"Why?"

"Cause the whole thing's based on Jesus Christ dying for us," I say. "It's all about having faith in what happens to you after you're dead and gone. Which is something you can't possibly imagine, regardless of what anyone tries to tell you. But that's the selling point, right? No personal responsibility. Everything is pre-ordained, set into motion with the quick flick of a switch. Nobody needs to worry because they're already covered."

"Or screwed."

I laugh. "True. I just think people would benefit more from focusing on the life they have rather than the one that's being sold to them."

"Absolutely," she says. "But I can totally understand their point of view. I mean, here's this God who supposedly loves us and is all-forgiving. What's more comforting than that? It's such a nice, warm thought. Makes everyone feel special. Helps them tread water when they're in too deep."

"So you don't believe in God?"

"No, I do," she says. "Though I severely doubt if he's anything like most of these religions say he is. Don't get me wrong, I think God cares about us, but I don't think he's nearly as concerned about what we believe as we are."

"Yeah, but don't you think that people lean on him a bit too much?" I ask her. "This easy excuse to finger point and hate? Whenever something bad happens, people immediately shout, 'Oh, God did it!' If an earthquake wipes out ten thousand people in Mexico City, people say it's because God hates margaritas and homosexuals. It's ridiculous."

"Well, of course it is," she says. "But it's equally hard to explain to someone in central Kansas, after a tornado blows through his town seven times, that God didn't destroy schools and homes because he was pissed about global warming. You'll never do it. Something that big, something that out of control, will always make people feel helpless and insignificant. That's why people fumble for answers and then sit down to create their own. And that, my friend, is what Christians call faith. It's an ointment for uncertainty."

I sit down beside her. "It's just hard for me to have faith in something I can't see."

"What about ninjas?" she asks me. "Ever seen one?"

"Uh...no."

"Then how do you know they exist?"

"Everyone knows they exist." I stare at her for a few seconds. "Wait. What's your point?"

"I'm not disputing the existence of actual ninjas, but you said your dad met some in Iraq. And obviously you've never hung out with any, so doesn't your belief in ninjas stem from having faith in your father? Sort of like a Christian's belief in God?"

"My father wouldn't lie to me," I say. "Sure, he may have exaggerated some of his stories, maybe embellished a few plot points here and there, but he had a lot of things he needed to tell me. He wasn't just doing cartwheels and performing magic tricks."

I can feel myself getting frustrated, the anger spreading inside me, growing larger and larger like an ink spot. Mellisa doesn't know a damn thing about me or my family. It must be so easy for her to sit there and critique my life, clutching her stomach as if it pains her to be so sweet and helpful.

"Don't blow a gasket," she says. "I'm just playing Devil's advocate." She brushes away a thin piece of hair that's strayed to her lips. "I think it's good to question what other people tell us, don't you? Otherwise we wouldn't be motivated to think for ourselves."

Neither one of us says anything, and after a minute I peer into her shrouded face. I can just barely detect her cocky smile, the way she holds her head high as if every word she says is without dispute. I want to knock down every single question she asks me. I want to hide behind a brick wall of childhood memories. But just when I start to open my mouth I think about my father, and all those cloudy days that he tracked into our lives like muddy footprints on a clean carpet.

I remember him shouting in the basement and cutting up his army fatigues with a pair of pruning shears. I remember one morning, in the middle of winter, when he ran down the street in his bathrobe, chasing after an intruder who had supposedly broken into the house to steal his gun collection. But most of all, I remember how he lulled me to sleep every night with a handful of stories, slinging them around my bedroom in all directions, over and over until they were garbled and patchy and soaked with whiskey.

Since his death, the truth has been hammering away at the plated door of my conscience. I've always known that there's something terrible on the other side of that door, and ninjutsu is the constant wedge that keeps it from splintering open to heap even more disappointments upon a poor, defenseless kid who only wants to be happy with a life he didn't choose.

Right at this moment I feel lost and disoriented, all these bad thoughts creeping around inside my head like a burglar. And standing on the church steps in the middle of a snowstorm, staring into a massive whiteout, all aspects of my life seem to blur together with no discernable structure or boundaries.

Mellisa stands up and wipes the snow off her pants. "It was nice chatting with you, Tim. Maybe I'll see you around, at school or wherever."

"Sure," I say, forcing a smile. "Merry Christmas."

She pats me on the back. "Cheer up. I'm sure Santa will leave you something good under the Christmas tree."

"Doubtful," I say. "I didn't ask for anything, so I'm expecting nothing."

"Think positive," she says. "Don't you believe that everything happens for a reason?"

"No, I think people create a reason for everything that happens."

She rewraps her scarf and zips up her puffy red jacket. "I hope I didn't bore you too much with my constant rambling."

"Not at all," I tell her. "It was a lot more exciting than the snooze fest inside." I smile, for real this time. "If you had a money basket, I'd definitely toss a dollar into it."

"And I'd let you, too."

As she starts to walk away, I take a step forward. "Hey, you don't think...I mean...well...you don't think the ninjas are...stupid, do you?"

She turns to face me, and for a few seconds she doesn't say anything. Then she takes my hand and squeezes it. "Tim," she says, "if the ninjas are really that important to you, then how can they be stupid?"

I stand there on the top step, not sure what to say, not even sure whether I should move forward or backward. But just when I decide to head back inside, the front doors of the church burst open with the force of a prison breakout, and the entire congregation charges headfirst into the freezing wind and snow, singing *Silent Night*.

Peering through the restless mob, I watch Mellisa muscle her way into the church. The light from the novena candles spills outside in warm yellow splotches, and the gentle organ music flows into the empty streets. She dodges her way through the swelling crowd, weaving past a frenzy of parents who rush toward their cars with sleepy faces, eager to speed home so they can tuck their children into bed and spend the rest of the night assembling expensive toys that will most likely be broken by the time Christmas dinner is over.

7.
The Meat in Youth

It's eleven thirty at night, and I'm staring at my hands. Why not? In the dim light of a halogen lamp they look so small and unfamiliar, like gloves I've swiped from the lost and found. Sitting at my desk, I lean forward to inspect each finger, starting with the bitten nail before moving down to the hairy knuckle. I scan the surface area, searching for wrinkles or liver spots, maybe small open sores that could be the onset of Ebola or Hantavirus. Every muscle spasm is a larval infestation, every pimple a threat of ringworm. So I poke, probe, and prod until I'm satisfied.

But what if I missed something?

All night long I've been thinking about death and mortality. Pathetic, I know, but this is what New Year's Eve does to me. In less than a month I'll be eighteen years old, and in less than six months I'll finish high school. Then it's off to college. U-Mass Amherst is my safety school, but I'm banking on either NYU or Northwestern. Both are top business schools in the country, and I'm hoping to secure some important contacts to help me finance my sprawling dojo in the White Mountains of New Hampshire. I need to hightail it out of this boring seaside town before I go bonkers. I want alpine huts and wide, looping trails instead of high-rise condos and steaming pavement. I want fresh country air, not filthy breezes blowing in from the dregs of Beantown.

With graduation looming, I'm hoping the laws of fate hold true. Everyone who gets bullied speeds out of town to become rich and famous while all the jocks stick around to sell real estate or work at the gas station, listening to their chain-smoking wives nag them as they sit in their tatty recliners and drink cases of Miller High Life.

Earlier tonight we ordered Chinese food, another New Year's tradition started by my father, and I couldn't wait to break open my fortune cookie and unfold that waxy strip of paper. Lately, I've been looking for positive affirmations, something to bring the surrounding landscape into a sharper focus, and I'm not above getting it from crispy cookies that look more like sickle cells than tiny vessels of infinite wisdom.

It read: YOU SHALL SOON MAKE LONG, OVERDUE PERSONAL

DECISION.

Granted, that's a fairly vague statement, but since I know there will be tons of important choices to make in the upcoming year, I'm wondering which earth-shattering event the fortune cookie is referring to. Selecting a respectable college, going to the stupid prom, or maybe asking out the Tae-Bo girl?

Of course, Mom had to pop my excitement with one of her needling comments, explaining that the fortune will only come true if I eat the cookie while the paper is still inside it. But I think that's complete bullshit. If I don't know what my fortune is, then how will I know if it comes true?

Maybe it's the MSG ramping up my adrenaline, but I keep thinking about my hopes and dreams, all of them unfolding before me like a pocket map, so many lines running in so many different directions. I'm anxious to unload all this potential I've been carrying, but sometimes I get scared that I'll be alone for the rest of my life, doomed to be some old man in a diner that everyone stares at and pities. I'm terrified I'll be a complete failure at everything I do, and that I won't live up to my father's expectations.

And then I realize that every year slips by faster than the previous one, and this thought depresses me even more. I probably have ten years left before my joints start to stiffen and little gray hairs sprout up on my already receding hairline. I need to make a difference while I'm still capable of forward motion. A ninja shouldn't break a hip trying to slide down an embankment. It's like Shakespeare said in some play he wrote. "A man loves the meat in his youth that he cannot endure in his age," which basically means that after a certain amount of time your body starts to fall apart like an old car that's been rusting in the junkyard.

Bottom line: I can keel over at any moment. I could ride my bike down Main Street and get plowed by a Mack truck, or I could eat dinner at Stonehenge Tavern and succumb to food poisoning. That's why this morning I paid a visit to www.deathclock.com and discovered that I probably won't die until Thursday, January 7th, 2075. Plus, my BMI is 22.

Then, after lunch, I researched cryonics, which is the process of freezing bodies after death. The current plan is to thaw me out in the future once technology finally catches up to all these science-fiction movies. That, or I'll be harvested for my DNA. Since I'm expecting to do great things, I figure my DNA will fetch a hefty price. At least among the intellectual elite.

I surfed the Internet and found four companies that will freeze my body. After deliberating for an hour, which mostly involved shaking my Magic 8-Ball, I settled on Alcor Life Extension Foundation, a non-profit organization in Scottsdale, Arizona. The price tag is $200,000, but they'll freeze my whole body, not just my head or torso. They also preserve the bodies in liquid nitrogen, which means that if the electricity goes out, I won't end up on the floor as a big gooey puddle.

I'm trying to get up the courage to ask my mother if she'll foot the bill, but she's been zoned out all day on the couch in the den. Any minute now, she'll call me downstairs to watch the ball drop in Times Square, though I'd rather lie on my bed and search my arms and legs for scabies. Every year we sit in silence, watch the crowds whoop and cheer, wish each other a Happy New Year, and then I creep away to bed while she pulls a bottle of wine from the folds of the couch and greets the New Year in much the same state she spent the previous one: plastered and depressed.

She usually tries making a top ten list, but passes out somewhere between numbers five and eight. The first few are total clichés: "Exercise More," "Floss Daily," and "Quit Smoking." I wonder if she actually thinks about them, or if she scribbles them down just to feel like another link in the chain of public hysteria. I'm hoping for one that reads "Be Nicer to Tim," but since I'm leaving for college next fall she probably figures there are more important resolutions to prioritize and then ignore.

I decide to create my own list, so I open my desk drawer and pull out a piece of notebook paper. I made some bold predictions last year, but maybe I didn't concentrate hard enough because no one in my family ever came through for me.

I sharpen one of my black warrior pencils and roll out a kink in my neck. Then I stare down at the white-lined sheet, trying to think of ten people who make a difference in my life.

Or are supposed to, anyway.

1. MY MOTHER
Last Year's Ranking: 2
Remains distraught over my father's suicide (almost ten years ago), but finally grasped the importance of live family members after long sessions with her therapist. She's still coasting on that life insurance money my grandparents left her after they both had heart attacks at their first Pilates class, Grandpa during and Grandma after. Went back to work as an accountant because soap operas were depressing, which forced her to abandon her three cocktail-hours every afternoon rule. When I told her my New Year's resolution was to exercise more, she suggested I grout the kitchen floor and clean out the shed. Says she wants to change her image, which could be the onset of a midlife crisis. Look for her to be more

"open" and "understanding" in 2014.

Pro: Actually let me drive her BMW (though all I did was back it out of the garage).

Con: Has started watching "A Makeover Story" on TLC.

2. MY FATHER

Last Year's Ranking: *1*

Slipped a notch since he pulled a no-show during the séance a few months back. I thought he might be haunting the upstairs bathroom until my mother convinced me that all the bangs and moans might just be El Niño fucking with a Santa Ana wind. Nevertheless, Dad continues to get props for befriending ninjas in Iraq, even if no tape recording or photo documentation exists. His presence permeates the entire house, yet starting a conversation about him is as hard as mastering a sacred Tibetan chant. Still, anticipate my mother finally dusting off her photo albums and giving me a history lesson.

Pro: He always did like spirits.

Con: As long as he could drink them out of a bottle.

3. LIZ

Last Year's Ranking: *4*

Got some press coverage after performing the Heimlich on that choking toddler in the supermarket. Still the most popular girl in school, especially now that she's lost her virginity to a bloodsucking freak. Has finally accepted her dyslexia as a congenital condition, but still transposes the numbers on her caller ID. When she informed me that Walt Disney was dyslexic, I told her his real name was Retlaw Yensid. Liz insists she's interested in politics and humanity, but said the same thing about the environment and then got fined for littering in the park. Look for her to run for student council so she can delegate and bitch at school like she does at home.

Pro: Reluctantly loaned me five bucks so I could buy a used copy of Eric Van Lustbader's classic novel *The Ninja*.

Con: Doesn't even know where Romania is on a map.

"Timothy," my mother shouts from downstairs. "Come watch the ball drop."

Putting on a T-shirt, I notice a mole on my chest that looks like the first stage of skin cancer. As I walk downstairs, I stab at it with my finger, twisting it around and rubbing the grainy texture. Could it be a birthmark? Or maybe a fungus? I'll have to measure it every day and see if it gets any bigger.

I'm so engrossed in the mole that I trip entering the living room and bang my shin against the coffee table.

My mother laughs. "Easy there, Frankenstein."

I sit on the couch and check the rest of my body, doing another sweep of all vital areas. Now I'm worried. My heart races and I feel a heat flash, which causes my skin to turn red, which scares me even further and initiates a scratching marathon that begins at my feet and ends with my mother smacking my hand away.

"Tim," she says, "are you doing cocaine?"

"No, why?"

"I read that cocaine addicts think insects are crawling under their skin, so they scratch and scratch until their skin becomes infected with sores."

"I think it's a mole," I say. "But I want to be sure. What if it's skin cancer?"

"It's not, okay? Trust me."

"But how do you know?"

"Because I'm a mother, alright?"

I grab some pistachios off the coffee table and crack them open, dumping the shells into her overflowing ashtray. She hates it when I do that. "Where's Liz?" I ask her.

My mother lights up a cigarette and blows a smoke ring into the air. "Your sister is at a party. With Emil."

Emil, Romania's answer to Leonardo DiCaprio. The first time he came over I asked him to stand in front of a mirror, just to be sure. My sister says he's cultured. So is bacteria.

"A party! What gives, Mom? You never let me go to any parties when I was a sophomore."

"You were never invited to any."

"Whatever. At least you know she'll be home before the sun comes up."

My mother shoots me a disapproving look. "Leave Emil alone. Your sister is very happy." She takes another drag off her cigarette. "Besides, he gets her out of the house, which means I don't have to listen to you two bicker all night long."

I move away from the cloud of smoke. "Why don't you quit? You know I have asthma. My lungs are probably black and slimy from all your Marlboros." I cough. "See, I'm already having difficulty breathing."

"Don't be dramatic, Tim."

"Dad had lung cancer. What happens if you get it, too?"

She blows another smoke ring into the air. "I'll be more appreciative if I survive. Your father just viewed it as a stay of execution."

I grab another handful of pistachios. "So what's your wish for the new year, Mom?"

"Over the counter Xanax," she says.

"Have you ever heard of addiction?" I ask her.

"Have you ever heard of children?"

I ignore her and continue my medical examination. My legs appear fine, but I see a few flakes on my arm that could be either eczema or the result of too much scratching. I lift my arm to my nose and sniff. I read somewhere that a strong, pungent odor, not unlike burnt bacon, can sometimes be the result of cancer cells. But there's no oozing pus, and no red welts, so it might just be that I need to cut my fingernails.

"Will you stop squirming around," my mother says. "Jesus Christ! You're a poster boy for Ritalin." She lights another cigarette and increases the volume on the television. The screams from Times Square are deafening. Everywhere I look, people are hugging and kissing and drinking cheap beer out of huge plastic cups. Their shouts are all garbled, just quick blasts of frigid air, and their red noses shine like Rudolph's in the glare of all the camera lights.

"Your father and I spent New Year's there, once," she says. "In Times Square. Right on the corner of Forty-Fifth and Broadway. It was so cold that night. Your father wore this huge bearskin coat that Jack bought him for Christmas. I had to huddle inside that thing for almost three hours, freezing my ass off."

She laughs. "The fur tickled my nose, and I kept sneezing all over your father's flannel shirt. At the end of the night I couldn't even feel my toes. Temperature must have been close to zero. I had to go to the bathroom so bad I peed in a cup and threw it in a garbage can."

"Was this before you were married?"

"No. It was right after he got back from Iraq. He wanted to do something special, so I suggested Times Square, which was an absolute nightmare. One million people stuffed inside a mile-long radius. I was a little worried about how he might react in such a giant crowd, but if it bothered him, the man never showed it. He was still the same silly bastard I fell in love with the day we met at Old Silver Beach."

"Dad could always make me laugh," I tell her, and suddenly I remember him sitting around the dinner table, cracking jokes until Liz and I laughed so hard the milk dribbled out of our noses. Until my sides hurt so much I thought I was going to throw up.

"Earlier that day," she says, "he bought us matching flasks at some trinket store in Manhattan, and before we left the hotel he made a batch of White Russians, and, boy, were they strong. We drank 'em all night long, singing and toasting and swaying with the crowd. Everyone was drunk and wishing each other a Happy New Year, patting each other on the back as if we were all best friends." She crushes her cigarette into the ashtray and leans back, shaking her head. "The future looked so different then," she says, her voice breaking. "We thought we were catching the sunrise."

4. THE TAE-BO GIRL
Last Year's Ranking: 3
It's been over a year, but I still want to climb over the counter whenever she saunters into the video store. Her spandex outfit makes me yearn for the softcore Skinemax section, but instead I've started learning Tae-Bo during my ten-minute breaks. Last November she thanked me for erasing five months worth of late fees, and then she actually waved goodbye. Plus, she drives a Mazda, which means she understands the importance of Asian consumerism. Has a habit of not making eye-to-eye contact, but her tangle of brunette hair looks great sweaty, and those labored breaths drive me into a sexual frenzy. In the next year, look for her to finally introduce herself and then blush when I ask her to dinner.
Pro: Has said, "You're cute."
Con: She wasn't talking to me.

5. UNCLE JACK
Last Year's Ranking: 5
Got extra respect for wearing a T-shirt to Thanksgiving dinner reading "I Hump on a First Date." Works in Boston as a cook at Magnolias Restaurant, but has yet to offer me a free meal. Says the spicy Cajun food gets him through the long cold winters. As my mother's only brother, he earns the right to tease her about all that money she spent on Liz's plastic surgery. He's pretty much the only male figure in my life, but he's always blindsiding me with cheesy advice that insults my intelligence ("Never fry bacon naked"). He got into some legal trouble last year with that underage girl, but

made a solid comeback with his best friend's wife. Bonus: He hates Emil.

Pro: He settled out of court.

Con: "She looked 18!"

6. WYNN

Last Year's Ranking: *8*

Gained some ground after admitting that *Fist of Fury* is a pretty decent flick, especially the end scene when Bruce Lee delivers an awesome flying kick that knocks Suzuki out of the room. Though skeptical of the Asian persuasion, he almost convinced me that he'd seen a ninja in his backyard, but it turns out he was just tripping on acid. Still, his detailed description of how the ninja glided across his lawn and disappeared into the bushes was spot on. Despite the constant barrage of "your mother" jokes, he's actually quite sensitive. He understands my obsession with the Tae-Bo girl, but warns me that restraining orders can be a pain in the ass. Look for him to finish writing his screenplay sometime next summer, but continue working at the video store with a heightened sense of apathy.

Pro: Just got his first raise.

Con: After two years.

On TV, the announcers broadcast the last few minutes of 2013. A live band is onstage, screaming into the crowd as electric guitars slash through scraps of colored confetti. Ryan Seacrest is waltzing around with his microphone, interviewing actors and musicians, and now Dick Clark pops up for his obligatory cameo, smiling from ABC headquarters while he wishes everyone a Happy New Year.

"Poor, Dick Clark," I say. "He looks like nine miles of bad road."

"Someday you'll be old, too," she tells me. "You'll have wrinkles and arthritis and angina, and you won't be able to roll over without slipping a disc in your back."

My mother is such a buzzkill. It's bad enough knowing that death is inevitable without having her remind me in the midst of a national celebration. Most kids my age are scared of rejection or commitment, but I'm scared shitless of the Grim Reaper, and not just because he hides his skeletal face and carries a scythe.

I'm pretty sure my phobia started when I was five-years-old, on a hazy afternoon in August when I was swimming in my grandparents' in-ground pool. We'd gone to the Cape for a family vacation, and Mom had convinced Dad to come along for the trip. He was already unraveling by that point, but my mother's voice, so soft and tender, carved his heart like a cow into rib roasts. The whole time we were at my grandparents' house, from the moment we stepped out of the car until the moment we sped away, he acted the perfect gentleman. He smiled, cleared the dishes off the supper table, and spoke short cordial phrases like a proper son-in-law.

That particular afternoon, my father was golfing with Gramps, and Liz was shopping with Grandma. My mother and I were lazing around the pool. I was splashing in the water. She was tanning in a lounge chair. I'd spent the better part of three days inside that enormous pool. Having recently watched *The Wizard of Oz*, I honestly believed that as long as I lingered near some form of water, the Wicked Witch of the West could never capture me. Lying in bed at night, I'd collect saliva in my mouth, always hopeful that I could spit in her face if she snuck into my room.

Not being tall enough to reach the pool floor with my feet, I wore my "buddy," a white Styrofoam bubble that I clipped around my waist with a bright blue belt. My buddy made me look like a mini Quasimodo, and it scratched red welts into my skin, but that was totally okay. Awkward and clunky, bulky and itchy, it was fully responsible for my life once I entered the water.

I'd been swimming in the pool all morning, thrashing around like a lunatic and making loud guttural noises, slapping the water as hard as I could with the palms of my hands. My mother kept reminding me that such behavior was inappropriate during pool time.

"What if you were really drowning?" she asked me. "What if nobody came to help you because they thought you were joking?"

My response: a loud waterlogged scream followed by a long plume of water that shot out my mouth and splashed onto the concrete next to her lounge chair. I laughed, flailed my arms in every direction, and made a ridiculous face as though I'd been shot in the chest.

My mother shook her head and continued reading the newest issue of *People*, abandoning her "Don't Cry Wolf" speech for the spoils of celebrity gossip.

When Gramps and my father arrived home, I leapt out of the water, cast off my buddy, and ran across the lawn to greet them. After a piggyback ride and bear-hug, I sprinted back through the wooden gate and charged toward the water with such speed that my feet barely touched the hot concrete. I dove into the shallow end of the pool and executed a perfect cannonball. It was only in mid-air that I realized I had forgotten to strap my buddy back on. I sank straight to the bottom and my feet hit the pool floor. Instinctively, I pushed up with my toes. When my head broke the surface, I sucked in as much air as possible, gurgled out a half-choked scream, and sank beneath the water again.

The last time I went under, my knees hit the tiled floor. Then the world went black. My lungs burned, and my nose stung from the chlorine. I tried to cough, and swallowed water. While my mother read her magazine, I lay at the bottom of the pool, curled into the fetal position like a dead bug on a windowsill. This sudden hush must have prompted her to glance up a few seconds later, only to find me lying motionless in the shallow end. She dove in and carried me to the top step, administering CPR until I coughed up water.

For the next two months I wore my buddy constantly. Whether at the dinner table or in bed, I clasped it around my waist, holding onto the frayed straps like they were umbilical cords. My buddy became my protector, with the reasoning that as long as I wore it I'd be impervious to harm. But when I broke my arm two months later while climbing an oak tree in the back yard, I ripped it off and threw it into the trash.

I never swam in that pool again.

Like the Ghost of Christmas Past, this memory revisits me every New Year's Eve, creeping into my thoughts like really tenacious ivy. And whenever I think of death, I remember the vinyl lining on the pool floor, as soft and smooth as the inside of a seashell. I remember the terror and confusion as my mouth and nose filled up with water and I struggled to rise to the surface. I remember my mother's screams, distorted and metallic, sinking down to me in sharp bursts. And this last burst explodes with such intensity that I nearly jump off the sofa, my ears ringing and my heart pounding as I realize that Mom has unloaded the champagne cork into one of the family portraits on top of the TV center.

She pours a glass of Korbel and hands it to me. "Drink up, Tim. Not much longer before another year goes bye-bye."

"I don't want another year."

"Don't be silly," she says. "Young people want everything. That's why it's called being young. You just need to take some initiative and quit moping around the house. Otherwise you'll wind up as some forty-year-old loser who sits in his mother's basement and watches old reruns of *Bonanza* every night." She lights another cigarette. "But don't worry, sweetie. I'm sure that once you unlock the mysteries of the universe you'll finally become this great warrior who dropkicks evil with throwing stars and nunchucks."

"Stop mocking me, Mom. I'm a ninja. When will you get that?"
"I'm not mocking you, honey. I'm doting."

7. SADAKO TAKANO
Last Year's Ranking: *Unranked*
My first Asian girlfriend, and still holds a special place in my heart, even if she did dump me over the Internet. I'd hoped her silence was the result of an ill-fated accident involving a pair of chopsticks, but deep down I knew she ate with a fork. I keep trying to chase down love, and I still have dating options (basically any woman who hasn't met me yet), but how can you ever really know someone? Although Sadako taught me that love is a harsh mistress, I know that someday I will find my special Kunoichi (female ninja).
Pro: Supplied more whack off material than a double issue of *Asian Babes.*
Con: I'm pretty sure I have carpal tunnel in my right hand.

8. THE NINJA
Last Year's Ranking: 9
With the enormous popularity of feng shui, look for ninjas to appear in film and television as well as music, poetry, and the occasional minimalist photo. The Iraq conflict continues to be a thorn in America's side, so anticipate Uncle Sam's use of the ninja as a covert spy, although any and all inquiries will be hushed up by The State Department. By summer, expect a ninja exhibit at the Guggenheim, a *Shogun* marathon on TNT, and a bumper sticker that says DON'T F**K WITH NINJAS. More will follow, but be patient, grasshopper. Be patient.
Pro: Crouching Tiger, Hidden Dragon.
Con: Cheerleader Ninjas.

9. ME
Last Year's Ranking: 7
Look for me to channel my energy more constructively in 2014. So far I've been unlucky with the ladies, but in the next year I plan to pursue a woman who speaks English and shares the same zip code. Liz says I'm depriving a village somewhere of an idiot, and Mom seems to think I'm self-absorbed, but neither of them are grappling with greatness, so what the hell do they know? I guess I need to put my priorities in order before I graduate high school, which means

more meditation and less Asia Carrera videos. If I can be stealthy as ninja in jungle, then look for me to unearth secret of my father's past and become warrior he always dreamed I'd become.

Pro: This is my moment. I can feel it.

Con: Didn't I say the same thing last year?

On television I watch the crowd cheer as the final sixty seconds of 2013 disappear forever. "Fifty-nine, fifty-eight, fifty-seven, fifty-six!" It's the most depressing sound I've ever heard, and in another year I'll have to hear it all over again.

I stare at the crowd and wonder how many of those people will be dead in a year. Diseases. Murders. Accidents. Suicides. What would all those people do differently if they knew they had less than three hundred and sixty-five days left to live?

I drink some more champagne. "Do you ever think about death, Mom?"

"Why?" she says. "No point in egging it on."

"But aren't you scared of dying? Of not knowing what happens after you take your last breath?" I sound like a broken record, and I pretty much feel like one, too, but this is what New Year's Eve does to me.

My mother doesn't say anything, and I'm wondering if I said something to upset her. Then she turns to me, and I see tears in her eyes. She places her hand on top of mine and says to me, in a choked voice, "Tim, the death of your father remains so hurtful that only my own death will bring closure."

I lean forward and stare at the wall, trying to choke down the lump in my throat. I try swallowing a sip of champagne, but I gag and it comes out my nose, a twenty-four proof nasal douche.

All these years I assumed my mother was past grief. I assumed she didn't talk about my father because she wanted to spite me.

The ball reaches its descent and the crowd explodes in cheers. "2014" flashes across the television screen in bright neon letters while confetti rains down in thick clusters, mixing together with the steady snowfall. All across Times Square people laugh and shake hands and hold each other tight, waving to the camera as the endless possibilities of a brand new year bring them closer together.

I want to yell, "What the fuck are you so happy about? Go check your bathrooms for dead fathers before you utter another drunken phrase."

Mom wipes her eyes and pours herself another glass of Korbel.

I sink back into the couch, and on TV Cal Worthington sells used cars at discount prices. "A brand new Ford F-150 at below sticker price!"

"Happy New Year, Tim," she says, chugging the rest of her champagne.

I swallow hard, the roar of the crowd still buzzing in my ears. "Happy New Year, Mom."

8.
A Drunk and Stormy Night

Today is my eighteenth birthday, and I don't think there's any possibility of staying sober tonight. I'm hanging out in the living room, waiting for Wynn to arrive with a case of whichever beer is currently on sale. I have the entire house to myself because Mom and Liz drove into Boston for the night, and they won't be back until midnight. They're meeting Uncle Jack for dinner at Magnolias, and then they have tickets for some opera that's supposed to be cathartic. Before she left, Mom cornered me in the kitchen and expressed her complete trust in me. Then she lectured me for twenty minutes on rules and respect.

"Normally, I wouldn't leave you alone in the house, Tim. Especially because there's lots of flammable material. But it's your eighteenth birthday, and...well...I feel like in the past few weeks we've really started to build a solid relationship."

"That's gross, Mom. You make it sound like we're dating."

"Liz and I will be back by midnight," she said, "so I expect everything to be cleaned up by the time we get home. Trash picked up. Music turned off. Call my cell if you have any problems. The first aid card is on the refrigerator, and the fire extinguisher is under the sink. And please don't try any ninja moves. I don't want to come home and find police tape blocking the doorway."

From outside in the driveway my sister honked the horn. Not once or twice, but a steady stream that quickly became annoying. You'd think that wearing a three-thousand dollar beak would make her grateful. Even on my birthday she's still trying to be the center of attention.

"Have fun tonight." Mom kissed my cheek, and I blushed. I couldn't tell if she was worried about me, or worried about her priceless objet d'arts scattered throughout the house. Either way, she seemed to be showing genuine concern.

Some might take it as highly suspicious behavior.

Others might take it as a positive sign.

I couldn't take it at all, so I headed into the living room to wait for the beer.

At five o'clock I hear a car door slam. I open the front door to find Wynn carrying a case of Coors Light. Standing behind him is a girl I've never met, holding a bottle of Smirnoff.

"Happy birthday, Tim!" He trudges into the house, wipes his feet on the mat, and hurries into the kitchen before I can even say hello. The girl walks inside and takes off her jacket, which she hands to me as if I'm a doorman at the Ritz Carlton.

I toss it onto the back of the coat rack where it slides off the hook and lands on the floor. "Um...hey. How's it going?"

Wynn comes out of the kitchen and throws me a beer. He's already opened one for himself. "Tim, this is my friend, Stormy." He puts his arm around a buxom blonde with long curly hair, a Medici nose, and freckles that look like Iroquois war paint.

"Happy birthday," Stormy says, shaking my hand. "It's nice to meet you." She's wearing purple jeans, a purple blouse, purple eye shadow, and purple lipstick. She looks like a hypothermia victim.

"So, Tim," she says, holding up the bottle of vodka, "I hear you're quite the party animal."

I give Wynn a dirty look.

"That's right!" he yells, punching me on the arm. "It's not a party unless something gets broken or somebody gets naked."

As if agreeing with him, Stormy twirls around and shakes her hips. Then, while I'm trying not to stare at her ass, she grinds her crotch into my leg and says, "Will you be my lusting crush of a man, Tim?"

"Sure," I say, directing her toward the kitchen. "I'm game."

She caresses my cheek and hurries down the hallway to make herself a drink.

Wynn sidles up next to me. "So? What do you think of Stormy?"

I twist the cap off my beer and chug half of it. "She's a little hottie. How did you two meet?"

"Over the Internet. While I was doing research for *Fetus Dreams*."

"Are you dating her?"

"Nope. She's as single as Kraft cheese."

"How old is she? Where does she live? Does she have a boyfriend?"

"Whoa." He pats me on the back. "All questions will be answered in an orderly fashion. For now, just relax, drink your beer, and enjoy this intimate play date."

"Intimate?"

"Yeah, it means informal warmth or privacy of a very personal nature."

"I know what it means."

"It's your birthday, the big one-eight, so lighten up and enjoy your gift." He winks at me. "Which is nonrefundable, I might add."

I'm about to take a large sip of beer, but the bottle misses my mouth completely. Coors Light splashes down my chin and stains the front of my Hattori Hanzo T-shirt. "Wait a second!" I glance down the hallway. "Are you telling me she's a prostitute?"

"Don't be insulting, Tim. They're called women of independent means. In fact, I've been thinking of writing a screenplay about a..."

"Great," I say. "My eighteenth birthday is a made for TV movie."

He takes a swig of beer and puts his arm around me. "I put some serious thought into this. And she was not cheap, my friend."

"Serious thought? You drove into Boston and gift-wrapped a purple hooker."

"First off, I did not drive into Boston. I looked up an escort service in the yellow pages. And I've heard this is the Tiger Woods of escort services."

"From who?"

"From an Internet site. But it's a reliable one. They do all their own graphics."

"What if she has a disease?"

"She doesn't. I already asked her."

"Are you delusional? She's a fucking hooker. Do you really think she's going to open up and admit that she has herpes? She could be dropping syphilis all over the kitchen floor for all we know."

Wynn finishes his beer and puts the empty bottle on my mother's curio chest. "Your imagination needs to lose a few pounds."

"This is supposed to be a quiet birthday party. Not an orgy where we slather each other with baby oil."

"Technically, that's called a Russian Salad Party."

I chug the rest of my beer and stare off down the hallway. "So why are you here? Don't you think it's a little awkward if I'm unwrapping my gift and you're standing around with your thumb up your ass?"

"Actually, I was kind of hoping I could play Xbox while you're upstairs taking care of business."

Just then Stormy returns with two more beers, a bowl of Doritos, and a large vodka tonic that's sloshing around inside one of Mom's domino martini, black stem cocktail glasses.

Wynn and I each take another beer, and then we all move into the living room. Wynn sits on the couch, shuffling through a stack of Xbox games, while Stormy finds the stereo and turns on the classic rock station. She sinks into the loveseat and throws her feet over the arm of the chair. I sit on the hassock and try not to stare at her boobs.

I'm torn between wanting to have sex tonight, but also conscious of the fact that leading a hooker into my bedroom isn't exactly a moral accomplishment. Would I feel sleazy afterwards? Would I be contributing to prostitution as a nationwide problem, or would I be extending financial aid to a nice girl who probably needs a few extra bucks for rent? I try telling myself that Stormy is probably a student at Tufts or Harvard. She probably works as an escort to pay for all her textbooks, or maybe to send money back home to a single parent who's dying of cancer.

She says, "Tim, when you first saw me, did you imagine what I might look like naked?"

"Yes," I tell her, "but only the top half." Which is true.

Wynn grabs a handful of Doritos. "I'm a firm believer that you can respect and admire women while mentally undressing them."

She runs her tongue around the rim of the martini glass. "Do you have a girlfriend, Tim?"

"Well...I'm kind of working on that," I tell her. "It's an ongoing project."

She leans forward, and my eyes trail down her blouse. "And what does she do, this mysterious woman?"

"I'm hoping me, but for the moment just Tae-Bo."

"So you haven't slept with her yet?"

I blush and take another sip of beer. "I don't like to kiss and tell."

Wynn laughs. "You don't kiss, Tim, so you have nothing to tell."

I flip him off, mostly because he's right. I've only kissed one girl, and that was Colleen Kohn, sophomore year. We'd been seeing each other for about a month, and I'd heard from my sister, who heard from her best friend, who heard from Colleen's best friend, that Colleen really wanted me to kiss her. Apparently five kiss-less dates were beginning to wear thin, and she was developing some sort of complex. So I took her by the hand one afternoon and led her into my back yard. The sun was just beginning to set behind the evergreen trees, and a sprinkler was throwing arcs of water onto the flower garden. I steered her behind the shed and we sat down on an old sawhorse. I cupped her face in my hands like I'd seen heroes do in the movies, and I placed my mouth over hers like a suction cup. Our tongues connected in a sea of saliva, and I moved it around in every direction as the sprinkler dotted our faces with drops of water. At one point I nibbled her lower lip just to say I'd done it.

96

When our tongues collapsed from exhaustion, and we finally came up for air, I pulled away to find Colleen staring past me with a vacant look on her face, bored. She didn't say anything. She just got up and walked home. The next day she dumped me.

Stormy holds up her hands the way directors do when framing a shot, her fingers forming a perfect square as she moves them toward my face for a close-up. "You're such a handsome man, Tim. You should call up this Tae-Bo girl and ask her to dinner. Girls love it when a man takes the initiative. It's sexy, shows confidence."

I can't tell if Stormy is flirting with me because she really likes me, or because Wynn paid her in cash to like me. Still, I can't deny that I'm attracted to her. In fact, knowing that she's a hooker is a huge turn on. I'll bet she looks delicious in fishnet stockings and crotchless panties. She's most likely a skilled lover, and I definitely want a girl that takes control, whether it's unfettered lovemaking or raucous, wall-to-wall spanking. And while she seems like a super nice girl, I'll probably double wrap my penis just to be on the safe side.

Stormy pulls a Maraschino cherry out of the empty martini glass and eats it, squeezing the fruit between her perfectly straight teeth until it pops and sticky, red juice dribbles down her chin. Then she ties the stem into a knot with her tongue, staring at me the entire time while she swings her foot in slow circles and hums along to Steely Dan.

I clap, and she holds the stem high in the air.

"All you need is a talented tongue and a lot of practice." She drops the stem into Mom's ashtray. "What about you, Tim? Any bragging rights you want to exercise?"

"I have ninja tongue," I tell her. "I can break a board in half with this bad boy." I stick out my tongue and curl it for emphasis.

"Good to know." She walks over to the stereo. "What do you say we slip in some mood music and get our sexy on?"

Wynn leans forward and lowers his voice. "Way to raise the bar, dumbass. Twenty bucks says that tongue comment comes back to haunt you. I'll bet you sprain it going down on her."

Stormy starts dancing in front of the stereo, flipping through a mess of CDs strewn across the top of the entertainment center. Wynn looks at me and motions toward Stormy, mouthing something I can't understand while he spanks the air with the palm of his hand, spilling half his beer all over the couch. I figure Mom won't notice. She's dropped enough drinks to pickle it twenty times over.

I rest my beer between my legs. I hear heavy drums and bass. It's

The Gold Experience, my favorite Prince album. I start playing the air guitar while Stormy stands over me, screaming the lyrics. "I'd rather do you after school like some homework. Ah... am I gettin' you hot? I'd rather wait 'til everyone's fast asleep, then do it in the kitchen on the table top." Her long hair swishes through the air, her belly button winking at me as her blouse ripples up and down.

As soon as I finish my beer, Stormy gives me another. She runs her hand through my hair and returns to the love seat. Sipping her vodka tonic, she kicks off her black boots to reveal the sexiest pair of fishnet stockings I have ever seen.

Of course, they're purple. Jackpot.

She watches me, perhaps expecting that I'll take her hand and escort her upstairs to my secret love lair. Right now I have a hard-on as big as the Washington Monument. I know Wynn is wondering when I'll complete the transaction, but I'm nervous as hell that I won't deliver an Oscar-nominated performance. Some guys can last as long as a feature film. I can barely make it through the Jeopardy theme song.

Wynn collects the empty bottles. He grabs Stormy's martini glass. "I'm making another beer run. Anyone want anything?" He gives me a stern look and nudges me with his elbow, almost tripping over the ottoman as he rushes out of the room. If he keeps pestering me, I'll Kung Pow him with one of the sofa cushions.

I turn toward Stormy, watching as she lip synchs to Prince, her purple toes curled over the arm of the love seat. Her whole aura is relaxing me, although it's probably just the cheap beer I'm pouring down my throat. I tell myself that ninjas probably sleep with hookers all the time, especially given the shortage of beautiful women in the jungle. Since ninjas live solitary lives, they must find it difficult to develop intimate relationships. Instead, they experience fleeting moments of passion. They scavenge quick glances, and relish the occasional, lingering touch. Plus, ninjas don't carry iPhones when they're on a mission, so they can't watch anime porn while running across rooftops.

According to my sister's newest issue of *Cosmo*, engaging in an active sex life helps reduce stress, burn calories, boost the immune system, and build self-esteem. And considering how often ninjas engage in espionage and hand-to-hand combat, and sneak into misty valleys to infiltrate hidden fortresses, it makes sense that they would want their bodies to be in tip-top shape. Which means that in addition to a daily regimen of push-ups and power smoothies, ninjas must cultivate their chakras with frequent interludes of S-E-X.

Bottom line: If I don't want to be a flabby ninja, then I need to respect my body. And if it's telling me to rumble between the sheets, then who am I to argue?

Wynn returns with four more beers and another vodka tonic that he hands to Stormy. He puts my beers on the coffee table and flops down on the couch. "I feel sorry for people who don't drink," he says, "because when they wake up in the morning, that's the best they're going to feel all day."

Stormy stands up. "Come on, birthday boy." She grabs my hand and hauls me off the hassock. "How about we go upstairs and find a dark, comfy corner?"

I burp and open another beer, knowing that I couldn't make a sensible decision right now if my life depended on it.

Wynn turns on the TV and grabs one of the Xbox controllers. I pocket an extra beer and follow Stormy upstairs. When we get to the top of the landing, I automatically turn left. But she turns right and tugs on my arm, leading the charge into my mother's bedroom.

"This isn't my room," I tell her.

"Oh, that's even better." She closes the door and turns on a small lamp beside the bed. "It's more kinky, more dangerous."

She pushes me onto the waterbed and I sink into the calico down comforter. I take the beer out of my pocket and place it on the nightstand. Then I chug the one I'm still holding. When she's not looking, I scoot over to the edge of the bed and hold the bottle up to the light, checking my reflection to make sure I look somewhat presentable. I narrow my eyes and mess up my hair, trying for the bad boy image, but then realize this whole affair is strictly a business deal, so Stormy probably doesn't give a damn what I look like.

She gets on top of me and runs a hand through my tangled hair. She kisses me on the lips, sliding her tongue between my teeth. Her tongue is warm and confident, twisting around mine in slow and steady thrusts. She's only the second girl I've ever kissed, and I have to smile at the fact that in the past thirty seconds my sexual history has doubled.

"Have you ever been to Fenway Park?" I ask her.

She bites my neck. "Do you want to have sex, or do you want to talk?"

"Chatting is the new foreplay," I tell her. Actually, I'm stalling because I'm trying really hard to remember everything I've ever read about sex. I'm trying to recall pressure points, massage techniques, and obscure positions. Stormy has probably slept with hundreds of men, and I don't want to embarrass myself by giving a lame performance that will make me the laughing stock of every escort service in Boston.

She starts nibbling on my ear. "You like older women, Tim?"

"Are they more experienced?"

She winks. "Honey, by the time I'm through with you, you'll never look at a high school girl again. They're just training wheels. It's time you graduated to something that moves with a little more pickup."

"So...uh...where do you work in Boston?"

"At an escort service. Helps pay my way through grad school. I'm working on a Master's degree in counseling."

I can't imagine Stormy sitting in the front row of some crowded college classroom, raising her hand to ask questions and taking diligent notes on white-lined paper that smells faintly of perfume. Then again, if I saw her walking down Newbury Street, I'd never guess that she moonlights as the Queen of the Night. On campus she has to be timely and studious; off-campus she has to be tempting and seductive. She's living in two separate worlds, and she seems to be in complete control of both, which is something I'm still trying to figure out.

I always thought it would be empowering to lead a double life cloaked in secrecy and machismo. To command constant attention and always have the upper hand, no matter how bleak the situation looks. Ninjas can be anyone they want at any given time. One minute they're patient healers, coaxing herbs from the ground with revered hymns, and the next they're liable to flip out and hammer fist your sternum. They can appear as peasants or priests, businessmen or factory workers. They blend in with the landscape; they hide in the shadows.

But maybe I don't want to hide in the shadows anymore. Because that's what my father did. And now he's dead.

Stormy sits up and takes off my shirt. The room is cold and my nipples immediately harden. I'm not sure what I should do next, so I kick off my shoes. She reaches down and pulls my socks off, then unzips my jeans and tugs them off, too. Trying to ease the process, I take off my boxer shorts and toss them by the doorway so I won't forget to put them back on after my time runs out.

Or after we both climax.

Or however this whole thing works.

She kisses my mouth, and then my chin, and then my neck, and then she scoots down lower and runs her tongue all the way down the center of my chest like she's a surgeon marking an incision line. She smiles and brushes back her hair. Then she positions herself between my legs and gazes down at my dick, which stands at attention, as hard as a tent peg.

She stands up at the foot of the bed. "Are you ready to see me naked, Tim?"

I lean against the headboard and nod. "Yes, please."

She removes her blouse and drops it on the floor. Then she unclasps her bra and tosses it on my mother's bureau. Her nipples are hard, the areola pink and swollen. She turns around, sliding off her jeans, and then she bends over so I can admire the purple thong that accentuates her ass. She must have bought it in London because it reads "Mind the Gap." In response, I reach out and give her two light slaps, one on each cheek.

She tells me I'm bad and steps out of her jeans. They puddle at her feet. She peels off her fishnet stockings, then places one foot on the bed, arching her back as two manicured fingers twirl through a small tuft of hair that curls above her vagina, right next to a sandy birthmark in the shape of Florida.

I lean over and start sucking her purple toes, massaging her calf because it's the only part of her body I can reach. She collapses on the bed and kisses my lips, her breasts covered in sweat, the droplets spilling onto my chest. I sit up and pull at her thong, tugging until I get it past her knees, at which point she lifts her feet and the thong zooms right off, smacking me square in the face. I almost somersault backwards onto the floor, but I manage to keep upright. Trying to be cool, I twirl her panties over my head, but they slip loose and fly into the television set on the dresser.

We pull back the comforter and slide under the sheets. Reaching over the edge of the bed, she fiddles with her jeans and pulls a Trojan from the back pocket. She tears open the packet with her teeth and pulls out the condom, which looks small and slimy like a snake's skin.

After I've been equipped for battle, Stormy eases herself onto me. My eyes open in surprise as her warmth fills my body like a blast of hot air.

"Wow," she whispers, "it's like blasting off into space, isn't it?" She moves backwards and forwards, up and down. "Start gently and slowly, okay, and then pump me faster. Alternate your rhythm. Tease me with your hands."

As Stormy begins to undulate, I pinch both her nipples, twisting them right and left like I'm dialing a combination lock. My bladder starts to burn, and the rocking motion of the water bed makes me nauseous. My pelvis is about to explode, and I'm experiencing heat flashes in my chest, shooting up my throat as if I've just eaten an entire carton of spicy Thai shrimp.

I'm also sweating, and I think my legs are about to spasm, which could be the onset of heart palpitations. I feel seasick, and I wonder if my mother has any Dramamine in the medicine cabinet. I consider calling for a time out, but now Stormy is moving faster, bucking her hips while I'm trying to be supportive by yelling out, "Oh, yeah," and "That's it, baby." But it's hard to hear anything because she's screaming up at the ceiling and punching the headboard.

Her hair is in my face, and it tickles my nose, so I blow it away, trying not to sneeze all over her. But now her hair is in my mouth, and I can taste her hairspray. I think it's Aqua Net. Like my grandmother used.

I can feel my orgasm building, which is making me nervous. My heart beats faster and my toes curl. I try to remain calm, sucking in a deep breath as I count to ten backwards and imagine getting my balls slammed in a car door, or having my arm mauled by a Rottweiler. I really want to impress Stormy with my war face, so I'm gritting my teeth as hard as I can and grabbing fistfuls of the comforter.

I consider asking if she wants to switch positions, but I think I'd be too nervous on top. What if I thrust too hard and damage some of her internal organs? Or what if I just miss completely and end up jabbing her inner thigh for the next five minutes? She wants an orgasm, not a purple bruise to match the rest of her outfit.

Just when I'm starting to think that maybe I can keep going and going and going, she leans forward, straightens her back, and tilts her entire body ever so slightly.

Time freezes. There is only me and Stormy, drifting through space on a king-size waterbed, our legs entwined as I thrust into her with eighteen years of confusion and frustration. Then, with one long groan, I ejaculate, holding myself inside her until I stop shaking and catch my breath. She collapses on top of me, her face flushed and sweaty. When she tries to get off, I laugh and pull her closer to my chest.

"Don't," I tell her. "It tickles. Give me a minute."

We lie there, waiting. In a few minutes I deflate, and Stormy rolls off of me. I remove the condom and a trickle of semen drips out the bottom and soaks into my mother's damask ivory sheet. I smile and hold the condom high in the air, not sure if I should hand it to Stormy for safekeeping, or run into the bathroom and flush it down the toilet.

She snatches it out of my hand, wraps it up in a few tissues, and makes a three-pointer into the garbage can by the side of the bed. Then she drinks the rest of my beer and snuggles up beside me.

Lying here in bed, my arms wrapped around a beautiful woman, I feel like a new man. For so long I've been trying to shed old skin and assume a new identity, obsessed with leading a secret and dangerous life, and tonight I feel like my father's spirit was guiding me toward the knowledge that I haven't been living a complete one, and that if you follow someone else, then you're just ignoring your own path. I've been dominated my entire life, first by Dad's presence and then by his absence, but now, with my heart roaring in my ears, and Stormy's quiet breaths rising and falling in sync, I'm ready to listen to myself.

I run my fingers along the small of Stormy's back. I caress her ass and plant kisses on her salty lips, soft and calculated, letting them linger in succession like the experienced lover I've now become.

"That was awesome," I whisper. "How was it for you?"

Pressing my head against her breast, she sighs and says, "Tim, you could be the keynote speaker at the convention for the worst lovers in history."

9.
Love in the Time of Chlamydia

At seven o'clock this morning I woke up with a headache and swore I was going to die. Since then, all morning long, everything has been smelling like ammonia. What began as morning swells of panic have quickly escalated into tidal waves of anxiety. I'm not sick or feverish. It's more of a nauseous feeling that's been festering in the pit of my stomach ever since I lost my virginity a few weeks ago.

This morning, while walking to calculus, the lingering scent of perfume reminded me of embalming fluid. Later, in the middle of Spanish, I gagged on the scent of Megan Lawson's menthol cough drops. I had to excuse myself and run for the water fountain, which is embarrassing in any language. During advanced biology we dissected fetal pigs, and the formaldehyde seemed to soak into my clothes and skin. I swore I could feel it dissolving my mucous membranes, irritating my eyes and burning the back of my throat.

Now it's one-thirty in the afternoon, the last period of the day, and I'm doubled over a book rack in the school library, making out with a bottle of Evian and cursing the venereal Gods for inflicting me with Chlamydia, or maybe even the clap.

I haven't been tested yet, but I just know there's something wrong. The tip of my dick burns, and there's more sensitivity than usual. It constantly aches, too, like a dull throbbing after you hit your thumb with a hammer. I've been drinking gallons of water every day, examining the color of my piss and checking for discharge. So far, I'm pus free. I did consider the possibility that I might have a urinary tract infection, so as an extra precaution I've been chugging cranberry juice, going to bed two hours early, and popping a shitload of vitamin C pills.

Then again, I might just be paranoid. After all, I did use a condom. And I did take a shower right after she left, which is supposed to help minimize the risk of catching an STD. I should have asked her to explain her medical history, but that's a hard topic to bridge when a naked woman is bucking her hips like a wild bronco and jiggling her perfect C-cups right in my face.

Not having any experience with post-coital goodbyes, I gave her a five-dollar tip, and now I'm hoping she didn't give me anything in return. I've read that lots of people who have chlamydia don't have any symptoms, which means I could definitely be a future candidate for blisters and skin lesions. I guess these physical effects could be purely psychological, but how does that explain the headaches and the diarrhea? Either way, it's hard to relax when your dick feels like it's caught in a waffle iron.

I've been flipping through my sister's magazines, everything from *Cosmo* to *Country Woman*, trying to find some STD articles, and I've been surfing the Internet for information regarding STD symptoms. Supposedly, they appear within one to three weeks, which means I'm still at risk for some painful urination. I hope I don't need surgery or a blood transfusion, though I did read somewhere that the liquid inside young coconuts can be used as a substitute for blood plasma.

Hidden away in the stacks, I drink Evian and continue rifling through the bookshelves. I've already flipped through most of the magazines, so now I'm hoping to find answers in the reference section. I'd expect most of these books to be covered in dust, but it looks like they're examined on a fairly regular basis. Apparently, in addition to signing up for the math club and the physics club and the drama club, as well as joining a bunch of underperforming sports teams, most of my fellow classmates are regular members of Club Mydia.

Three titles intrigue me, so I pull them off the shelf: *Color Atlas and Synopsis of Sexually Transmitted Diseases, ABC of Sexually Transmitted Diseases,* and *Chlamydia: Intracellular Biology, Pathogenesis, and Immunity*. I carry the books over to a small table in the corner and open my loose-leaf folder, ready to take some self-soothing notes and convince myself that I still have many fruitful years left to engage in mind-blowing sex, preferably with women who don't:

1. orgasm all over my mother's comforter
2. require cash up front.
3. leave bruises when they "playfully" hit me.

The main problem is that I don't know anyone who's ever had a sexually transmitted disease, and there aren't any local support groups I can check out, or a 1-800 number I can call, so I feel alienated from the rest of society, even though I know that more than three million people share my agony.

Skimming through the books, I can't seem to find anything interesting or useful, although the glossy, color pages are fun to touch. They're so soft and shiny, which is probably why I keep running my fingers over their smooth surface. To be honest, I'm actually feeling a little bit sick to my stomach. Most of these STD pictures are just plain gross, nothing but blisters and scabs and sores that look like chunks of moldy food after they've gone a few rounds through the trash compactor.

I drink more water and remind myself that as of right now I'm not showing any symptoms. This calms me somewhat, and I actually experience less of a burning sensation in the tip of my dick. I wonder if I should go to the doctor and get one of those STD tests. It would definitely calm me down to know that my dick isn't rotting from the inside out, or that it won't fall on the floor suddenly while I'm playing dodgeball in the gym.

Actually, getting a test seems like a pretty solid course of action, but somehow I'm sure my mother would find out, and then I'd be subjected to endless crying jags in which she'd question her skills as a parent while cursing the day she bore me.

While I'm imagining my mother's reaction, and searching through a worn copy of *ABC of Sexually Transmitted Diseases*, someone taps me on the back. I glance up to find Mellisa Wright peering over my shoulder, staring at the open book with a smirk on her face. On the page is a group of detailed pictures illustrating the various effects of chlamydia, such as inflammation of the rectum, pink eye, and epididymitis.

"Hey, Tim." She looks around at the mess of books. "Let me guess. You're either studying for a health exam, or you're reminiscing over a hot date?"

I close the book and cover my face with my hands. I want to crawl under the table and hide, just me and my one liter bottle of Evian.

She drops her backpack on the floor and sits down across from me. She doesn't even ask if I want company. "You're probably overreacting," she says. "Trust me, I have two older brothers. If you used protection, you'll be fine."

I never know when it will strike, but lately there have been times when I know for sure I won't escape from a long conversation. When I know it's going to throw me down on the floor and just beat the ever-loving shit out of me. Like right now.

"I hardly know you," I say, glancing around the library. "Can we please not discuss my sexual history?"

"How long ago did you have sex?" she asks.

I stack the books in a pile and look around for the nearest exit, which is currently being blocked by a bunch of giggling freshman girls. Mellisa crosses her legs and smoothes out her skirt, placing both hands across her knee. Obviously, she has nothing better to do. I wish I had that problem.

"A few weeks ago, alright." I lower my voice and take another sip of water. "Can we talk about something else?"

"Didn't you use a condom? Hell, you can get one for a dollar in the boy's bathroom."

"I did use a condom." I point to all the books on the table. "I'm just taking precautions."

"The *condom* was the precaution, Tim." She smiles, and for the first time I notice how attractive she is. The last time we talked it was on the front steps at Our Lady Star of the Sea. Bundled up in a winter jacket, she wore a baseball cap that hid her pretty face. But now I can see her strawberry blonde hair, fluffed out over her shoulders, her split ends clinging to a red cardigan sweater. Her cheeks still look flushed, and I wonder if she's constantly excited or just in love with blusher.

Glancing down at her notebook, I see her name written in the upper right-hand corner. "Is your name spelled wrong? Isn't there supposed to be one L and a double S?"

"Traditionally," she says, "but my dad's name is Mel, and my mom's name is Lisa, so they just combined the two. Easier than flipping through all those baby books."

Trying to be discreet, I check to see if she's wearing sandals. She's not, although I wouldn't expect it in the middle of February, which is another reason why I hate winter. Still, I wonder if she paints her toenails, and if she does, what color. My guess: emerald green.

Mellisa leans forward. "I didn't know you had a girlfriend, Tim."

"I don't."

"Just a weekend lover, then?"

"It was a spontaneous act," I tell her. "Like moving your furniture around because you're sick of how your bedroom looks."

I look over toward the exit again, but the glee club is still clumped together with their hands on their hips, trying to decide what color dresses they should wear to the Valentine's Day dance. I can't stand Valentine's Day. For most people, it's twenty-four hours of syrupy Hallmark cards stuffed with roses and chocolates. For me, it's a pointless day when insecure people use their overcharged credit cards to buy accolades and attention. It's just another reminder that Cupid enjoys pissing all over my heart.

"If your bedroom set is so passé," she says, "then maybe you should shop for new furniture." She winks at me. "Just stay away from the discount bin, okay?"

Even though I'm mortified, I can't help but smile. She seems so confident and in control. Christmas Eve, I noticed it in her voice, but now I can see it in her features, the way her hands slice through the air in search of a point, or how she leans forward to talk, her chin jutting out as if she's not afraid of anything in the whole wide world.

"Relationships would be a helluva lot easier, and a lot less aggravating, if you could just collect all the pieces yourself and then assemble the product you want."

"But where's the fun in that?" she asks me. "A relationship is supposed to suck ass every once in a while."

"Says who?"

"Tim, there's no such thing as a perfect relationship. Any couple that tells you they never argue is completely full of shit. They're either lying, or they both have really bad communication skills."

"I guess I'm just picky. Kind of like how I am with M&Ms. I only like the green ones, but I can't buy just the green ones, so I have to buy five other shitty colors, too."

"You have a weird way of connecting the dots," she says. "First, you can't compartmentalize your life. You can't separate your emotions into itty bitty piles and then choose which ones you want to sample. Second, all the colors taste the same."

"Trust me, the green ones taste better. I'm pretty sure it's the dye they use."

"I heard that the green ones make you horny."

"Beats me. I just know they taste better."

"Is green your favorite color?"

"Yeah, so?"

"Maybe that's why you like them so much. Or maybe it's because the green M&M character is a sexy lady."

"She is a hot piece of hard candy shell, but I still stand by my assertion that the green ones taste better."

"Hmmm...it's probably just in your head."

"Yeah...well...I get that a lot."

Mellisa puts her elbows on the table. "Course, I'm not that picky. I don't mind a little crazy thrown into the mix, or even a little clinginess. As long as he isn't psychotic and tries to run me over with his car, it's all good."

I push back my chair and steal another look toward the exit. Those dorky girls aren't going anywhere. Now they're talking about candlelit dinners and expensive jewelry, about how much weight they'll each have to lose after they gorge themselves silly on Whitman's samplers, and sugary conversation hearts, and gift-wrapped bags of milk chocolate roses.

"Love is just another way to bleed," I tell her.

"You're just in a grumpy mood. Being in love is completely numbing, like being caught in the middle of a thunderstorm."

"Right. And then you get zapped by lightning."

She rolls her eyes. "There's nothing wrong with opening yourself up so someone can get close enough to take a peek inside."

"I don't want to feel that exposed. Next thing you know, you're getting into a shouting match over whether cats or dogs make better companions. Then you have a nervous breakdown because some girl dumped you at the prom. Like Bruce Young."

"Bruce Young can't find his own car in the parking lot. He's a blueprint for idiots."

"Yeah, but remember how he lost all that weight because he was so stressed out? And then he was all miserable and unhappy?"

"He's bipolar."

"Exactly. He's used to being manic depressive. As soon as he wakes up in the morning he's picking out moods instead of clothes."

She laughs. "And how is that different from being so freaked out that you wind up in the school library thinking there's a forest fire between your legs?"

I'd forgotten about my shaky condition, but now my stomach starts to cramp up, followed by a burning sensation that singes my groin and radiates outward until the tip of my penis explodes in blazing pain, like a dying ember that flares up again with a blast of fresh air.

"Are you okay?" she asks.

I'm squirming around in my seat, trying to reach below the table so I can thrust my hand inside my jeans. My goal is to build some breathing room for my little warrior, which I'm hoping will ease the constant pressure and get rid of this awful throbbing. I've been doing this for the past two weeks and the only thing it's done is to make me look like a compulsive crotch-grabber.

"I'm fine." I drink more Evian. "These chairs are really uncomfortable."

"If you're obsessing this bad, then you should go see a doctor? Sure, he'll have to shove a Q-tip into your dick, but at least you'll be worry free."

"No way. I read an article in *Men's Health* that said it hurts like hell. Said it's like shoving a baseball bat through a keyhole."

Mellisa says, "How come people whine about how much they hate being alone, and poor me and all that bullshit, constantly griping about how badly they want to be in some brilliant fairy-tale romance, but then, as soon as they find something worth grabbing, they just turn tail and run away?"

"You're asking the wrong guy," I tell her. "Lately, my moral compass is a needle stuck in a piece of cork."

"Maybe it's all these ridiculous expectations we cart around. People have these laundry lists of personal needs they want filled. Like 'has to cook for me' or 'has to like horror films,' and you know they'll never be completely happy until they find someone who can check off every single need on that list."

I shrug. "Some will, some won't. So what?"

"So don't be flippant. All I'm saying is that sometimes people are too choosy." She grins. "It's called an M&M complex."

I scoot my chair closer to the table and lean forward. "Alright, smarty pants. What kind of man are you looking for?"

She thinks for a second. "I want a man who can fill in all my blanks."

"Good luck finding one in this town." I glance around the library. "Most of these idiots have enough trouble finding a number two pencil, let alone filling out an entire Scantron sheet."

"Don't you want a steady girlfriend?" she asks me. "So you don't have to keep coming back to the library every couple of weeks."

"That's why I can't wait to graduate and get the hell out of here. I need to live in a place where I don't have any history."

Mellisa looks down at the table and starts picking at her thumbnail. "What schools have you applied to?"

"U-Mass Amherst, Holy Cross, NYU, Bowdoin, and Northwestern."

"Feeling the draw of the big city?"

"Why not? Can't you see me eating a double-decker club sandwich in some outdoor cafe or hailing a cab during rush hour? Maybe hanging out at Starbucks, or giving spare change to the homeless."

She laughs. "I applied to U-Mass, too. Plus Colby, Georgetown, and James Madison. But I'm fairly certain I'll wind up in Virginia. JMU has a really good theatre program."

"A thespian, huh?"

"Yep. I had a role last year in *Prelude to a Kiss*. I don't suppose you saw it?"

"Sorry. I don't get out much."

"Is that because you're a ninja?"

"No, it's because I'm not very popular."

"Well, I'm not one of those artsy chicks, so don't worry. I don't have any crazy hip tattoos or nipple piercings. And I hate tofu."

"I don't like it either," I tell her. "Something about the texture. Makes me think of *Soylent Green.*"

Mellisa looks out the window. It's one-forty-five, and all the buses are starting to line up in the parking lot. "I'd love to spend an entire year traveling around the globe," she says. "Learning all sorts of customs and eating exotic foods. It must be great to be that spontaneous, to just take off in any direction."

"I haven't been anywhere," I say, suddenly feeling like a small town boy who's afraid to cross the street. Sure, I've visited a few other states, mostly in New England, but I've yet to cross any major borders.

"Last year I went to Spain," she says. "With the Spanish club. I filled three huge photo albums with pictures from Madrid, Salamanca and Barcelona. I even got this awesome close-up of Saint Teresa's finger. They keep it at her convent in this huge glass case. It's all moldy and shriveled. Really gross, but worth the price of admission."

"A few years ago I got my passport," I tell her, "and then I spent the next three months making detailed lists of every major site I wanted to visit, like Mount Fuji and the Great Wall. I even called the airlines so I could compare ticket prices for Tokyo, Shanghai, and Beijing." I close my loose-leaf folder and slide the pencil stub behind my ear. "Mom finally nixed the idea. She got super pissed when she started getting loads of junk mail every week about places she'd never heard of."

Mellisa pushes out her chair and stretches her legs. "Where would you go if you could escape for a few weeks?"

"Probably, Tahiti," I say. "Right now I need crystal blue water and clear skies. I need sunny hours, and white-hot sand that burns the soles of my feet." I smile and take a sip of Evian. "My idea of a vacation is chilling in a hammock and gorging on huge slices of pineapple while the juice drips down my chin. I want to eat jumbo shrimp and steak tips marinated in teriyaki sauce. I want to drink piña coladas that are served to me inside massive, hollowed out coconuts."

It feels good to dream, even if I can still smell the floor wax. Even if I can still hear the librarian stamping the pile of outgoing books. Here, on this imaginary beach in Tahiti, I can breathe in the salty air and see for miles in every direction. There aren't any bodies on the bathroom floor, or foggy nightmares that wrap me up in crazy parents and worn-out angels.

These last few weeks have been a steady stream of doubt and apprehension, and my ego is bruised from constantly getting bitch-slapped by reality. But sitting here in the middle of the library, basking on some far-off tropical paradise, I can actually taste a better life.

"When I was a kid," I tell her, "my parents always talked about traveling. Dad wanted to visit Ireland. He wanted to drink a pint of Guinness in Dublin and kiss the Blarney stone in Cork. His dream was to play eighteen holes of golf on the southwest coast. But Mom wanted to visit Sicily. She always talked about taking the train through the countryside and eating nothing but pasta and gelato. She wanted to visit the Palazzo dei Normanni and then tour the catacombs in Palermo. My Uncle Jack toured them once, said the air is cold and smells like wet dog. He said there are mummies all over the place, some with their skin still intact, even babies wrapped up in little bandages."

Mellisa smiles. "Your parents sound pretty cool."

"Not really. In fact, they're constant reminders that the world contains too few happy endings."

She leans forward, her face in her hands. "Did they ever go?"

"Nah. Dad got sick with lung cancer. Just started coughing up blood one morning. Mom told us the doctors would have to rip out one of his lungs." I drink more Evian and stare out the window. "A few months later they operated on him, and when he came home I thought he was a ghost. He'd lost all this weight, and his skin looked papery and crinkly. He stayed in bed for almost two weeks, doped up on codeine, slurping homemade chicken soup from an old china bowl he once used as an ashtray."

"That's a real bummer," she says.

"He never could catch a break. Even from himself." I push out my chair and stand up. "Anyway, I should really get going. Nice seeing you again."

Mellisa opens her backpack and takes out a piece of paper. She scribbles something down, tears the page in half, and hands it to me. It's her telephone number. She even drew a tiny heart above the 'i' in her first name, which is cheesy as hell, and so 1990s, but it's still kind of sexy. Plus, she shaded it in, which I guess means she *really* likes me.

"Call me sometime," she says. "We can see a movie, or drive into Boston for the afternoon."

I put the scrap of paper in my pocket. I want to ask her if this will be an actual date, or if we'll just be hanging out as friends. Or if we'll be hanging out as friends with the possibility of labeling it a date depending on what happens as the night goes on. I can't keep track of all these different dating guidelines. When to hold her hand. When to open the door. When to say she looks gorgeous. When to laugh at her jokes. When to use my tongue or kiss her on the lips.

"How come you like me?" I ask her.

"Because you're unpredictable," she says. "And you're cute."

"But you're not freaked out?"

She grabs her backpack off the floor. "I gave you my number so we could go out together. Not so we could have wild sex in the backseat of your car. And I really don't think you have an STD. I think you're just paranoid."

I take a long gulp from my bottle of Evian.

Mellisa points to the bright colored label. "Why are you always drinking bottled water?"

"I don't trust town water. Too many toxic metals. Ninjas say spring water is the elixir of life."

"Ah, the ninjas." She nods as if this is an important point she should have remembered. "And what do they know about love?"

I glance over at the stack of books I've left on the table. "Apparently, not very much."

When she doesn't say anything, I pick up my loose-leaf folder, shake her hand, and say goodbye for the second time. Walking away, I put my hand in my pocket and touch the slip of paper, making sure that our conversation was real and not some dream that will poof away in a wisp of acrid smoke.

I step into the hallway and turn around, offering her one last wave. She smiles and waves back, following behind me with that yellow backpack slung over her shoulder. Pushing through the double doors, I realize that my headache is gone, and that I'm actually hungry. When I get home I think I'll make a grilled cheese sandwich and relax on the couch, maybe watch a rerun of MacGyver. And just to be safe, I'll stop by the bathroom to make sure that my dick hasn't turned into Mr. Hyde.

Some days I feel like the dog, and some days I feel like the hydrant, but if I can survive another four days without searching my body for boils, or convincing myself that I'm dying of some heinous multi-syllabic disease, then I should be free of imminent danger and ready to resume a normal life.

Whatever that might be.

I'm almost to the front door when Mellisa yells, "Hey, Tim. Do you know what 'Evian' spells backwards?"

I glance down at the bottle, rearranging the letters in my head as I pass out of the building and into the parking lot, past the endless row of school buses and into a bright winter sun that reflects off the snow banks to momentarily blind me.

10

The Tae-Bo Girl

I'm starting to wonder if love and I will be doomed forever to a tragic existence. It's depressing, I know, but this is how I feel when I walk into the video store on a rainy Saturday night in March, about a month after Valentine's Day. My conversation with Mellisa has bolstered my self-confidence, or at least nudged it in the right direction, but I still haven't picked up the phone to call her. I keep saying how much I want a steady girlfriend, and I know I shouldn't be picky, but for some reason I just can't stop thinking about the Tae-Bo girl.

The time has come for action, which is why I've finally decided to approach her and express my undying devotion. I've spent all day rehearsing lines that are sure to make her swoon like a sixteenth-century maiden, and I even ironed my yellow and blue golf shirt. But as soon as I walk through the doors of Blockbuster Video I become short of breath. I want to turn right around and run for the parking lot.

Wynn follows me into the store and takes off his coat. "Rain makes me want to do three things," he says. "Have sex, eat Chinese food, and sleep."

I stuff my jacket under the counter. "Don't talk to me about sex, okay? Or relationships. In fact, I don't want to talk about women at all."

He pats me on the back. "Why the sad face, sunshine?"

I log onto the computer and open a Sprite. It's just past six, and the usual weekend crowd won't barge through the doors until at least eight o'clock. "Tell me, Wynn. What kind of woman do you want?"

He laughs. "Do you even know what *you* want, Tim? I mean, you screwed a call girl, scored digits from a cutie, and now you're pining away for some exercise chick. Christ, your love life looks like a Chinese fire drill."

"Hey, the birthday hooker was your idea."

"You need to stop spinning the bottle and just pick someone. Look at me. I've been seeing Suzie for almost six months."

"I didn't know you had a girlfriend. How come you never talk about her?"

He smacks me on the side of the head. "I do, dumbass. But you never listen. You're too busy talking about yourself."

"Is she as smart as you?"

"Of course not. But she is an existentialist. I've never dated one of those."

"She's a right wing terrorist?"

He punches me on the arm. "Not an extremist, you idiot. An existentialist. She believes in individual existence and free will."

"How old is she?"

"Nineteen."

I give him a high five. "Going after the younger ladies, huh?"

"Priorities, my man. I don't want a chick with cobwebs between her legs. Besides, a younger girl can chug Coors Light all night long, eat a chalupa supreme from Taco Bell, and not wear it on her ass the next morning."

We stare up at the promos on the television, watching a long parade of fast-paced action trailers and overproduced music videos. We've been playing them all for the last few months, and we know every single one by heart. They've become part of our environment now, rotating every half hour, and we don't even notice them unless we happen to look up at one of the half dozen TV screens scattered throughout the store. Sometimes we'll catch ourselves mouthing cheesy lines from a stupid movie preview, or singing along to some R&B song.

"What if the Tae-Bo girl says yes?" I ask him. "Should I take her to a matinee? Or buy her dinner in a fancy restaurant?"

"Nix the movies," he tells me. "Nobody respects the cinema as an art form. Suzie and I went to the movies last week and everyone around us spent the entire time texting and talking. There's even a reminder before the movie begins that tells everyone to shut the fuck up and sit still. This whole group of dumbass kids sitting in front of us started texting as soon as the opening credits rolled. And don't even get me started on the cost. Eighteen dollars for two tickets? It's a goddamn rip-off. I paid twenty-five dollars for two large popcorns, a couple of root beers, and a box of Junior Mints. I can get a halfway decent blowjob for that amount in any major U.S. city."

I stare at the computer screen, watching the cursor flash every three seconds.

"Why don't you ride into Chinatown next weekend and snag yourself a cute little Asian."

"I need a break from Asia," I tell him. "Every time I turn east, that entire continent gives me the finger."

What I really need is some alone time, so I wander into the Drama section and start placing the returned videos back on the shelf. A few are out of alphabetical order, so I reorganize them just to make myself feel better. I want to hide in Comedy until midnight, only emerging from my cinematic burrow when Wynn locks the door and I don't have to worry about the distinct possibility of rejection.

Now I'm edgy and nervous, so I run into the bathroom and splash water on my face. I practice my introduction and comb my hair. Then I bite my thumbnail until it bleeds. Then I chat with a few customers. I even try working the register, but Wynn tells me to go away after fifteen minutes because all I'm doing is staring at the door and mumbling under my breath, hitting random keys and screwing up every transaction.

It's not until nine-thirty, while I'm blocking videos in Horror, that the Tae-Bo girl finally walks into the store.

She's wearing a gray sweat suit and a pair of red flip flops. Her toes are painted orange, and I notice she's chipped some nail polish on the big toe of her left foot. A set of keys is hanging from a yellow lanyard around her neck. Usually, she ties her hair back, but tonight it's draped over her shoulders. She looks perfect, just as I saw her last weekend, and the weekend before that, and the weekend before that. Watching her disappear into Action/Adventure, I'm depressed to think that her anticipated appearance every Saturday night is one of the only constants in my otherwise tumultuous life.

I follow her past the Dirty Harry movies, wiping beads of sweat from my forehead as I check my nose for any loose stragglers. I tuck in my shirt and put on some mint chapstick.

Then I stick my hands in my pockets.

Then I hook them into the belt loops of my khakis.

Then I cross my arms and walk the perimeter of the store.

When that doesn't feel right, I decide to untuck my shirt and mess up my hair. I even try leaning against the candy rack in a mock GQ pose.

But I still feel like a dork, so I comb my hair and tuck in my shirt again. Plus, my stomach is nauseous, so I stand off in the corner and practice some ninja breathing exercises. I press my tongue against the roof of my mouth, in harmony with my pulse, trying to burn off any toxins and impurities that might render me a babbling idiot. I do this for about five minutes. Then, when I feel calm and collected, I close my eyes and visualize our entire conversation, every sentence scrolling through my mind like pages in a script.

I'm really hoping that, for once, my expectations will collide with reality.

Fifteen minutes later, after I've stepped outside for some fresh air, and bitten off every single fingernail, I finally walk over to the Tae-Bo girl. She's kneeling down, looking at a copy of *Live Free or Die Hard*. When she doesn't notice me, I brush up against her and clear my throat.

She glances up. "Oh, hi."

"Hi. Do you...uh....need help finding anything?"

"No, thanks," she says. "I'm just looking"

I wonder what she looks like naked, or if she can tie a cherry stem into a knot with her tongue. "I...uh...don't mean to bother you, but could we talk for a second?"

She puts the movie back on the shelf and stands up. "Shit! Is this about those late fees?"

"No." I hold out my hand. "We haven't been properly introduced. I'm Tim Dimmick."

She shakes my hand. Her palm is soft and smooth, pulsing with the scent of Aloe Vera.

"I don't want to make you feel uncomfortable," I tell her, "but there's definitely a connection between us, and...well...I think we'd be fools not to capitalize on it."

Her eyes narrow. "Are you serious?"

"Well...yeah." I don't know what else to say, so I look over at Wynn. He smiles and gives me thumbs up. "Do you want to...maybe...go out for a romantic dinner? We could do surf and turf. Or we could do Chinese. You're not allergic to MSG, are you?"

She looks around the store. "Am I on some reality show?"

I place my hand on her shoulder, hoping she'll sense the deep spiritual connection that I've been thriving on for the past fourteen months. Instead, she makes one of those disgusting "Uggh" sounds and recoils from my hand as though it's an agitated copperhead ready to lunge at her throat.

"We don't have to go to a restaurant," I say. "We can chill out at my house and play X-box, or drive to Devereux Beach and watch the sunset."

She takes a step back. "You're really freaking me out."

"Give me at least one chance."

Silence.

"Please?"

She shoves me into the aisle and puts her hand in her purse. "Stay the hell away from me."

This is not how I expected our conversation to end. I fully expected to copy down her address and phone number and escort her outside, maybe even fasten her seatbelt and wave to her as she drove out of the parking lot. I wanted her to blush and giggle and fall into my arms.

Instead, she's flat out rejecting me.

Actually, she's sprinting for the exit.

"Wait!" I shout.

She flings open the door and rushes outside. I charge past Wynn, who stands at the checkout counter with his mouth hanging open and a video scanner in his hand. Up until now I haven't felt like a love-crazed stalker, but all that changes when I dash outside and she sprays me with mace. Her aim is perfect. My eyes and nose are saturated with the stinging liquid, and I collapse on the pavement, writhing in pain and screaming obscenities. I can't see, I can't breathe, and my face feels like it's being flambéed by an atomic hydrogen blowtorch.

I lunge forward into the parking lot and vomit all over the asphalt. "Don't throw us away," I gasp, straining to see through my burning tears. "Let me show you a good time."

"Fuck you, dipshit!"

Coughing and retching, I reach out my hand in the direction of her voice. "I want to be with you until the end of the world."

She walks over, gives me one good kick in the ribs, and spits on my face. "Then I wish the world would end."

Luckily, there are no other customers in the store. Wynn hurries outside and leads me into the bathroom where I spend the next twenty minutes dousing my face with cold water and rinsing the mace out of my bloodshot eyes. My clothes stink, my skin burns, and my chest hurts where she kicked me. Thank God the flip-flop was plastic.

When I return to the counter, Wynn laughs. "You made the Hall of Shame tonight, Dimmick. I give your performance five stars."

"I can't believe it. I thought for sure she'd agree to at least one date."

"You were doing fine until you opened your mouth." He leans against the counter and smiles. "My favorite part was when she hosed you. You just dropped to the ground and started screaming like a little girl."

I know I have a black belt in failed relationships, but I honestly thought that girls were obligated to grant every man a default date, no matter how awkward his pimping skills. I thought all girls *wanted* to be chased.

Shows what I know.

In the past year I've called the psychic hotline, organized a disastrous séance, and slept with a prostitute. Some track record. All I ever wanted was to feel needed and loved, but now all I want to do is go home, crawl into bed, and listen to The Smiths.

I glance up to see my face reflected in the glass window. My hair is reaching out in every direction and my eyes are still watering. Plus, my nose is bleeding and there are pieces of gravel embedded in my cheek. Moving closer to the window, I realize how exhausted and defeated I look. My entire life has been nothing more than a series of unexpected pitfalls, and I'm officially tired of climbing out of one hole only to fall into a deeper one farther on down the road.

I turn to Wynn. "I need to see the Tae-Bo girl. Right now."

"Are you crazy? She turned you into the Elephant Man."

"To err is human," I tell him, "to forgive is divine."

"Yeah, well, to touch an electrified fence is painful, but to do it twice is fucking stupid."

"I acted like a complete idiot, I realize that, but the best thing for me to do is to drive over to her house and apologize."

He shakes his head. "Bad idea. She just sprayed you with mace. Who knows what she'll do if you ring her doorbell."

I punch him on the arm. "Why can't you agree with me that this is a good idea?"

"Because if I agreed with you, then we'd both be wrong."

"I screwed up. I know that. But I need this."

He stares down at the floor.

"Now is my chance to man up and fix this whole crazy mess." I pat him on the back. "So can I borrow your car?"

"It's the busiest night of the week. You can't just leave your shift. Besides, you don't even know where she lives."

I tap the computer. "But I know her name. I'll just pull up her membership info and get her address. She lives right here in Swampscott. I'll be back in thirty minutes. An hour, tops."

"Tim, the girl wants you to stay away from her."

"How do you know that?"

"Because she said, 'Stay the hell away from me.'"

I hold out my hand. "Give me your keys. I need to salvage whatever dignity I have left."

He laughs. "Trust me, it's not worth the gas mileage."

"If you don't help me, I'll tell Brian about that time you made out with a customer in the break room because she didn't want to pay her late fees."

119

"You knew about that?"

"Yeah."

He tosses me his keys. "Make sure you fill it up with gas, alright?"

***

After punching up her information, I scribble her address on the back of a Dairy Queen receipt. Then I comb my hair, button up my winter jacket, and rush outside. Wynn drives a 1985 Yugo. It's got over two hundred thousand miles on it, and the engine rattles like a maraca, but it's still in good condition. I plug in his GPS and type in her address: 42 Elmwood Road near Linscott Park. It's only a few miles away, maybe a ten minute drive, which leaves me plenty of time to figure out how I can apologize like a gentleman without being assaulted for the second time in as many hours.

I park the car a few houses down, shutting the door quietly so I won't piss off any pain in the ass neighbors. I'm feeling jumpy and anxious, and the last thing I need is for some cranky old man to run outside in his underwear and wake the entire block with a lot of yelling and screaming. For the most part, the street is fairly quiet. Nothing but a few cars driving past, the wind gusting through the trees, and a small dog barking and running around in circles.

I need to be cautious approaching her house, so I decide to go into stealth mode. I flex my knees and control my breathing, creeping down the sidewalk like a drunken crab. I'm staying on the balls of my feet and sliding across an enormous sheet of ice, which is how I end up slamming into a mailbox and tearing a hole in my khakis. Plus, my eyes are still watering from the mace, so everything looks hazy.

Moving off the sidewalk, I take a few deep breaths and try to maintain perfect balance, but it's dark, and I keep slipping on the ice. I'm glad I'm wearing my blue Blockbuster shirt because it's helping to hide me. Most people think ninjas wear black, but black is ineffective because it makes you more visible, which is why ninjas actually wear dark blue. Of course, my tan khakis aren't doing much to help the effort, but they're so dirty at this point that it probably doesn't even matter.

I run across someone's lawn and sneak around an elm tree, tripping over an exposed root. Then I hide among some evergreen shrubs so I can blow into my cupped hands and flip up my collar. There's a thin layer of snow on the ground, and I forgot my gloves at the video store, so already my fingers are frozen.

I scan the neighborhood for any random lights or passers-by, keeping my hands in front of me to detect any possible obstructions. I take in more deep breaths to avoid muscle tension, and then I drop to my hands and knees. I look both ways, roll across an icy driveway, and somersault over a soggy newspaper that someone left in the middle of his yard.

When I arrive at the Tae-Bo girl's house I tiptoe past her Corolla and crawl along the grass, cutting my hand on a sprinkler and stepping in a big pile of dog shit. I reach the walkway and inch my way over to her front door. Looking through the window I can see her sitting on the sofa. She's watching *Scrubs*, her bare feet propped up on a pillow and a bowl of popcorn resting on her stomach. I knock on the door and scuff my foot against the welcome mat a few times. Then I grab a stick and poke at the bottom of my sneaker, trying to scrape away any leftover shit.

She opens the door and jumps back before I can even say hello. I'm afraid she might slam the door in my face, or whip out a shotgun and kill me on the spot. Instead, when I take a step forward to apologize, she charges outside, punches me in the jaw, and shoves me into the shrubbery.

"Hey, asshole..." She gives me another kick in the ribs. "....I told you to leave me alone."

I pull myself up, brushing snow and twigs off my jacket. Part of me really wants to give her a hug, but I don't want to take the chance. She's liable to whack me over the head and give me a Harry Potter scar.

"I'm not here to hurt you or anything," I tell her. "I just wanted to apologize for what happened earlier at the video store."

"I said I didn't want you..." She wrinkles her nose. "Is that dog shit?" She switches on the outside light and stares at the huge glob of shit I've smeared all over her parents' mat. She looks at my bleeding hand, then down at my ripped khakis. "Jesus Christ! You look like you've been crawling around in a sewer."

"No, I haven't. Well, sort of. I've been crawling, but..."

"I don't know what your problem is," she says, "but I'm sure it's hard to pronounce."

"Do you want to talk about it?" I ask her. "I could come inside."

"You have one minute to leave, or I'm calling the police." She slams the door and locks it.

I move into the middle of the front yard and gaze up at the second story windows. Sure enough, a light comes on in a corner bedroom. I run back to the driveway and pick up a handful of small stones. I sprint across the lawn and stand underneath her window, throwing them against the glass as hard as I can. By now everyone in the neighborhood has switched on their porch lights. My mouth is dry and my knee throbs. I smell like mace and dog shit, and to cap it all off I have an audience of middle-age cranks shouting obscenities.

Staring up at her window, I remember John Cusack holding up that boom box in *Say Anything*, stoic as hell while Peter Gabriel belts out *In Your Eyes*. And while I'm standing on her lawn, shivering in the night air, and bleeding from multiple wounds, I really wish I loved someone so intensely that there was nothing left to do but break open the night with a medley of top 40 hits, romancing her with the kind of lyrics that seem to define every single relationship I've never been a part of.

"Fine," I shout. "I'm leaving." I drop the rest of the stones. "And just so there are no hard feelings, the next time you come into the store I'll give you a free rental."

She flings the window open. "I called the police. They'll be here any minute. If I were you, I'd start running."

Tired and sore, I put my hands in my pocket and head for Wynn's car. As I'm halfway down the street a police cruiser skids to a halt in front of the curb, lights flashing and sirens blaring. The officer catches me off guard, and in a moment of panic I decide to run for it.

He gives chase, waving his nightstick and yelling for me to stop, but then he slips on the ice and lands flat on his back. I double over, laughing hysterically, and by the time I catch my breath he's found his footing and tackled me in the grass.

He identifies himself as Officer Lavelle. His voice is a booming cannon, deep and raspy as though his vocal cords are stonewashed.

"This is a total misunderstanding," I tell him. "If you'll let me explain, I can clear all of this up in, like, two minutes."

Ignoring me, he slaps on the handcuffs and marches me back to his cruiser. He leans me up against the passenger side door and reaches into my back pocket for my wallet. Removing my license, he instructs me not to move, which is difficult seeing as how my entire body is shivering and my legs are crossed because I'm trying not to piss my pants.

I keep apologizing, but Officer Lavelle gets into his cruiser and fiddles around with the dashboard computer. Five minutes later he steps out of the car, puts my license back in my wallet, and says, "You're under arrest, Mr. Dimmick."

"Seriously? For what?"

"Trespassing," he says. "Along with disturbing the peace. We received a call that you were harassing a young woman, and that you refused to leave the property when she asked you."

"This is crazy. There are people committing actual crimes, and you're busting me for being romantic?"

He opens the car door. "Watch your head, please." He pushes me into the back seat. It smells like beer and cigarettes. I wonder if anyone has ever died inside a police car.

"You have the right to remain silent," he tells me. "Anything you say can and will be used against you in a court of law. You have the right to an attorney. If you cannot afford an attorney, one will be appointed for you. Do you understand these rights?"

"What about the car?" I ask him. "It's my coworker's. How is he supposed to get home?"

"You can call your parents after we get to the station."

"What about the Tae-Bo girl? She sprayed me with mace. And kicked me in the ribs. Twice, in fact." I twist around in my seat. The handcuffs are hurting my wrists, and I think I smell urine in the floorboards.

"Relax," he says. "You're giving me a headache."

"But I was trying to do the right thing. This isn't my fault."

He shrugs. "I didn't say it was your fault. I said I was blaming you."

I thought police officers were supposed to serve and protect, not demean and ignore. Here I am, practically dying in his back seat, and he's acting like I only have a few cuts and bruises. What if one of my ribs is cracked and I start hemorrhaging? What if that gash on my hand becomes infected with pus and develops into gangrene?

Officer Lavelle gets into the cruiser and starts the ignition. He picks up a large cup of steaming coffee from Dunkin Donuts and removes the lid. He blows across the surface for a couple of seconds and takes a long satisfying sip, which makes me hate him even more.

I kick at the back of his seat with my shit-covered sneaker. "But I was trying to apologize," I yell through the metal divider.

"That was your first mistake," he says, as he pulls out onto the street. "And you're lucky I don't cite you for it, either."

***

I've never been to jail before, but I have seen *Lock Up* with Sylvester Stallone, and I know that one wrong move could cost me an arm or a leg. I wonder if they'll interrogate me with sodium pentathol, or if they'll throw me in a padded cell and beat me with wooden chairs. Maybe I'm just being paranoid, but I've never seen the inside of a police station, and when faced with the unknown my mind has a tendency to conjure up

123

worst case scenarios.

As a soldier, my father knew all about worst case scenarios. During his time in the Middle East, he watched cars explode and buildings collapse, chunks of wreckage strewn across the sand like rusted metal in a junkyard. He saw anti-tank mines scattered throughout Iraqi villages, and children lying dead on the side of a dusty road, their legs crushed under the wheels of desert patrol vehicles. He was engaged in a firefight on the border of Kuwait, and wounded in the leg by shrapnel. Later, near the Battle of Khafji, his skull was fractured when his convoy got attacked by a suicide bomber.

My father returned home with his arms full of stories. He shared them with me one at a time, pulling them out of his pocket like a magic trick that never gets old. He asked me to be his second in command and showed me his scar, a half moon ridge of bumpy white flesh that felt soft and hot whenever I touched it.

He even tried to build a trench in the backyard. A perimeter, he told me. For concealment and protection, he told my mother. Every night he'd stand on the back porch, aiming the garden hose into a two foot hole filled with dirty water, finally retreating indoors when Mom cleaned out the basement and gave him full reign over the dusty spider webs and corners caked with mold.

And now, walking into the police station, I feel like I've disappointed Dad for the umpteenth time. He survived a war and multiple injuries, but I can't even romance a girl or deliver a late-night apology.

I flex my muscles and try to look tough, but with all the blood and torn clothes I look like someone has just beaten the crap out of me in a downtown bar. If someone approaches me and wants to fight, I'll probably just collapse on the ground and beg for a quick death.

I have one phone call to make, and I'm not sure if I should call Wynn or my mother. If I call Wynn, he'll probably just end up calling Mom, so I might as well risk the category-five storm that's sure to erupt on the other end of the line.

I look at my watch. It's 10:58. Mom hates to be woken up this late. It's one of her major pet peeves.

Again, I think about calling Wynn, but there's no way he can pick me up. He also has no one to help him close the video store, which will really piss him off. Right now he's probably wondering whether I'm locked in a holding cell, getting laid, or trying to free myself from the wreckage of a horrible accident.

Nah. He's probably drafting an outline for his next film.

Officer Lavelle removes the handcuffs and sits me down at his desk. He gives me a glass of water, which I gulp down in five seconds. When I ask for more, he refills the glass and hands me some chewable aspirin. I stretch out my arms and tuck in my shirt, which is wet and muddy and ripped at the bottom. I wipe blood off my face from where I cut my upper lip when he tackled me in the grass. Right now, I'd like to crawl into a bathtub and slide down the drain.

He motions toward the phone. "Dial like a man."

I shake my head and look down at the floor.

"Tell her you'll be fined for disturbing the peace," he says, "but we won't charge you with a misdemeanor."

I stare at the numbers on the phone, watching them rise off the keypad. The rest of the room blurs together, dissolving into a bunch of fuzzy gray lines until all I can see is Mom's cell number looming before me like a portentous combination to Satan's gym locker. "My mother's going to kill me."

"Probably," he says. "But don't come crawling to me for sympathy because I'm fresh out. I'm a divorced, middle-aged man with restless leg syndrome."

"I don't even know what that is."

He points to the phone. "Just make the call."

After he leaves, I watch the second hand run laps around the clock. I have no idea what I'll stutter when Mom asks me for an explanation. It seems like all I've been doing lately is collecting bad decisions, and their weight is crushing me to the point where I can't even breathe. I want to be strong and assertive, like I know Dad would want, but right now I feel twisted up inside, like a giant pretzel.

And right then and there I want to call Mellisa. I want to talk to her about traveling and M&Ms and stupid stuff that only matters because we want it to, and because we don't care what anyone else thinks. The rest of the school treats me like an imbecile, but she actually sought me out and gave me her telephone number.

So why haven't I called her?

But deep down, I know exactly why I shoved that tiny slip of paper into the back of my desk drawer. Like that night at Our Lady Star of the Sea, she made me question things I don't want to know. She exuded compassion, and I responded with indifference. I'm not used to someone displaying a genuine interest in me, and it scared me so much that I tried to find solace in the Tae-Bo girl, a woman who acts just like my mother and sister: apathetic, impassive, and contemptuous.

I take the phone off the hook and hold it against my ear, listening to the dial tone. I have no idea what my mother will say, but I know she'll never let me forget that I made her get out of bed and drive to the police station. It's not even a misdemeanor, and she'll probably pay the fine in cash, but I'm sure she'll act like it's first degree murder. She'll use this as ammunition for the rest of my life, even reminding me on her deathbed that besides my father's suicide her biggest disappointment was that I'd harassed some poor girl and embarrassed my whole family.

She answers on the fourth ring. "Hello!"

"Mom, it's me."

"Timothy!" she yells. "What's wrong? Are you okay?"

"I'm fine." I take a deep breath and count to ten. "I'm at the Swampscott police station."

Silence.

Then: "What the hell are you doing at the Swampscott police station?"

"Um...well...I got fined for trespassing. And...uh...also for disturbing the peace."

"You're supposed to be at work!" she shouts into the phone.

"I only left for a few minutes. I needed to talk to a girl. It was an emergency."

I hear her light a cigarette. She's definitely walking downstairs to fix herself a drink.

"How did you get to her house?" she asks me. "Because the last time I checked, you don't have access to a car."

"I borrowed Wynn's."

"Which is where at the moment?"

"At the Tae-Bo girl's house."

"At the Tae-what house?" I hear ice rattling in the background, bottles being opened, harsh fizzing, and then a spoon being stirred into a glass. Vodka tonic, most likely. "Tell me something, Einstein. How is Wynn supposed to get home if his car is sitting in somebody's neighborhood?"

"I don't know. Maybe the police can drive him home."

"Did you ever consider the fact that you might get fired for leaving work?"

"I won't get fired, Mom. Wynn said he'd cover for me. Besides, I can always find another job."

"Right. As long as they don't require a background check."

"It's not even a misdemeanor," I tell her. "It's just a fine. Maybe a hundred dollars."

"My son is a criminal," she says, though it sounds like she's addressing her drink instead of me.

"Mom, the officer said you can drive over here and pick me up."

Then she starts crying. Hard chest sobs that practically shake the phone. "I don't know what to do with you, Tim. I've tried everything."

"Look, I know I screwed up, but I promise it won't happen again."

"Are you on speed?"

"Why do you always assume I'm on drugs?"

"Because you're constantly making stupid decisions. And stupid people usually do drugs. And if A equals B and B equals C, then you do the math, Mister straight-A student sitting in a police station at 11:00 pm."

"I don't want to argue with you, Mom."

"Sometimes I think you've only got two brain cells," she tells me. "One is in a wheelchair and the other one is pushing."

"Look, I'm tired and I'm bleeding and I'm..."

"What? Why are you bleeding? Did the police whack you with one of those nightstick thingies?"

"No. I cut myself on a sprinkler. And I ripped my pants."

"What the hell were you doing? Crawling around like a serial rapist?"

"Get real, Mom."

"Jesus Christ, Tim, please tell me you weren't peeping in on some poor girl in her underwear?"

"Can we please talk about this at home?"

I hear ice cubes drop into her glass. Then she takes a minute-long sip and says, "I'm not picking you up."

"What?"

"I'm not picking you up. It's late and I'm tired, and I don't feel like getting dressed and driving all the way to Swampscott."

"It's fifteen minutes."

"Sorry. Maybe a night in the slammer will give you some time to think."

"You're not coming?"

"Put the officer on the phone."

"You're really not coming?"

She crunches on an ice cube. "Sleep tight. Don't let the bed bugs bite."

I can't believe my mother is leaving me in prison for the night. She's the one person I'm supposed to depend on for anything.

"You're a bitch," I say, and drop the phone on the desk.

For the next ten minutes Officer Lavelle speaks with my mother while I wait in the hallway. I watch the weekend drunks pour into the police station and stagger past me. Occasionally, I glance over at Officer Lavelle as he paces back and forth in front of his desk. He laughs a few times (which doesn't make me feel any better), then he looks at me a few times (which makes me feel even worse), and finally he hangs up. When he steps into the hallway I hand him the car keys.

"One of the officers will drive your friend to his car," he tells me. "That way he won't be inconvenienced by your dumbass decision making."

He takes me into a dingy bathroom where I wash my face and wipe away the excess blood on my leg. I notice there are still twigs and leaves in my hair. He offers me peroxide, which I dab onto my cuts and bruises. After I towel myself dry, he leads me down a dim hallway. My leg throbs, so I limp behind him like a young Igor. The whole place smells moldy and damp, and I immediately think of my bedroom closet. I see the paramedic rushing upstairs, and that blonde-haired angel drowning in dirty water, surrounded by shards of broken glass.

When we reach the last cell, Officer Lavelle opens the door and smiles. "It's not the Holiday Inn," he says, "but it won't be the worst night's sleep you've ever had, either."

Inside is a rusty sink and toilet, a stack of magazines that looks to be covered with a decade's worth of bodily fluids, and a bunk bed that probably houses more infectious diseases than Mass General Hospital. At this moment I feel more alone than I've ever felt in my entire life.

I step into the cell and the door swings shut behind me.

Officer Lavelle slides his key into the lock. "Breakfast is at eight," he says, laughing, "so try to be on time, okay." He gives a half-hearted wave and walks away, his heavy footsteps echoing down the corridor.

I grab a ratty pillow from the top bunk and crouch down at the foot of the bed. I press it against my chest, and gag on the smell of urine and old cotton. I unfold a coarse wool blanket that's lying on the dirty floor and wrap it around my shoulders. Then, trying not to cry, I squeeze myself into a corner of the cell, listening as Officer Lavelle switches off the overhead light.

The darkness smothers me, and I fight to breathe. Through the bars I can barely see the Exit sign at the end of the corridor. The panel is broken in the middle, and flickers of fluorescent light emanate through miles of empty blackness. A few cells down, someone is snoring. I hear the faint tapping of claws against the concrete floor, and something scurries under the bed. My sink is leaking.

I wonder. Will anyone care if I hang myself with my shoelaces? Or slit my wrists with a strip of metal from the bed frame? Will anyone care if I dive off the top bunk and crack my skull open on the edge of the sink?

All pointless questions, seeing as how I'm such a coward. I can't even solicit my mother's sympathy, or appeal to her maternal instincts. I wasn't strong enough to demand that she put on some clothes and drive down to the police station to pick me up.

She, on the other hand, had no problem abandoning me. She didn't even give me a second thought. She probably finished her drink, rolled over, and went back to la la land.

And what about my father? His ninjas, which once seemed so strong and forceful, now seem as flimsy as paper dolls.

Shivering under my blanket, I look up at the thick steel bars that loom over me, locking me into this cramped and tiny cell where the only protection I need is from myself. I cross my arms and hang my head, squeezing the pillow as it erupts into a stinking cloud of mold and dust mites. Water continues to drip from the rusted sink, and I count each splash until, cramped and sore, I finally fall asleep, knees hugging my chest as I try to convince myself that I still have a little fight left inside of me.

11.
Do Zombies Shit?

One of the officers wakes me up at seven o'clock the next morning. I open my eyes to find myself lying on the cold cement floor, my face pressed against the bars while a string of drool dribbles down my chin. My arms are still wrapped around the moldy pillow, and the wool blanket is tucked between my legs like we're on a first name basis.

I stand up and stretch, leaning against the wall as I listen to my knees pop. My back is sore and I have a splitting headache. My nose is stuffy. Plus, I have to go to the bathroom, but I'm scared to use the toilet because I'm afraid I might catch herpes.

"Breakfast," the officer says. He unlocks the cell door and hands me a cafeteria tray with what looks like food on it.

Luckily, I'm not a big breakfast eater. Not that I was expecting an all-you-can-eat buffet, but my morning meal consists of cold cereal and powdered milk, runny eggs that look like an open sore, and a Dixie cup full of warm apple juice. I sit down on the bed, take a few bites of cereal, and almost throw up. The corn flakes are soggy and the milk is clumpy. When I go to drink the apple juice I find a hair floating in it. But I don't want to be rude, so I dump the food in the toilet and try to look grateful.

For the next couple of hours I sit on the bed and stare at all the graffiti that's splattered across the walls. The entire room is like a grungy library for weekend drunks and lovelorn teenagers. To the left of the sink someone drew a broken heart, a large machete sticking out of its jagged center, the edge of the blade dripping with blood. To the right, someone drew a huge dick with a smiley face, and on the floor someone sketched a massive cross and wrote "God is Coming Soon...and he's Bringing Doughnuts." Above the toilet someone else scribbled "I'd rip off your balls if I had a microscope."

Feeling rebellious, I pick up the dented fork and scratch my own timely message into the cracked wall opposite me: "The food here ~~fucking~~ sucks." It takes me almost forty-five minutes to complete my masterpiece, and my fingers are red and swollen, but now I officially feel like a juvenile delinquent.

Mom finally arrives at nine-thirty. She doesn't look at me when I enter the hallway. She just pays my ticket and walks out the door. I follow her into the parking lot and get in the car, hoping she won't reach over and backhand me. Instead, she tosses me a wet wipe. "Wash your face," she says. "You look like a poor excuse for a criminal."

I rip open the towelette and run it along my forehead. I wipe down my sweaty neck and scrub behind my ears. "Thanks for picking me up, Mom."

She turns on the radio.

"I'm sorry."

She rolls down the window and lights a cigarette. She doesn't bother to blow the smoke out the window.

The entire ride home she stares straight ahead, chain-smoking and humming along to "Crocodile Rock" and "Hotel California." Every time I cough or try to say something she either turns up the volume or honks her horn to yell at a passing car. When we pull into the driveway she grabs her purse and says, "You're grounded. Until April vacation. And if you ever pull this shit again, it'll take years for the police to find your body." She slams the door and heads toward the house, then stops, walks around to my side of the car, and says, "You owe me eighty-five dollars for that ticket, mister. And you will pay me back."

I nod, look down at my torn Blockbuster shirt, and realize how awful I smell.

Mom slams the front door when she enters the house. Feeling chicken shit, I decide to wait around for a few minutes before getting out of the car. I'm afraid she might be lurking around the corner with a pickaxe, a shovel, and a heavy duty garbage bag.

After fifteen minutes I start to feel safe again. I jump out of the car, hurry inside, and run up the stairs as fast as I can. I'm halfway down the hallway when Liz walks out of her bedroom. When she sees me, she stands right in front of me and starts laughing. She pumps her fist in the air and claps as loud as she can.

"Bravo, Tim. How was your night in the big house? Did you get a tattoo? Or a new cuddle buddy?"

"Shut up, Liz. I'm not in the mood."

"Speaking of cuddle buddy, that girl Mellisa called again. That's the second time in two weeks."

"Yeah, fine. Whatever."

"I know you have a long list of admirers," she says, "most of whom probably don't speak English, but it wouldn't kill you to pick up the phone and call her back."

"Thanks, Dr. Phil. Now run along and color code your barrettes."

"You should be more appreciative, Tim. I almost baked you a loaf of bread with an emery board hidden inside it. In case you wanted to break out of prison and make a dozen more stupid mistakes."

"Piss off."

"When Dad told you to culture yourself, he didn't mean down at the local jail with a bunch of drunken degenerates."

"Go away," I tell her. "I'm tired. All I want to do is take a hot shower and watch TV."

"Have fun," she says. "Just remember not to bend over for the soap."

I shove past her and walk into the bathroom. I brush my teeth and gargle with Listerine. I strip off my dirty clothes and toss them into the hamper. Then I turn on the shower and set the dial as hot as I can take it, standing directly underneath the pounding pressure to let the water scald my face and chest. When my skin is red and itchy, I grab a bar of Irish Spring and scrub every inch of my body until I'm dizzy from the heat. I can still smell the mold from the pillow, the way the bedding reeked of wet dog.

Twenty minutes later, after I've fogged up the bathroom mirror and my fingers are wrinkled and pruned, I towel myself dry and trudge back to my bedroom. Sitting at my desk are a chocolate-chip granola bar, two aspirin, and a glass of orange juice. Mom must have brought them in while I was washing away a night's worth of bad memories. I pop the aspirin in my mouth, chug down the juice, and devour the granola bar. All in about thirty seconds.

Feeling less hungry, and somewhat normal again, I put on a clean pair of boxer shorts and start rummaging through every desk drawer, looking for that slip of paper with Mellisa's phone number. I find it ten minutes later, still folded in half from when she handed it to me in the library over a month ago. I see the little heart she drew above her first name, shaded in red, and I remember the way she smiled when she reached across the table to drop it in the palm of my hand.

I pick up the phone and lie on my bed, taking a deep breath as I dial her number.

"Hello?"

"Uh..." I sit up and freeze, my mouth hanging open as I stare down at the floor. It's definitely a girl's voice, but I can't tell if it's Mellisa's. I'm really bad at recognizing someone on the other end of the line. What if it's her mom? Or her sister? I don't even know if she has a sister. Or a mom. For all I know, her parents could be divorced? Or dead like mine.

These are things I like to know before I pick up the phone and start jawing away.

"Hello?" she says again.

I consider taking a guess, but I'd hate to embarrass myself before the conversation even begins. "Hi, may I speak with Mellisa, please?"

"This is she."

"Hi, Mellisa. It's Tim."

"Hey, Tim." She sounds excited, which is definitely a positive. "Nice to hear from you. I was wondering when you'd give me a ring."

"I wasn't ignoring you," I tell her. "I had some things I needed to take care of." I sound cryptic, but I definitely can't tell her about my video store obsession. Or about my night in jail. It's bad enough she caught me freaking out in the middle of a pointless STD mess. Slap a misdemeanor on top of that and I might as well hang up the phone right now. "So...how are you?"

"Great, thanks. You?

I yawn and rub my eyes. "I'm surviving."

"You sound pretty tired."

"I didn't get much sleep last night."

She laughs. "Too much kung fu fighting?"

"Something like that."

"You should take a nice, long nap."

I look at the clock. "It's ten-thirty in the morning."

"Yeah, but it's Sunday. The one day of the week when people expect you to sit on your ass and be totally lazy."

"That's true," I tell her. "I got nowhere to go, and all day to get there."

"Drink a glass of warm milk. It sounds gross, but trust me, there's a chemical in it that makes you super sleepy. Then get some lavender oil. Pour a few drops onto a handkerchief and rub it against your nose. You'll sleep like a baby."

"I've never understood that saying. Babies are always waking up every couple of hours, especially newborns. Right? They almost never sleep eight hours straight, and when they do wake up they're hungry and pissed off and crying. So wouldn't you say 'I slept like a baby' only if you had a horrible night's sleep?"

"The fact that you're even asking that question proves you need to crawl into bed and catch some Z's," she says. "Besides, if you don't reenergize yourself, you'll be a pretty anemic ninja. And then you won't be much use to anybody."

"I've already hit that point." She doesn't say anything, so I'm wondering if I've made her feel uncomfortable with my moodiness and self-deprecation. I can sense the conversation starting to slip away. "So anyway...I...uh. This isn't...I mean. I hope I'm not..."

"Trying to make sense?"

I smile. "This isn't a bad time, is it? You're not busy, are you?"

"I'm leaving in a couple of minutes to go shopping with my mom."

"Oh. Well, I won't keep you. I was just wondering if..." I cross my fingers. "...you wanted to go out sometime?"

"I'd love to. What did you have in mind?"

Oops. I didn't realize I was supposed to have a game plan this early. Was I supposed to have already made reservations? Was I supposed to have bought two tickets to the hottest new show at The Orpheum, or written her a free-verse love poem? Maybe I should drive down to Barnes & Noble and buy *Relationships for Dummies*.

"Honestly, I hadn't thought about it," I tell her. "Dinner? A movie?"

"Hmmm. Let's get out of Marblehead. I'm a firm believer that a first date should be an adventure. So I vote we take a trip into Boston. We could go to the aquarium? Check out some of the exhibits?"

"Sounds great. Maybe afterwards we can grab some dinner. Or walk around the city. Not the whole city, obviously, but...."

"When should we knuckle down and do this? Next weekend?"

"I wish, but I can't. I sort of got grounded this morning."

"For what?"

"It's complicated. Let's just say I wasn't thinking clearly and I really pissed off my mom. She's probably writing me out of her will as we speak."

"How long are you grounded for?"

"Till April vacation."

"Fine. Give me a call when your sentence is over and we'll lock it down. Who knows, maybe you'll get out early for good behavior."

I start picking at the frayed comforter. "Should I plan all this out and then get back to you? I can research the restaurants downtown. Do you have a favorite food? Do you have any allergies? What time should I pick you up? I'll need to get directions to your house."

"You have plenty of time to knock this out of the ballpark," she says, "so don't stress out."

"I wish it was that easy, but I have all these questions bouncing around in my head, and whenever I try to answer them, it's like a huge mushroom cloud fills the horizon."

"That's because you're asking the wrong questions."

"What do you mean?"

"Do zombies shit?"

Maybe I'm so exhausted that I'm starting to hallucinate. "Did you just ask me if..."

"Yeah, now answer the question. Do zombies shit?"

"I don't know. I've never thought about it before."

"Of course you haven't. That's because most people ask the same old, boring, generic questions, like how can zombies walk or run when they're decomposed, or suffering from rigor mortis. Or, how can some of them talk if they don't have a brain in their friggin' head, especially if their head is cut off from their body?"

"That's actually a good point," I tell her. "Their intestines probably aren't working, so wouldn't all that flesh just sit in their stomachs? Plus, what happens if they don't have a stomach? Where does all that food go?"

"Exactly. It's such a crucial question, but most people don't even think to ask it. If zombies do take a dump, then how come we never see them doing it?"

"It is kind of a private moment."

"Not to a zombie. They'll rip you apart in front of a packed crowd and not care who's watching. But if they can't drop a deuce every couple of days, then why don't they get all fat and bloated? With all those arms and legs and brains they're chomping on, wouldn't they get weighed down with raw flesh?"

"But if that were the case, zombies wouldn't be very exciting to watch. They'd just roll around on the ground like rotten sausages."

"My point exactly," she says. "Sometimes the most obvious question is the one you never think to ask."

"Good call."

"You're welcome. Take me out to dinner and we'll call it even. And I'm sure...." She pauses. "Tim, I gotta go."

"Okay. Have fun shopping. I'll talk to you later."

"Give me a ring whenever you want. And get some rest, too. I want you in tip-top shape for our date."

"Yes, sir."

I hang up the phone and smile, thinking that maybe the world doesn't suck quite so bad. Last night I felt musty and stale, ready to stick a fork in myself, but now I feel like I've been pumped full of fresh air.

My body is sore and exhausted, and I can't stop yawning. Plus, my muscles are tight and achy, and my upper lip is still swollen and bruised. I pull down the shades and crawl into bed, inhaling the citrusy smell of Downy as I bury my face in a twisted tangle of soft, clean sheets.

When I finally fall asleep, I dream of zombies. But they're not fighting over bloody arms and legs, or chasing after me with outstretched hands. They're not chewing on strips of fat and gristle, or ripping apart fresh, juicy brains. Instead, they're rushing through my front door, belching and farting, their faces scrunched up and their eyes bulging out. They're cramming into my bathroom as fast as they can, bent over at the waist and fighting each other for the use of a single toilet. And as I stand there laughing, tears rolling down my face, they shove me away and drop their pants, squatting like toads so they can push with all their might, trying to expel some intestinal obstruction that's been breaking them down with constant cramps and chronic indigestion.

12.
You Kiss like Your Father

I always swore I would never go to therapy.

Not because I'm scared, but because it looks really boring. At least in the movies. All you do is lie back on a smelly leather couch and stare up at the ceiling, whining and crying because your needs aren't being met, or because you suck at commitment, or because you can't eat one potato chip without gorging on the entire bag.

So you fork over hundreds of dollars a month, and reveal your innermost secrets and desires, only to discover that the real reason you're miserable is because you have way too many needs, or the reason you can't carry a relationship is because you're totally selfish, or the reason you're fat is because you eat too much junk food.

Duh.

For years my mother has been nagging me to set up an appointment with one of these self-righteous shrinks. Usually, whenever she brings up the topic, I get all huffy and tell her I don't want to be another case study locked inside a file cabinet. I tell her I don't want to twiddle my thumbs while some psychobabbling moron jots down my issues in a little black notebook.

But all that changed last week when Mom came into my room and said, "You're seeing a therapist next week." She handed me a slip of paper with a phone number written down in her usual chicken scratch. "His name is Dr. Wayne. He comes highly recommended." She crossed her arms. "You will see him at least once. Do you understand?"

I nodded. She was visibly upset, and her hands were clenched into fists. Her eyes were cutting edge lasers, and her mouth was set in a thin, hard line. She was armed and dangerous, and there was no way I was going to make a stink about therapy and cry foul play.

Mom and I haven't spoken much since my episode with the Tae-Bo girl. Every meal feels like a funeral procession, and when she wants me to do any chores she simply writes her demands on a dry erase board she stuck to my bedroom door. I'm still pissed that she left me in jail for the night. She's still pissed that I trespassed on private property and got fined eighty dollars for disturbing the peace. To make matters worse, Brian fired me from the video store.

Pretty much all I've been doing is sitting in my bedroom and thinking about my fucked up life. The only thing that could depress me even more is if the sky suddenly darkened and all the animals started lining up two by two. Even Liz noticed my intense brooding, and as a sign of détente, she brought me a dish of mint chocolate-chip ice cream and asked if I wanted to hang out in the living room with her and Emil and watch reruns of *Lost*.

Which is where I wish I was right now.

Because even though Emil is a complete douchebag, at least I can choose whether or not I want to talk to him.

Dr. Wayne, on the other hand, probably won't let me take a nap or chew my fingernails or stare out the window. In fact, he hasn't stopped talking since I walked into his office. As soon as he saw me, he pumped his fist in the air and shouted, "Welcome to my crib, T-dogg!"

I wasn't expecting a white, upper-class psychologist to be ghetto, but Dr. Wayne is a total wigger. Short and tubby, with a child molester mustache, he looks like Ron Jeremy, but acts like Jay-Z, wearing his hair in a pompadour and sporting gold chains around his pimpled neck. At first I thought he had a nervous tic, maybe a twitchy neck spasm, because he seems to bob his head whenever he opens his mouth, as if secretly humming the tune to some hardcore rap song.

And let's not forget the pimped-out office. There's a Ja Rule CD sitting on one of the bookshelves, a set of blue and lime green curtains that looks like something out of a 1970s blaxploitation flick, and behind his desk is a huge poster of Tupac Shakur. The heading reads 2PACALYPSE NOW, and below it the rap legend smokes a cigarette, eyebrows raised as he flashes "the gangsta look."

In a basket by the door he keeps assorted goodies for various age groups: a stuffed Barney, nude GI Joes, a Hello Kitty mirror, a Nerf basketball, and a family of homemade sock puppets that looks like a casting call for *The Hills Have Eyes*. I'm hoping he doesn't make me act out my embarrassing arrest with freaky sock puppets and a naked action figure.

After an awkward introduction, which includes a lame attempt at a high-five, I lie down on a black leather couch and stare up at the rotating fan, counting all the tiny cracks that spider web across the ceiling. My heart is pounding and my throat is dry, but I don't want Dr. Wayne to think I'm soft, so I whistle and say, "Pretty pimped-out pad, dude."

Across from me, in an aging swivel chair, my hip hop therapist nods his head and says, "Thanks. My dissertation was on rap music and cognitive therapy, hence the laid-back decor."

"How is rap music beneficial?" I ask him. "Isn't it all about guns and drugs, and bitches and ho's?"

"Actually, it's known as rap therapy," he says. "Using music to help kids develop their social skills."

"Like, what kind?"

"Mostly how to interact with others in positive ways. Personally, I like to focus on anger management and decision-making. How to establish a value judgment that's not based on violence. Or how to be in a loving relationship without being clingy and controlling."

"No kidding? Does it work?"

"Absolutely. For a lot of kids, especially the ones struggling with self-identity, rap therapy helps to boost their confidence. It improves their verbal and nonverbal communication skills. Not to mention it's fun to listen to, right?"

"Word," I say, although he's too busy gloating to catch my sarcasm.

"If you're really interested," he says, "you should check out my new book. It's a great resource for people struggling with depression and self-identity, especially adolescents. Of course, that's my professional opinion. It's not like I'm insisting you buy it."

"Right."

According to his website, which I pored over before coming here this afternoon, he recently published his first book, titled *You Kiss like Your Father*. It's a bunch of case studies about messed-up teenagers dealing with drug and alcohol addiction, domestic violence, sexual abuse, and tragic deaths in their immediate family. Naturally, at the end of each story, he rides in on a blinged-out horse to save the day, blasting Tupac and Notorious B.I.G. until the beats and lyrics bitch slap those suburban punks into forgiveness and acceptance.

"So...uh...how are sales?" I ask him.

"The literary world is a fickle animal, Tim. You have to be patient."

Which means his book sucks and no one wants to buy it.

Dr. Wayne flips open a dollar ninety-nine notepad from Office Depot. "So, Tim, how are you feeling today?"

I smile. "With my hands, as usual."

He stares at me for a second. "How about emotionally?"

"Great," I say, giving him thumbs-up. "I'm living the dream."

He lays the notepad on his knee and holds up a finger. "First, let me start off by saying that it's perfectly normal to be nervous. Just because you're in therapy doesn't mean there's something wrong with you. Okay?"

"Sure."

"Second, any information that you share with me today is strictly confidential."

"What about my mom?"

"Not even your mom. She can badger me all she wants, but I won't tell her a thing. You have my word on that."

I nod. It's kind of hard to hate Dr. Wayne. He seems so excited to have me in his office, like we're old college buddies about to swap dirty jokes and listen to gangsta rap.

"How long will this last?" I ask him.

"Forty-five, fifty minutes."

"How long have you been a therapist?"

"About seven years."

"Do you see a lot of nut jobs?"

He laughs. "Tim, the people who come to see me are all normal. They're not weird or neurotic. They don't smear walls with their own feces. They just need someone who will sit down and listen. Someone who'll remind them to stay positive and keep rockin'."

I nod again.

Dr. Wayne clears his throat and straightens his tie. It's an ugly patchwork of green, red, and yellow splotches, like maybe it had once been white and during an intense therapy session someone had puked on it.

"So, Tim," he says, "what do *you* expect to get out of this session?"

"My mother off my back."

He looks hurt. "This is your time to shine, so try being honest instead of disagreeable."

"Fine. I know I'm not perfect, and...well...I guess I do have a few issues I've been carting around, but...."

"...Do you want to talk about your father?" he asks me.

"I don't know," I say, watching a fly buzz overhead. "Do you want to talk about Snoop Dogg?"

"During the patient's first session, I typically like to have a normal face-to-face conversation."

"Okay. Then let's talk about all the jerks who throw their cigarette butts on the beach. Does that bother you, too? Cause it really pisses me off."

He tents his fingers and presses them to his chin. "What specific issues do you think you have?"

"I'm not depressed or suicidal, alright?"

"I didn't say you were."

"You had a tone."

He takes a ballpoint pen out of his shirt pocket and writes something down. "Why are you here, Tim?"

"Because my mother was hell-bent on making me come."

"Why would she do that?"

"I don't know."

"Sure you do," he says. "Tell me."

I ignore him and look around the room. Off to my left is an enormous poster of Sigmund Freud, a profile shot reading "What's on Man's Mind?" No points for guessing, but given Freud's sexual obsessions, I'm guessing fellatio and a backrub followed by wine and caviar. I imagine Dr. Freud and his libido ravishing the nymphet Lolita in a green meadow, her snow-white bobby socks hanging from a tree and an empty bottle of Riesling spinning lazily in a Viennese wind.

"Tim?" Dr. Wayne snaps his fingers. "Why does your mother want you to see a therapist?"

He's patient, I have to give him that much. "Maybe because of my father's death."

"What? I couldn't hear you."

He heard me, the asshole. "Because of my father's death."

"Tell me how he died."

I want to haul off and punch Dr. Wayne square in the nose. "Isn't all that information in my file?"

"It might be," he says, "but I want to hear it from you."

"He killed himself. When I was eight-years-old. Satisfied?"

"Do you remember how you felt at the time?"

I sit up and look toward the open window. There's a cool breeze blowing in from the ocean, and I want to run outside and stand on the sidewalk, my arms spread wide open as cars drive up and down Main Street, forming a mile-long ribbon of businessmen in sleek Mercedes Benzes, parents and kids stuffed into minivans, and college students idling along in beat-up Pintos and rusty Volvos. I want that thundering commotion to rally inside my head, to drive away all memories of a terrible night that, ten years later, is still pushing me around like some bully on a playground.

"Tim?" He waves his hand in front of my face. "Do you remember being scared? Or sad? Or confused?"

"Probably all three," I tell him. "His death hit me pretty hard. Like an emotional drive by."

"Yes!" He pumps his fist in the air. "Score one for the T-dogg! Way to open up during our first jam session."

"That was totally life-changing," I say. "Can I go now?"

"Don't cheapen the moment." He chews on the end of his ballpoint pen. "Losing one's father is incredibly tough, at any age. And suicide only complicates the equation."

"Equation? Doc, did you see me bring an abacus in here? My dad blew his head off. This isn't Speak & Math. My mom doesn't pay you a hundred dollars an hour to sit around and do word problems."

He takes the pen out of his mouth, and a long string of drool drips onto his white collared shirt, which is dotted with food stains. He wipes away the drool with his stubby thumb, then wipes his thumb on the underside of his dusty chair.

Gross.

I grab a handful of Andes mints out of a cheap plastic bowl. I eat five of them while Dr. Wayne scribbles in his black notepad, occasionally muttering to himself as he bites his bottom lip and crosses out random lines with large, ferocious strokes.

I want to lean forward to see what he's writing. I know I'm being flippant and pigheaded, but I don't want to come off as some high-strung, angry nerd who needs to be doped up on antipsychotic drugs. Maybe he's mentioning that I'm at risk to stick my head in the oven. Or that I'm a future serial killer, susceptible to wild tantrums whenever cute girls reject me, or prone to crying jags whenever a stranger invades my personal space?

Or maybe he's bored and jotting down his top ten favorite rap songs.

But two can play at that game. So while Dr. Wayne defames me in shorthand, I make a mental list of the top ten things that piss me off even more than coming to therapy.

1. Girls who dress like guys (If you're a transvestite, you get a free pass.)
2. People who drive with their dog on their lap (There are safer ways to find a cuddle buddy; besides, you already have an airbag.)
3. Football players who dance in the end zone (You're not being paid millions of dollars to act like an imbecile.)
4. Telemarketers (Next time you call, I'll waste fifteen minutes of your time by trying to sell you all the shit in the back of my closet.)
5. Finding a hair in my food (There are better ways to get protein.)
6. Straws (No one looks cool sucking liquid through a flimsy piece

142

of plastic.)

7. Tanning booths (Why don't you just inject cancer directly into your body?)

8. Guys who drive around with faux testicles on the back of their pickup truck (If you're that self-conscious about the size of your dick, then pay for a penis enlargement.)

9. Cheerleaders who starve themselves (You can't survive on just gossip.)

10. Tight clothes on fat chicks (Be proud of yourself, but please know your size.)

I eat more mints and stare at Dr. Wayne. On the left side of his face is a deep red birthmark in the shape of a turtle. I spotted it when I first walked in, but resisted the urge to touch it. I know it's rude to gawk, so I try looking everywhere else in the room except at his birthmark, which is the first place my eyes keep landing. I try looking outside, but the leaves are turning green, which makes me think of turtles. I try thinking about winter, but then I remember turtleneck sweaters. All roads lead back to that amphibious decoration, and the more I stare, the more obvious it is that his port wine stain captivates me.

I wonder what turtle soup tastes like. Probably chicken.

Dr. Wayne glances up. "What are you thinking about, Tim?"

"The Galapagos," I say, grinning.

"Interesting." He scribbles more notes, probably suggesting that since islands symbolize solitude and isolation, I'm a lonely young man who craves maternal love and peer-bonding.

I look down at my watch. "What's next on the agenda? This is exhilarating, but Spike TV is running an all-day James Bond marathon."

He flips to a new page. "Tell me about the ninjas."

I shrug. "There's not much to tell. Dad was a soldier fighting in Iraq, he happened to meet some ninjas, case closed."

"I didn't realize there were ninjas in Iraq."

"That's why they're called ninjas," I tell him. "Because you never know when or where they'll suddenly pop up."

"And where did your father meet these ninjas? By the side of the road? At a farmer's market?"

"In the VA Hospital."

He jots down a few sentences. "Why did they choose to reveal themselves to your father? Why not the doctor? Or one of the nurses?"

"They knew he had potential. That he was trustworthy."

"Were the ninjas on vacation, or was this a business trip to recruit new members?"

I can't tell if his question is meant to sound snarky, or if he's genuinely interested. "Ninjas are concerned about all the corruption they see, like war and greed and the decline of family values. They want to be protectors and make the world a better place."

"And they thought your father could be an important ally?"

"Yep. They spent weeks teaching him their beliefs and philosophies."

"What kind of philosophies?"

"Like the importance of using positive energy to conquer fear. Or the importance of using your mind to solve problems instead of resorting to senseless violence."

"So being a ninja isn't just about killing whoever's standing next to you?"

I ball up all the Andes wrappers and look around for a trashcan. Finding none, I throw the wad onto the coffee table in front of me. "It's the art of survival," I tell him. "It's about weathering hardships, and dodging all the crap that life throws at you."

"And how does a ninja survive?" he asks me. "By using swords and spears, or poisonous mushrooms?"

"If need be. But only in self-defense."

"What's the standard gear?"

"The uniform, obviously. Which is usually blue, but it can also be white if the terrain is snowy. Toss in a few throwing stars, a sword, maybe a satchel full of nuts and berries."

"Do you drink your own urine?"

"Whoa! Why would you even ask me that?"

"I watched a documentary recently, and it said that a lot of Asians drink their own urine because it enhances their beauty and cures certain diseases."

"Ninjas don't drink their own pee," I tell him.

"What if they're stranded in the jungle and dying of thirst?"

"They make a divining rod and dig up some water."

"Supposedly, it's all the rage in India," he says. "Holy men have been chugging their own urine for thousands of years."

"Look what good it's done them. They're still a third-world country."

"Apparently they drink the midstream. The guy they interviewed said people mix it in their orange juice or serve it over cereal."

144

Now I feel nauseous. I can't imagine pouring a hot cup of piss into a bowl of Cinnamon Toast Crunch. I'd have to douse it with sugar just to hide the bitter aftertaste.

"I know it sounds crazy," he says, "but you'd be surprised at some of the weird ideas people embrace."

"Speaking of weird, do you ever watch *Sábado Gigante*?"

"Is that a movie?"

"No, it's a TV show."

"Portuguese, right?"

"Actually, I think it's Spanish for 'gigantic Saturday.'"

He shakes his head. "I'm not trying to steamroll you, but I'm pretty sure it's Portuguese. It means 'salacious gigolo.'"

"No, it means the sixth day of the week. Which is gigantic. Like my knowledge of foreign TV shows."

"I have a Ph.D.," he says.

"I have the Spanish channel."

He shrugs. "Fine. Let's just agree to disagree."

"Whatever." I stretch out my legs and put my feet on the coffee table. "Anyway, *Sábado Gigante* is basically a four hour version of the gong show where contestants perform all these crazy-ass stunts. I saw a guy suck up water through his nose and then squirt it out his eye so he could write calligraphy on a piece of paper. And another guy lit a hundred firecrackers that were taped to his chest."

Dr. Wayne smiles. "Sounds fascinating and bizarre. I can definitely see the attraction."

"I like that there are people in this world who applaud individuality," I tell him. "And I like knowing I'm not the only person who chooses to highlight his uniqueness. Even if I never get any credit for it."

"Is it possible, Tim, that what you view as daring and commendable is really nothing more than a self-gratifying act by someone who's trying to fill a void in their life?"

I want to grab Dr. Wayne by his bulging love handles and chuck him out the second story window. "You think you're so superior, don't you?"

He doesn't say anything, which annoys me even more.

"You think you can break me down with your cryptic questions?" I lean forward and point my finger to let him know I mean business. "All you care about is busting me wide open so you can take a look inside and collect material for your next book, which will probably tank."

Silence.

"You have no frigging clue how I feel, sitting there all high and mighty in your stupid ghetto suit from Walmart."

He waits a minute before speaking, letting me reposition myself on the couch so I can eat another fistful of mints.

"Tim, you need to realize that your father's death is still hurting your mother and sister. And you haven't come to terms with it yet, either. It's called psychological trauma."

"Wow! Did you read about that in the newest issue of *Psychology Today*?"

He pinches the bridge of his nose. "Is there anyone else you can talk to? Maybe a friend at school, or...."

"Do imaginary friends count?"

"Now you're being a smartass."

"It's better than being a dumbass."

"What about a girlfriend?" he asks me. "Got one of those?"

"Kind of. We've been talking a lot on the phone, but we haven't actually gone on an official date yet. I guess you could say I'm leasing with an option to buy."

"Jump on that," he says. "Women don't like to wait."

Like he would know.

"We're going out in April," I tell him. "After my mother paroles me."

"What's her name?"

"Mellisa."

"That's Greek," he says. "It means honeybee. According to mythology, she was a nymph who discovered the taste of honey and fed it to the infant Zeus."

I give him a round of applause. "Congratulations on knowing something that no one else even remotely cares about."

He leans back in his chair, putting his hands behind his head like he's trying to look cool. "Is Mellisa aware of your wacky family drama?"

"Don't be condescending."

Dr. Wayne doesn't say anything, which makes me wonder if he's egging me on. Maybe he's trying to wind me up real good until I have a string of choked-up epiphanies and start bawling into his suede sofa cushion. Maybe he'll keep prying me with questions until I leap up and announce I can't possibly survive unless I see him every week for the next six months.

"Let me ask you something," he finally says. "And be honest. Are you happy with your life?"

"Hell, yeah," I shout. "My mother is a functioning alcoholic who prefers shopping over spending time with her own son. My sister is a prima donna who's probably possessed by a bitchy ghost. I just lost my shitty job at the video store because I got arrested for trespassing. Kids at school make fun of me because they think I'm a basket case. I lost my virginity to a hooker, who I'm pretty sure overcharged me. Oh, and my Dad killed himself. So, yeah, my entire life is pretty much one gigantic cluster fuck. Every time I think I've hit rock bottom, life throws me a shovel and tells me to keep on digging."

I stand up and walk over to his desk, fighting back a gusher of tears, coughing as I try to control my breathing and calm my nerves.

Dr. Wayne doesn't say a word.

I start playing with the Newton's cradle, watching the metal balls swing back and forth, listening to each tinny click as I focus my eyes on the harsh glare of sunlight on silver.

"Tim, what do you want most?"

"I don't know." I bite off the top of my thumbnail and spit it onto the carpet. "I guess I just want to be totally indispensable. That's not wrong is it? To believe that I'm meant to do great things?"

"I'm all for having big dreams," he says, "but you have to make sure they're your own dreams, and that you're not just borrowing them from someone else."

"But I have a responsibility."

"Sure, to yourself."

"What about to my father?"

Dr. Wayne shakes his head. "Sorry, but I don't believe you have a moral obligation here."

"What about all the stories he told me? All those secrets he shared with me?"

He leans forward to look me in the eye. "I'm probably not the first to tell you this, but you're not a horrible son if you admit that your father needed counseling."

I shake my head and choke back another round of tears, shutting my eyes tight as I try to ignore that peripheral intrusion of traumatized parents and drowning angels, of stalking Mean Men and bloody bathrooms.

An hour ago I thought I had all the answers.

But now?

I'm not even sure if I understood all the questions.

My throat feels tight, and I swallow. "His death wasn't meaningless."

"Is that what you're afraid of most?"

"Who says I'm afraid?"

"Don't play superhero with me. Everyone is afraid of something. That's what defines bravery. Not the absence of fear, but having the courage to face it."

"Sounds fishy."

"Tupac once said 'All I'm trying to do is survive and make good out of the dirty, nasty, unbelievable lifestyle that they gave me.' I think that's a good example..."

"How is that a good example?" I ask him. "Tupac got gunned down in cold blood."

"I realize that. Instead of changing his dirty, nasty, unbelievable, lifestyle, he swung it over his shoulder and brought it into the recording studio. And it ended up inciting a rap war and getting him killed."

"What's your point?"

"Music isn't reality, Tim. It's a representation of reality. You can't pretend your life is a hard-edged rap song, or a glamorous Hollywood musical. You can't waste time pretending to be your favorite character in the hope that one day you'll suddenly transform into him and just march your way toward a better life."

I stare outside as the daylight dwindles, watching a bank of clouds drift out of town toward Marblehead Bay. Up the street I see my mother coming over the hill in her Beamer. She pulls up next to the curb and honks the horn twice. She lights a cigarette and blows a trail of smoke out the window. Peering closer, I see the backseat is loaded with boxes and bags, ribbons overflowing into the front seat, every purchase lined up neatly as though set in a display case.

I turn to Dr. Wayne. "Translate."

He walks over to me. "Sorry, my man, but at the end of the day, you're just going to have to take a long, hard look in the mirror and make all your own decisions. And then, whether you like it or not, you'll have to follow through with them the best you can."

And that, I want to tell him as I slam the door and bolt for the stairs, is what I'm most afraid of.

When I get inside the car, wheezing and out of breath, my mother says, "How was therapy?"

"Fine." I push away a jumbled mess of shiny gold ribbons and red felt bows. I couldn't care less about the week's bargain basement splurges, but I desperately need a motherly fix. "What did you buy?" I ask her.

She hesitates, mid-drag, eyebrows raised, and flicks her half-smoked cigarette out the window. She reaches into the backseat and opens box after box, sharing her shopping adventures while she holds up blouses and skirts and vests and sweaters. She drapes them over the steering wheel and lays them out on the dashboard.

I hang my head, my temples throbbing as I stroke layer after layer of cotton and leather and cashmere. I want to turn on the radio and just close my eyes, or maybe bang my head into the glove compartment, but all I can do is slink down in my seat and inhale the smoky air as plastic bags ripple in the wind and sales receipts flutter at my feet.

My mother parades through her weekly raiment carnival, her words swathed in dollar signs, and in the approaching darkness, as twilight shadows rap on the windows, her flashy wardrobe is a soothing opiate to all the grotesque images still dancing behind my eyes.

13.

The Insane Clown Posse

We're cleaning out the upstairs guest room in my grandparents' house, Liz and I. We're rifling through drawers and closets, and tossing armfuls of junk into stacks of cardboard boxes. Moving through the room, I touch silk damask curtains and hand-stitched Oriental rugs, leaving my grubby fingerprints on Tibetan singing bowls and a glass coffee table. I climb atop a California-king size bed covered in linens and a down duvet, and I gaze up at the oak bookcase in which my grandparents housed classic novels they never read, my eyes swimming across the stone turtle figurines that guard each shelf.

No one lives here now, but Mom still refuses to sell it. Once a year she hires a cleaning crew to shampoo the rugs and polish the floors, to rake the yard and water the flowers. But this year, perhaps feeling thrifty, she ordered Liz and me to drive down to Cape Cod for the weekend and kick off her spring cleaning frenzy.

According to her, we're supposed to scrub the funk and box the junk.

School is out for April vacation, so neither one of us wants to waste our time cutting apart massive cobwebs, or chasing crickets across the countertop with rolled up newspapers. Granted, it's just for two days, and I probably wouldn't do anything anyway except sit at home and mope, but it's the idea of performing manual labor that really irks me, especially when I know it's only because Mom is still mad at me. I thought I had served my time by agreeing to visit with Dr. Wayne, but apparently Mom won't be satisfied unless I'm tired and sore and sweating profusely like a prisoner on a chain gang.

Even though they've been dead for three years, I can still smell Grandpa's rum and maple tobacco. I can still smell Grandma's favorite perfume: *Savon Adoucissant au Miel*. Like a ghostly presence, these scents follow me from room to room, clinging to curtains and clothes. I smell perfume on the couch downstairs where Grandma crocheted after dinner. I smell whiffs of tobacco whenever I open one of Grandpa's books, the pages brittle from his constant thumbing.

My grandparents collected everything imaginable, from clocks, pictures, and coins to magazines, coffee cups, and the obituaries of all their friends. Instead of family members, they doted on lavish antiques, filling the house with vintage moonshine jugs, a bronze statue of Amelia Earhart, and drawers full of broken jewelry. The rooms are full of Baccarat and Aubusson carpets, and everything is tucked away behind panes of beveled glass. Old Christmas cards are shoved into plastic shopping bags, and winter jackets fill the closets like cotton balls stuffed into medicine jars. Even their yard is littered with pink flamingos and lawn gnomes.

Because the house is boarded up eight months out of the year, everything has a spoiled and stagnant feel about it. The air is dank and musty, and the heat vents are rusted over from years of salt corrosion. The toilets are cracked and chipped, and the windows are streaked with grime. I never enjoyed staying here as a child, and I like it even less now. This heavy silence keeps drawing me into the darkest parts of the house, into those cramped spaces where the Mean Man still waits with his out-stretched hands.

Liz trips over a pile of moldy sports jackets. "You'd think Grandma and Grandpa would have tossed out some of this stuff, or at least had a garage sale."

"They didn't come upstairs that much. Gout and arthritis."

"Well, they could have at least done some rearranging. What's that called, Tim? Fuck Shit?"

"It's feng shui," I tell her. "It's supposed to enlarge your personal space and make you feel better about your life."

She laughs. "So basically you move your desk under a window and suddenly the whole world is peaches and cream?"

"That's the idea."

"Dad should have tried it," she says. "Then maybe he wouldn't have gotten depressed and gone into the bathroom."

"Don't talk about Dad," I yell, wanting to smash my fist into her three thousand dollar rhinoplasty. What I wouldn't give right now to feel that euphoric crack as muscles and tendons collapse under the force of a powerful jab.

She sits down on the edge of the bed. "I miss him just as much as you do, Tim. But I'm still pissed that he didn't think about us when he put the gun in his mouth."

Stumbling over a mound of half-filled cardboard boxes, I maneuver my way around a pile of dirty clothes so I can open the window and take in a breath of fresh air. I look down into the backyard, staring at the remnants of my grandparents' pool. I used to swim in it all the time when I was a kid, right up until the day I almost drowned. But after that traumatic moment, I was content to just sit on the top step, holding onto the chrome railing while I splashed my feet in shallow puddles. Like so many other things in my life, the pool is now empty and deserted. It's filled with wet leaves, a couple of lawn chairs, and a rusted out wheelbarrow. It looks like an enormous grave.

Early this morning, before we left for Cape Cod, Mom called me into the kitchen. She was still in her bathrobe, clutching a cup of coffee in one hand and wiping the sleep from her eyes with the other. I really wasn't sure what to expect when I sat down at the table, but I wasn't anticipating hugs and kisses. Even though she's finally started talking to me again, we still haven't said more than a few terse sentences.

So when I sat down I didn't even look at her. I was tired and hungry, and I didn't want her to reprimand me, or interrogate me, or ask me if I was on drugs.

In fact, all I've ever wanted is for her to lay her hand on top of mine and say, "Tim, I love you. I understand."

But she hasn't said those words since my father died.

She watched me eat breakfast, and then, in a surprising display of civility, passed me the grape jelly and handed me a butter knife. I just stared down at the kitchen table, counting all the crumbs that had fallen off my English muffin. I wondered how things might be different if Dad was still alive. I thought about my sister and me, and how we bicker and fight on a daily basis. I thought about my mother's grief, and about all those photo albums that remain empty after 2004.

"Tim," she said, "I know you're still upset about your night in jail, but you have no right to be angry with me. You're the one who got yourself into this mess. True, I haven't been the world's greatest parent, but..."

"Look, Mom, I appreciate..."

She held up her hand. "This is a lecture, not a debate. Besides, it wouldn't hurt you to listen for a change." She took a long sip of coffee. "I honestly don't know what to do with you anymore. Every time I turn around you're making a fool of yourself."

Her voice sounded old and tired, barely above a whisper.

"I know you won't believe this," she said, "but I really do have your best interests at heart."

I just nodded. All I wanted to do was crawl under the table, close my eyes, and stick my fingers in my ears.

"Someday you'll be man enough to realize that, Tim. And when that glorious day comes, I sure hope you'll be man enough to tell me."

As I sipped a cup of green tea, my ego beat to shit and limping out of the room, she reached into her pants pocket and handed me the keys to the Cape house. "I don't usually send you and Liz to spruce up the place," she said, "but I'm thinking of spending some time there this summer, so I want you to clean it up for me. And buy some air fresheners, too, so the place doesn't smell like a goddamn nursing home."

"Okay."

She handed me fifty dollars. "For food and gas. And eat some seafood, too. It's good for your brain."

I took the money and tucked it into my shirt pocket.

"I need you to do me a favor," she said. "In the basement are some boxes I left there years ago. Just personal belongings. They're probably piled in the corner, or shoved underneath that pool table your grandfather bought and then never used." She stirred more sugar into her coffee. "They're regular cardboard boxes, except they're wrapped up in duct tape. My name is written all over them in black magic marker. Grab them for me and load them into the car."

"Yeah, sure."

She drank the rest of her coffee and hummed along to the radio. When we were done eating, she got up and walked over to the kitchen sink to rinse off our dirty plates and load them into the dishwasher. The window was open, and she stared outside into the bright sunlight, smiling.

"I haven't seen a Saturday morning this beautiful in ages." She let out a long breath and poured herself another cup of coffee. "Who knows? It might just be a gorgeous weekend, after all."

***

After lunch, Liz and I tackle the den. Armed with Pledge and Windex, and a handful of wet rags, we scrub inches of dirt and grime off brown leather coasters and black walnut picture frames. We clean the Waterford crystal with strips of microfiber cloth, and we shine every maple bookcase, standing on our tiptoes so we can polish Grandma's set of ceramic angel figurines. Hollow and cheap, they're the only things she ever dusted, wiping them with a sponge soaked in ammonia until she could see her own reflection.

According to her, Liz and I each had our own guardian angel that would follow in our footsteps and keep us from harm. "So long as you pray," she said, "the angels will save you from all manner of wickedness and temptation." I wanted to believe her, and at night I would kneel down at the side of my bed to recite the Lord's Prayer. But why bother? I had tried talking to God for years, and the only response I got was a dead father.

But Grandma was harsh and relentless, like a shrunken, arthritic car salesman, and every time I came to visit she would steer me into the den and tell me the story of the angel at the sepulcher, insisting that haloed saints and winged seraphs would protect me from all the evils of the world. After Dad died I wanted to push her away, grab a hammer, and smash those stupid angels into a million little pieces. I was so frightened of their watchful eyes, fearful of their tiny pale hands pressed together in prayer. They used to stare down at me from the top shelf, grave and solemn, as if judging me for some unpardonable sin.

Now, gazing up at them, I notice how small they appear. Pushed back on the shelves, cracked and chipped, they look so clownish, so bruised and battered, as if they no longer have the energy to fake innocence by impersonating godliness. They're just a bunch of dusty knickknacks, their celestial light smothered by years of neglect.

I still want to topple every single one of them, laughing and cheering as hundreds of milky-white shards scatter across the hardwood floor like jagged pieces of bone. But I can't stand looking at their wide-eyed expressions, so I give them each a quick rubdown and flick them in the face with my index finger.

"Hey, Liz," I say, wiping a dead fly off the couch, "don't all these angels give you a sort of creepy, not so fresh feeling?"

"Right," she says, laughing. "Though probably not as disturbing as spending a night in the slammer."

I ignore her and scrub a brass lamp, swearing at a particular stain that won't lighten. After a few minutes my arm starts to hurt, so I admit defeat and wash the leather ottoman. When I'm done, I sweep dirt off the hardwood floor, dust off the first-edition books, and polish the entire northern hemisphere on the Mother of Pearl globe.

Liz sits down on the loveseat and tosses her dishrag into a bucket of dirty water. She stares at me, but doesn't say anything. She opens her mouth and starts to speak, then turns away to play with her split ends. She does this four or five times until I drop my sponge on the coffee table and lean against the doorframe, waiting.

"Were you scared that night?" she asks me. "When you were in jail?"

I thought she was going to say something snarky, so I was getting ready to make fun of her fake nails. Instead, I sit on the arm of the couch and shrug. "A little. It was pretty intense, but... I don't know...I guess it was more boring than anything else."

"What was the worst part?"

"I can't remember."

"Bullshit." She crosses her arms. "Come on. Thrill me."

I take a deep breath, staring down at all the nicks in the floor. "I guess it was just...feeling so utterly useless and insignificant. I mean, who else can I depend on? Dad handed me a crap load of advice, but I have no idea where to put it. And it's pretty obvious that Mom will never care about me."

"Tim, she cried all night long. She even got dressed and sat in her car for forty minutes."

"That's not the point!" I shout. "Mom would never abandon *you*."

"Is that what you're worried about? That Mom will just chuck you out of the house and change all the locks?"

"No. I'm just...I don't know..." I rub my temples. I can already feel the beginning of a massive headache. "I'm just scared that no matter what I do, I'll always feel this wretched and hopeless."

Liz gets up and walks over to the window, moving aside the curtain so she can gaze off into the backyard. "Do you know what I'm afraid of?"

This is something I should probably know, like her favorite color or her favorite TV show. But I don't know those either. Hell, I can barely remember her birthday, or the last time I gave her a hug. I'm not even sure where she wants to go to college, or what major she wants to pursue, or if she wants to get married someday and have a couple of yuppie kids.

"No idea," I tell her. And as I say this, as I'm staring at the back of her head, I realize she could be any stranger off the street, just another person I pass by without noticing, another person I completely disregard because she's not worth a moment's thought. In a way, it's sort of humiliating. After sixteen years, my sister and I hardly know each other. We've been too busy patching the holes in our lives with anger and resentment.

I take a few steps toward Liz, squinting in the bright sunlight, not really sure if I should pat her on the back and say something nice, or if I should stand here in the middle of the den with my arms folded. The room is quiet, and for a few seconds neither one of us speaks. I feel so edgy and restless, like the Mean Man is chasing me down the hallway, like I'm struggling for breath in the back of my closet, and I just want to run outside because I don't want to hear whatever it is she has to say. Instead, I want her to say, "Never mind" and pick up a wet dishrag so we can scrub away this uncomfortable silence with expensive household cleaners.

"I'm afraid of losing Mom," she says. "I already feel like half a person since Dad died."

"Well, at least you have a boyfriend," I tell her.

"Had. Emil and I broke up."

"Are you kidding me?" I'm trying to hide my excitement, but I have a smile as wide as the Yangtze River. "When did this happen?"

"Last night."

"What happened? Did he try to bite your neck?"

Liz turns away from the window. "I'd been thinking about dumping him for a while, but the other night we were watching *Jerry Maguire* and it made me think about our entire relationship. Remember that scene at the end when Jerry tells Dorothy that she completes him?"

"I try not to."

" Well, I was watching that scene, and I just started to get all freaky and emotional. Hot flashes, shortness of breath. Like, a serious sob-athon."

"Maybe you had food poisoning."

She walks over and smacks me on the arm. "Listen, dummy, I'm trying to tell you. I got upset because I realized Emil would never say that to me. He'd never be that honest and truthful even if he felt that way. But then, while he was trying to calm me down, I realized *I* would never say that to *him.*"

She stares at me as if I'm supposed to have a Eureka moment and suddenly understand whatever the fuck it is she's talking about.

"So I started thinking about the end of the school year, and how he'll fly back to Romania and forget all about me, and probably shack up with some dumb bitch..."

"Who looks like Elvira."

"...which is probably what's supposed to happen, but..."

"Wait a second. You broke up with your boyfriend based on a spontaneous decision you made while watching cable?"

"I got bored with him. Nothing felt new or exciting anymore. He was just a fad, like the newest iPhone or low-carb fast food. I liked having him around, and his accent was kind of sexy, but eventually the honeymoon stage ends, right?" She leans against the wall and peels off a fleck of paint with her fingernail. "I needed him for a little while, and I guess I'm okay with that, but now it just feels stale and repetitive."

"I wish someone needed me," I tell her. "Then maybe *I* wouldn't feel so stale and repetitive."

"Call that Mellisa girl. She's cute. And she probably doesn't carry mace."

"I called her a couple of weeks ago."

"No shit!" Liz stands in front of me, eyes wide open. "You actually dialed a girl's phone number? And spoke to her?"

"Yep." I think I'm blushing, but it might just be my allergies from all the dust.

"Voicemail doesn't count, Tim."

"Trust me, she was alive."

"Don't stand there smirking. Divulge some details."

"We talked for a few minutes, about school and the weather and all that cliché bullshit, and then I just straight-up asked her if she wanted to go out with me sometime. And she said that sounded awesome, so, yeah, it's definitely game on."

"Where are you taking her?"

"We'll probably drive into Boston for the day, maybe check out the aquarium. I guess I should buy her dinner, otherwise I'll look like a schmuck. I'm supposed to call her this week so we can set it up."

"Respect her personal space," Liz says, "and let her do most of the talking. And don't mention anything that has to do with ninjas, or throwing stars, or crane style kung fu."

"Don't worry," I tell her. "I won't make the same mistakes all over again."

"That's good," she says, patting me on the back, "but don't make any new ones either."

***

It's almost dinnertime, so while Liz is taking a nap on the freshly scrubbed and pine-scented couch, I decide to look for Mom's boxes. Still fighting off a headache, I walk into the kitchen and unlock the basement door, tugging on a rusted pull chain that hangs from the slanted ceiling. A dull yellowish haze trickles out of a bare and grimy light bulb, illuminating a five foot radius. I make sure to avoid that wobbly first step, which is warped and splintered, and then, wary of spiders and insects, I creep down the rickety stairs, my hands searching for cobwebs, my nose twitching from the damp, moldy smell. I haven't been down here since the summer after my father died, when I spent a rainy afternoon building forts out of cardboard boxes, pretending I was trapped underground and searching for buried treasure.

There are no windows, so I grab a flashlight from Grandpa's toolbox. I maneuver my way through the gloomy basement, tripping over dozens of boxes that are scattered everywhere in no particular order. They're stacked on top of the pool table, shoved into corners, and piled onto crooked shelves along with broken charms and dusty ornaments. I see lots of junk, but none of the boxes are wrapped up in duct tape, and none display my mother's name in black magic marker. I consider telling her that I couldn't find the boxes, and that I spent hours looking for them, but I know she won't believe me. Besides, she's been so angry these past few weeks that she'll probably disown me if I fail to deliver on this one simple request.

I finally decide to open every single box. The first few contain shirts, pants, and blouses, while those atop the pool table are loaded with tattered copies of Hemingway and Faulkner, and old editions of the Saturday Evening Post. On the shelves, they're filled with pencils, pens, and rusted staplers. In one box I find a spare set of Grandpa's false teeth, dotted brown with nicotine. Looking around at all these kooky keepsakes, it's no wonder that Dad always referred to Mom's side of the family as "the insane clown posse."

I swing the flashlight under the stairs where the light catches three emaciated boxes, stacked one on top of the other and surrounded by a nest of cobwebs. I pull down the first box and open it up, finding nothing but a bunch of old photo albums. Most of the pictures show Grandma and Grandpa gallivanting across America. They're posing at the Grand Canyon, standing beneath the St. Louis Arch, hugging and kissing at the Sears Tower, and smiling in front of Niagara Falls.

The second box contains my mother's wedding dress, which I recognize from all those glossy 8 x 10 pictures that sit atop our entertainment center. I remove the wedding dress, and underneath is a moth-eaten tuxedo that I assume belonged to my father. Like the dress, it's standard wedding attire, a dusty black and white with the bow-tie and cummerbund affair.

Inside the third box is a black leather-bound book. I open the cover to find it's another photo album, but this one is filled with pictures of my family, most of which I've never seen before. There's Mom and Liz standing next to a swing set at Castle Rock Park. There's Dad dressed in his army fatigues, smiling that gap-toothed grin as he waves to the camera from the top step of our front porch. There's even a picture of my parents on their wedding day, posing at the Spohr Gardens in Woods Hole, shrouded by daffodils and daylilies while Dad wraps Mom in a giant bear hug and kisses the nape of her neck.

And there are pictures of me. In one, I'm asleep on the couch with my mouth hanging open, my arms crossed over my chest while Rosie, who died years ago, nuzzles up beside me with her head in my lap. In another picture, Mom and Liz are laughing while Dad and I splash around in the ocean at Old Silver Beach. And in another, taken at night, the entire family is walking past a merry-go-round at the Barnstable County Fair. Mom and Dad eat cups of vanilla ice-cream drizzled with hot fudge and whipped cream while Liz and I stuff our mouths with sticky handfuls of blue cotton candy. The four of us are talking and laughing. We're smiling at the camera like a real family, just perfect examples of a life so sunny it hurts my eyes.

Shining my flashlight over the parade of pictures, I try to make out each and every detail, but the edges are faded and curled inward. Plus, there's an inch of filth caked onto the plastic sheets, all of which are cracked and brittle, not to mention moldy. I want to start at the beginning, so I push aside the three boxes and sit down on the cold cement floor. I balance the photo album on my lap and clean each page with the bottom of my T-shirt, rubbing the plastic in slow expanding circles to reveal patches of clarity I can gaze into like portholes on a ship. Then, huddled beneath the stairs, I flip through the pages one at a time, coughing and sneezing as these washed out pictures finally begin to take shape.

Photo: *James and Mary Dimmick stand on the Prudential skywalk in downtown Boston, holding hands as they stare off into a vast expanse of shimmering lights.*

James has just returned home from a tour of duty in Iraq. He is skittish around people, and wary of loud, sudden noises. He stands in the corner with a five dollar cocktail, nose pressed against the glass, sipping his frustration as he talks with Mary about going to college and earning a business degree. He wants to buy a house in Marblehead. He wants to live a normal life.

Mary kisses him on the lips, molding herself into his tough frame. She tells him she wants to plant a rose garden and edge it with ivy. She wants to become an accountant and raise a family. But more than that, she wants to steal her husband's pain and drown it in the Charles River.

James remains silent, staring at the skyline as dusk settles over him like a nylon-covered flak jacket. Try as he might, he can't shake the apprehension that somewhere in the darkness the enemy is waiting. He knows they will creep into his suburban foxhole with inhuman patience, eager to learn the secrets he has suffered since his awakening that night in the V.A. hospital.

Fifty floors down, a line of cars inch their way up Boylston Street. Pointing at their headlights, Mary tells James they are a procession of yellow ants. They remind him of explosions in the cool desert night.

Photo: *Returning home from the car dealership, Mary waves from the driver's seat of her brand new, white Saturn coupe.*

Thanks to her accounting job, Mary has saved enough money to buy her first car. With a brand new home, and a child on the way, she believes her life is finally stable. She is tired of kneeling by her bed at night to whisper novenas. She is tired of loving a shadow, a ghost that glides through her fingers when she reaches out to touch it.

For the past six months James has held a steady job as an auto mechanic. He is proud to bring home a weekly paycheck. He wants to put food on the table and plant a garden for his wife. He wants to buy toys for the baby and set up a nursery with stuffed animals and picture books. But despite his good intentions, he is unfocused and always late for work. In one week he will be fired for throwing a wrench at a customer.

Mary believes the therapy sessions are helping her husband cope with his nightmares, but doesn't know that he sometimes skips his appointments, or that he drives into Boston to wander the busy streets, charging into the noisy crowd to feel like he's a part of something greater. She is oblivious to packets of Thorazine stashed in the closet, to bottles of whiskey hidden in the basement.

James listens to a Harry Chapin song playing on the radio. He sings about the cat in the cradle and the silver spoon, about little boy blue and the man on the moon. He imagines being a dad, and he wonders how someone can separate the best and worst parts of himself when it comes to raising a child. Already, he feels a devastating pressure to be a fierce protector. He wants to establish ground rules. He wants to stockpile their house with countless stories.

Glancing over at Mary, James knows he must close his eyes and relax, but no matter how hard he tries, every expectation keeps snapping him to attention, driving him into the ground like a nail hammered into a coffin.

Photo: *Snoring in his recliner, a half empty bottle of beer by his side, James sleeps with his mouth wide open.*

Shrouded in the faint glow of a lamp, he dreams of driving through the desert in a beat-up patrol jeep. He sits in the passenger seat cradling his machine gun, a topographic map spread across his lap.

A rocket-propelled grenade rips open the dawn. A mortar explodes, spraying smoke and debris into the morning sky. James is thrown from the jeep, his lip sliced open on the cracked pavement. Then he awakens in the military hospital, bloodied and dehydrated, his head wrapped in thick bandages. The doctors check his pulse and monitor his fever. They dress his wounds and inject him with drugs.

In the middle of the night he overhears two soldiers discussing the film *One-Armed Swordsman*. He listens as they talk about the Shaw Brothers and Bruce Lee, about wire stunts and Hong Kong action. His blistered ears catch scraps of their conversation, and the word "ninja" cements itself to his mind. In his delirium, James believes a ninja has crept into his hospital room to enlighten him with prophetic visions.

When he wakes up, after three days of intense fever, he will have trouble remembering his home address and his telephone number, or the worried wife he left behind in Massachusetts. And when the doctors ask how he feels, he will squeeze his morphine pump and whisper the word "ninja," fading in and out of consciousness as he drifts toward an honorable discharge.

Photo: *Six months pregnant, Mary leans against an oak tree and pats her swollen belly.*

On Sunday afternoons, James drives her to Boston Esplanade where they lie in the shade and eat a picnic lunch. They drag their fingers across the cut grass and discuss baby names. She suggests Matthew and Elizabeth; he likes Timothy and Jennifer. Later, they walk along the river-bank, gazing up at the skyline as Mary takes her husband's hand, delighted that he is grounding himself in lawn maintenance and suburban pool parties, that he is cleaning out the garage and searching the classifieds for a regular part-time job.

Mary has always been his port of refuge, but while she is at work, James drives into Chinatown to search the stalls for exotic food and cheap trinkets. He buys ginseng and dried fish, mechanical crickets and bamboo back-scratchers. He takes them home and hides them in the basement. He needs these magic talismans to protect his family, to stop the big bad world from crashing down on them like a giant tsunami.

Mary watches people push strollers through the park, wiping runny noses and retying dirty shoelaces. She imagines waiting with outstretched arms at the bottom of a curvy slide, or struggling to sit on a tiny see-saw, her knees hunched up to her chin. But most of all, she envisions a home in which every room is piled high with blankets and buckets of toys, and puzzles and board games are scattered across the floor in a thin dusting of Johnson's baby powder.

Photo: *Two guns rest on a table in the basement, a .44 Magnum and a Glock 22.*

With a two-year-old son, and a daughter on the way, James buys the guns for protection. He is certain that intruders will sneak into his home and murder his family. He can hear them at night, tunneling through his brain while he sits alone in the darkness, cradling a half-empty bottle of Wild Turkey. He believes the enemy will creep onto his lawn in a Guerrilla attack. He believes they will ambush him during his morning shower, or sabotage his car while he's washing the dishes.

Sentenced to a long list of medications, James sketches a detailed map of the entire neighborhood, drawing large red Xs to mark any spot where he can crouch in the bushes to throw metal stars and set up bamboo traps. At night, he slips into the basement and examines his guns. Here, a cocking handle that's dented and scratched. There, a silver barrel that bulges out like a flexed muscle.

He hides them under a work table that's riddled with grooves, deep and ugly like the scars he sees when he watches himself in the bathroom mirror. He tells himself he's asserting his control, that there's more to being a father than just nursing scraped knees and shushing endless questions. An idealist, Mary believes in the strength of a smile and the force of a handshake. But James, who knows from experience that words can sometimes fail, believes his two loud-mouthed friends can be effective diplomats if given the right opportunity.

Photo: *It is Christmas morning, and Timothy clutches his father's gift, a snow globe resting on a mahogany base.*

In the center of the globe, a blonde-haired angel stands guard atop a fluffy white cloud, gazing up toward heaven. A small halo floats above her head, shrouding her cherubic face in a golden hue. Crystal blue tears are etched onto her cheeks. With outspread wings, she embraces two young children, a girl and a boy.

The children's bodies are dotted with snowflakes, glittery flecks of plastic that slide off their shoulders in a mini avalanche, sloshing against the sides of the glass as Timothy tosses his snow globe into the air and turns it upside down. He shakes it as hard as he can until the water becomes foamy, until the bubbles burst apart in dizzying splashes of white. He holds it up and laughs, mesmerized by this compact world that he can manipulate with a simple flick of his wrist.

James taps a thumbnail against the snow globe. "Those two kids are you and your sister. And I'm that angel. I might not be divine, but I will always be here to protect you. Whenever you feel scared or unsure, just give this a shake." He puts his arm around Timothy and gives him a quick squeeze. "You have to make your own luck in this world. Cause it's not something that just magically appears whenever you need it. You have to fight hard for it, and you have to believe that no one wants it more than you do."

I stand up, stretch my legs, and walk over to the pool table, dropping the photo album onto a moldy patch of ripped green felt. The hairs on the back of my neck are standing at attention, and I feel drops of sweat collecting on my forehead. I try closing my eyes and taking a deep breath, but all I keep seeing is that snow globe resting in the palm of my hand.

I want to run upstairs and wake Liz for dinner, but this picture is screaming up at me, so I reach down and pick up the photo album, shivering in the damp basement as I shine my flashlight on the musty page, staring down at that snow globe until the picture starts to grow fuzzy and I remember a different scene, this one late at night, so many years ago.

And now the lights are turning on in my brain, not murky like usual, but glaring like floodlights, blinding me with these bad thoughts I've been trying to dim for the past ten years. I want to fend them off with my allegiance to ninjutsu, but I'm so worn down that all I can do is just stand here while they trample over me.

I remember waking up to the sound of my parents shouting downstairs.

I remember a fist banging down on the kitchen table, and the Mean Man backing me into a corner.

I remember the shattering of broken glass.

Then everything else comes into focus. It happens in an instant, a surge of white, hot pain, as if someone has jammed his thumb into the soft spot right behind my eye.

I remember grabbing that snow globe off my nightstand, believing I could rush downstairs and fix everything with a wave of my hand, flourishing that winter wonderland in stunning slow-motion arcs, as if all the fairy-dust trapped inside could sprinkle my parents with patience and understanding.

I remember Dad shouting at Mom, flecks of spit flying out of his mouth.

I remember shards of broken glass, and dirty water trickling across the linoleum in sluggish streams.

And now I finally understand why Mom had to hide these pictures in the basement. And now, more than ever, I want to pick up the phone and tell her that it's okay. She tried to talk to me so many times, but I ignored her so I could make my own excuses about what happened that night when everything fell apart.

I always wanted Dad to be the ultimate warrior. I wanted him to have the answers nobody knew to the questions nobody asked. Instead, he tried to protect us with an armory of war stories, talking about Asia and ninjas like some people pop tranquilizers. But it wasn't enough to save his sanity, and eventually he collapsed under the karate chop of depression.

Leaning over the pool table, I continue flipping through the photo album. Every page is another bolted door that swings open, shoving me toward a past I've been trying to forget. With each faded picture, the missing gaps slide into place, and I realize that my father was not always the hero I revered. All these years I refused to believe that he had his faults, but now I know that he broke down under the stress of his own secrets, and he kept them hidden until there was nothing left to do except choke on a bullet.

Photo: *The Dimmick family grills hamburgers at Castle Rock Park.*

It's a Sunday afternoon. Liz sits in Mary's lap, eating a cheeseburger while her mother reads her *The Cat in the Hat*. Timothy and his father play tag, chasing each other in wide circles around the freshly mown field. Their jeans are smeared with dirt and grass, their mouths crusted with mustard and ketchup. James slows down so Timothy can tag him. He congratulates his son on being the fastest runner in Marblehead.

For the past two months they have come to the park every Sunday afternoon. Mary treasures this consistency. Every night she prays the storm clouds will pass over her family like an April shower, revealing blue skies as limitless as her patience. She believes in her own stock of guardian angels, and she trusts that her prayers have been answered. Last week, she received a raise at the accounting firm, and James has worked as a short order cook for eight months with no altercations. He has even quit smoking, and Mary teases him about the extra weight around his belly.

James returns to the barbeque pit. He flattens out a few more burgers and sprinkles them with basil and oregano. He prods the burgers with a steak knife, watching the fat hiss and spit, the flames rising up to singe the hair on his arms. As the burgers continue to sizzle, he presses them down with his spatula, watching the juices seep out like a wound that won't heal.

Photo: *At Mass General Hospital, Timothy and Liz stand beside their father's bed, horrified as he raises his left arm to reveal a ten-inch incision running lengthwise down the side of his chest.*

Recuperating from a thoracotomy to remove his left lung, James winces every time he draws in a breath. Mary kisses her husband and strokes his forehead. She says, "Keep fighting, babe. You beat the cancer. That means you're strong. That means you can beat anything."

Timothy hugs his father, who asks him to open the bedside window. "In case they come to see me," he whispers, his eyelids fluttering from the anesthesia.

Liz points at her father's stitches. She tells him they look like tiny railroad tracks. He smiles and says, "Choo choo, all aboard," cringing as bed sheets rub against brackish stitches that are swollen with pus, and weeping a thin clear fluid that smells faintly of almonds.

"Destination nowhere," he says, as he gazes out the window. "What a long and lonely ride."

James fingers the rubbery chest tube coiled by his side to drain excess blood and air. Timothy watches the fluid as it spirals down the tube and drips into a glass bottle on the floor. He stares at his father's incision, wanting to erase those tiny railroad tracks with a quick swipe of his hand, wanting to shake his father like an enormous Etch-a-Sketch.

More than anything, though, Timothy wants to ask the doctor for a Band-Aid.

But where is there a Band-Aid to cover a wound that large?

Photo: *Timothy sits on the kitchen counter while his father carves a Jack O'Lantern for Halloween.*

James cuts off the top of the pumpkin and scoops out the seeds. He reaches his hand inside and pulls out the pumpkin guts, long and stringy like battered intestines. He rinses the seeds in a colander, then blots them dry. He drops them into a frying pan with a few teaspoons of extra virgin olive oil.

Timothy drinks his hot chocolate. He watches the marshmallows float on the surface, bobbing up and down like the buoys in Boston Harbor. "Why do you fry the pumpkin seeds, Dad?"

"They keep your arteries from hardening," he says. "And in China, they're used to treat depression."

James opens a Coors Light and chugs half of it. He returns to the pumpkin with a damp dishrag and a black magic marker. He wipes down the front to remove any dirt and then crouches down to draw a ghostly face. He carves two triangles for the eyes, a check-mark nose, and a gaping, half moon smile with bits of clinging rind that look like decayed teeth.

He steps back to admire his patchwork creation, running a finger over the lopsided grin. "You see, son, if you want to be a true warrior, you have to rip apart the world around you. You have to sift through its guts to find all the important secrets."

"Like the pumpkin, Dad?"

"Exactly, son."

Timothy stares at the misshapen face. "But what if it's empty inside?"

Photo: *Sitting on a bed at Arbour Hospital, James welcomes his family as they arrive to take him home.*

It is a psychiatric hospital, and James Dimmick was admitted as a person in crisis. Mary drove him into Boston one night after she found him in the basement. He'd thrown up and lost consciousness, a gun in his hand and the word "NINJA" etched into the table with a soldering iron still plugged into the wall. According to the doctors, James suffers from post traumatic stress syndrome. He complains of headaches and dizziness, and occasional chest pain. He drinks too much and is addicted to painkillers.

Some of the doctors have suggested cognitive-behavioral therapy. Others suggest brief sessions of psychodynamic psychotherapy. They want to enter his mind and map the rocky terrain, exploring the most devastated areas as if they are Red Cross relief workers. They talk with Mary about possible medications, rattling off a long list of stats and side effects. They show her dozens of plastic bottles, every pill a different shape and color and texture: fluoxetine, venlafaxin, sertraline, mirtazapine, olanzapine, and quetiapine.

Timothy reaches into his jacket pocket and pulls out his snow globe. It's smudged with fingerprints and cracked on one side. The water has turned yellow. The base is chipped. Timothy leans forward and tucks the snow globe into his father's hand. He says, "Hold onto this, Dad. I've been shaking it every night, but I think there's still some luck left inside."

Photo: *James and Timothy stand on the shore at Old Silver Beach.*

Tired of balancing two kids, a battered husband, and a nervous breakdown, Mary decides to visit her parents. She is hesitant about bringing James, but she refuses to leave him alone for an entire weekend. He will spend it watching the History Channel, chugging tonic water, and sitting on the front porch in his bathrobe and slippers.

While James was recuperating in the hospital, Mary took a sledgehammer and demolished the basement. She swung as hard as she could in every direction, smashing his worktable and breaking his tool chest. She damaged a steel support post and crushed the aluminum racks, smiling as years of frustration erupted in clouds of drywall dust and sparks of dented metal. Later, she sold the gun and tossed every bullet into a heavy duty trash bag, hauling it to the dump where she spun around in circles like a ballerina, flinging her pain into a reeking landfill.

Timothy leans into his father's side, shivering as a cold wind whistles over the waves. The clouds gather in force as they hurry across the gray sky, stacked atop each other like black floor tiles. James reaches into his back pocket and removes a blue plastic bracelet. He is ashamed, but wants Timothy to learn from his mistakes. He wants to save his son any way he can, even at the expense of his own failing dignity.

Bending down, he digs a small hole with his hand and buries the bracelet. He covers it up and pats the sand, slow and gentle as if he doesn't have the strength to hurt anymore. He looks up at his eight-year-old son. He says, "Don't judge me, Timmy."

Photo: *In the darkened foyer, James takes a picture of himself in a silver antique mirror.*

Having forgotten to disable the camera's flash, the outline is blurred and murky. The picture is a close-up, chest high, in which James stands at attention. No smile. No gesture. The shadows on his face are hard and rigid, accented by three days of stubble. One eye is blank as it stares into itself; the other, obscured by a dull bluish light, gapes open like a black hole.

The mirror itself fills the entire frame, and James is trapped within its borders. Behind him, patches of gloom sneak through a front window. He looks faint and unclear, his mouth slightly open as if just now realizing, in mid-sentence, the futility of his condition.

Months after his death, Mary will see this picture after she finds a disposable camera hidden away in a junk drawer in the basement. She will develop the film on Tuesday morning, and by Tuesday night she will begin a long journey filled with anti-depressants and bottles of Merlot. Ensconced in her bedroom, she will spend weeks creating a family photo album, cramming all her grief into five-by-seven plastic slots.

Late one night, after her two children are tucked into bed, she will break down at the foot of the stairs, scattering dozens of pictures across the foyer. She blames herself for her husband's death. She believes she gave him one too many chances.

Hardened by this tragedy, she vows never to fail her children. Instead, she will banish the album to a crumpled box in her parents' basement, pushing it out of her mind so she can concentrate on repairing her broken family.

14.
Foul Weather Ninjas

I remember the night my father walked into my bedroom for the last time–the night he sat down beside me and whispered "Once upon a time."

It was the end of May, and it was still light outside. Kids were riding their bikes around the neighborhood, and the Red Sox were playing the Orioles on TV. All the windows were open, and a cloud of flies buzzed around the screen door in the kitchen. The entire house smelled like fresh cut grass.

Mom was in a particularly bad mood. She'd spent the better part of the day dusting furniture and washing curtains and vacuuming rugs. It didn't help that Liz and I were running around the house like a bunch of lunatics, shooting each other with elastic bands, or that Dad had been drinking Jameson since dinner, running down to the basement every half hour to clean his workbench and organize his tools.

When Mom came into my room and said, "Bedtime," I knew I should drop everything and listen, but I just wasn't looking forward to another week of getting up at six-thirty in the morning and riding a smelly school bus. I didn't want to learn about stratus clouds or practice cursive. I didn't want to sit inside a stuffy classroom decorated with blue crepe paper and slog my way through long division, or run the quarter mile in gym class. I just wanted to be down at the beach, building sand castles and swimming in the ocean, eating greasy cheeseburgers and throwing French fries to swooping seagulls.

I slipped into my pajamas and drank a glass of water. While Mom was tucking Liz into bed, and reading her *Goodnight Moon* for the umpteenth time, I crept downstairs and hid behind the couch in the living room. I played with my Matchbox cars, zooming them along the hardwood floor at full speed until they crashed into the baseboard and ricocheted into the hallway. When they flipped over, their wheels made fast zipping sounds.

My mother hollered at me to come upstairs and wash my face. "Get a move on," she yelled. "It's already eight-thirty."

Five minutes later: "Come on, Tim. You've stayed up long enough."

After ten minutes she came stomping down the stairs. "Put those cars away and get up to bed."

At nine o'clock she picked up the phone and threatened to call the Mean Man.

While I scrambled to collect my Matchbox cars, Dad knelt down beside me. "Hop on," he said. "I'll give you a ride."

I put my cars on the windowsill and climbed onto his back. He stood up and stuck out his arms like they were airplane wings. He raced around the living room, dive-bombing the couch and grazing the curtains, circling the coffee table as he skidded into the hallway and ran up the stairs two at a time. I held onto his neck, laughing and screaming and yelling for him to go faster.

In my room, he spun around and dropped me onto the bed. "Thank you for flying Dimmick Airlines." He took a dramatic bow. "Now it's time to get some sleep."

I could smell the whiskey on his breath, hot and strong. "Why do I have to go to bed if I'm not tired?"

He tousled my hair. "Because you have little construction workers in your body. And every night while you're asleep they open up their toolboxes and drive around in their little tractors, ironing out those aches and pains, and repairing any cuts or bruises you might have. But..." He held up a finger. "Only if you're asleep."

"Do you have any tractors in your body?" I asked him.

He touched the side of his chest. "Sure do. But mine only work part-time. And lately it seems like they've been on strike. That's what happens when you get old and rusty."

"Is that why you were in the hospital?"

"Sort of, yeah." He patted the bedspread. "Come on. Let's get you under these covers so you can catch some zzz's."

I slipped into bed. "Do ninjas ever sleep?"

"Absolutely. Where do you think they find the strength to climb trees and dig tunnels? A ninja can't be an effective warrior if he's always tired. How embarrassing would it be if a ninja fell asleep during a covert mission and his enemy snuck up behind him and dropped a scorpion down the back of his shirt?"

"Dad, do you really think I have what it takes to be a ninja?"

He smiled. "No question. But it doesn't happen overnight. It takes years to be a ninja. You have to be patient and attentive, and you have to learn how to see the world. Remember, what is a ninja's first objective?"

"To evade danger."

"And his second?"

"To maintain secrecy." I propped a pillow behind my head. "Is that why we never see them, except in the movies?"

"Exactly," he said. "Ninjutsu is an attitude. It's a way of life. It's about chugging along on the highway when everyone else is stalled out at the end of the driveway."

"You already told me that."

My father sat down on the edge of my bed. "Let me tell you a story about survival, Tim. Once upon a time, during the Franco-Prussian War, there was a small town in France that had been cut off from the rest of the country, and everyone had to survive on their own. There was hardly any food or water, but it was summer, so people were able to survive on plants and animals, whatever they could scrounge.

"But then winter came, and people began to realize they were running out of food. So they began eating the livestock. And after a few weeks there were no more cows or pigs or chickens. So they began to kill their pets. Dogs, cats, hamsters, anything alive that might have some meat on the bones. They butchered and ate them just to stay alive. Because they had to, otherwise they'd have died.

"And finally, when all the animals had been killed and eaten, there came a day when there was no more food. No fruits or vegetables or fresh meat. Nothing but dirty snow and piles of bones. There were constant blizzards, and the temperature dropped below freezing. And that's when people started to die of starvation. Dozens of them. Every day. And the bodies began to rot and smell, so people stacked them in a large pile at the edge of town because they were too weak and hungry to dig any graves.

"But that was the least of their problems, because there was still no food, so everyday more and more people collapsed and died." He looked me straight in the eye. "Do you know what they did next, Tim?"

I shook my head.

"They ate those dead bodies. They cut up their friends and family. They chopped all that meat off the bones, cooked it up, and divided it into rations. That's how they endured and made it through the war. Anyone who died became a meal so someone else could live."

"Gross." I looked down at my fingers, trying to imagine some skinny Frenchman eating them like spareribs. "So...uh...what do we taste like?"

"Probably chicken, but that's not the point. What's important is that sometimes you have to go through hell in order to survive. You have to do things you don't want to do, and you have to see things you don't want to see. That's why you're learning ninjutsu."

"Really?"

"Sure. At some point you'll have to charge onto the battlefield all by yourself, whether you want to or not. I won't always be here to steer you in the right direction."

"Dad, do you think I'm a fair weather ninja, or a foul weather ninja?"

He kissed me on the cheek and stood up. "You're the bravest kid I know, Tim. You can adapt to any climate, so quit worrying. Now get some sleep." He switched off my bedroom light and closed the door behind him.

After he left, I couldn't fall asleep. I kept imagining myself lost in a thick forest, chased down by a village of starving cannibals. I heard snapping twigs and rustling leaves, and knives being sharpened. I saw myself being dumped into an enormous black cauldron with beets and eggplant and all the vegetables I couldn't stand to eat.

I kept wondering how far I'd go to stay alive, wondering if I'd have the strength to keep plugging away on a steady diet of grass and woodchips, or if I'd give in to stomach cramps and boil my best friend. Could I trust myself to make sensible decisions in crazy and difficult times?

I needed to go to the bathroom, so I crept out of bed and snuck down the hall. And that's when I heard my parents arguing downstairs in the kitchen. Their voices were raised and sharp, and I heard Dad bang his fist on the counter.

I ran back to my bedroom, grabbed my snow globe off the nightstand, and tiptoed downstairs, careful to avoid the creaky treads. I stopped right outside the kitchen and stood still for a moment, then peered around the door frame. Dad was sitting at the table, his chin perched in his hand. He was staring down at the tablecloth, stabbing random crumbs with a soggy toothpick.

"...the hell do you get off tucking him into bed with a story about cannibalism?" My mother towered over him, arms spread out as if a great answer might crash right into her. "I was standing outside his bedroom door and even I had no idea what the hell you were trying to say. If he wakes up in the middle of the night screaming because he's had some terrible nightmare, it'll be your ass that gets out of bed to deal with the situation. Not me."

"For Chrissakes, Mary, he's a tough kid. He can handle a different perspective." Dad threw the toothpick across the table and stood up to face her. "This big blue marble we live on isn't quite as stable as you think. If it suddenly stopped moving, we'd all be swept into the atmosphere at a pleasant 1,100 miles per hour."

Mom groaned and rubbed her temples. "What does that even mean?"

"Tim needs to prepare for the unexpected so his entire life isn't one big skidmark."

"He doesn't understand your stories, Jim. He's not one of your war buddies. Fifth graders don't give a shit about politics, or culture, or who constructed the Great Wall. They play with action figures and cheat at board games. They eat lots of junk food and then throw up so they can laugh about it. Why can't you let him be normal, like every other kid in the neighborhood?"

"Because he's special, Mary. And because I don't trust the rest of the neighborhood. And neither should you."

"But he's malleable, too," she said. "And because he hangs on every word you say, he thinks all your stories are true, even the ones that sound completely ridiculous. I'm surprised he hasn't jumped out of his bedroom window and tried to fly around the neighborhood."

"Don't be over-dramatic. It's not like I'm teaching him how to kill or maim someone."

Mom grabbed a glass off the shelf and poured herself some water. "Do you really want your son going to school thinking there's a ninja hiding in his locker?" she asked him. "Do you have any idea how other kids will treat him if they know that you've filled his head with all this kung fu nonsense? They'll bully him, they'll make fun of him, and they'll pity him."

"Here's to pity." My father raised an imaginary glass into the air. "It's the only reason people do nice things for us."

"You're not setting him up for greatness, Jim. You're setting him up for a major ass beating. And I absolutely refuse to see that boy fall apart with some kind of complex. I've watched it happen to you, but I swear I won't let it happen to him."

"Don't make me out to be some crackpot, Mary. Have I ever hit you? Or the kids? Do I run around the house like a lunatic, smashing up the furniture and howling at the moon?"

"Fine, but digging a hole in the backyard, in the middle of the night, is not exactly a normal activity. And neither is schooling your son on how to be a black-belt ninja. He has enough trouble learning multiplication and division. He doesn't need this pressure. He shouldn't have to live up to your expectations."

Dad threw up his hands. "All I'm trying to do is watch over my loved ones. How can you condemn a man for wanting to protect his family?"

She put her hand on his shoulder and smiled. "We don't need protection, Jim. We just need someone who's dependable. Someone who can bring home a steady paycheck and help out around the house. The children need a father, and I need a husband. And right now you're neither."

The room was silent. Then she said, "Maybe we need to talk more about checking you into a VA hospital. I don't want to...you know that...but...I really don't know what else to say or do."

Mom had barely finished speaking when my father knocked her hand away and backed her against the counter, yelling, "You can't make me go, it's not safe there, why won't you trust me!" He kicked the dishwasher and grabbed her shoulders. He pounded the countertop with his fists. He spoke so fast that spit flew out of his mouth.

I didn't know if he was going to hit her, so I ran into the kitchen and wedged myself between them, holding out my arms to keep them apart. The room was quiet, just the faucet dripping into a sink full of dirty pans, and the sound of the ice cube maker as it buzzed and rattled in the back of the freezer. Mom and Dad looked down at me, surprised, and for a split second I wondered if either of them actually recognized me.

My mouth was dry, and my hands were trembling. I reached out and put a hand on Dad's chest. "Here." I held up my snow globe. "Shake it up." He stared at me, his face flushed and sweaty, his fists clenched. And then, without saying one word, he snatched the snow globe out of my hand and threw it to the floor as hard as he could.

The smash was thunderous, and I jumped back, banging into one of the chairs. Water splashed onto my bare feet. Pieces of glass slid under the table. Hundreds of tiny snowflakes scattered across the kitchen floor and stuck to the linoleum. The plastic angel was swept away in a tide of broken glass, covered in dust beneath the kitchen table.

I looked up at this hulking monster. It opened its mouth and a jumble of words spilled out. "Tim...I..." The monster moved toward me with slow, uncertain steps, but I shied away, afraid it might scrape its knuckles across my face. I slunk into the corner, coughing and hiccupping as I tried to catch my breath.

Before I could even register what was happening, Mom had lifted me into the air and carried me upstairs to my bedroom. She kept telling me to calm down and take deep breaths, but I couldn't stop crying. I felt guilty, believing that if I'd gone to sleep when I was supposed to, my snow globe might still be resting on my nightstand, and instead of fuming at opposite ends of the house, Mom and Dad would be sitting on the couch in the living room, watching TV and laughing at stupid commercials.

She tucked me into bed and handed me a tissue. I held onto her, afraid to let go. "Your father is sick," she said. "He didn't know what he was doing, like he was in a bad dream. Sometimes people don't think before they act, and then they do things that make them sad."

"Like the cannibals?"

She rubbed my back until I stopped crying. "Your father's been going through some hard times lately, and we need to give him a wide berth."

"Why was he mad at me?"

"He wasn't mad at you, Tim. He loves you very much. You know that, right?

The only thing I knew for sure was that my parents were fighting because Dad thought I was too normal, and Mom thought I wasn't normal enough.

"I promise we'll do everything we can to patch him up quick." She smiled. "Dad's not very much fun when he's doomy and gloomy, is he?"

"But what if he doesn't get better?" I asked her. "Ever."

She started to cry, and I felt terrible all over again. "Let's just try to stay positive, okay?"

I kissed her on the cheek. "I love you, Mom."

She switched off the light. "I love you, too, honey." She pulled the bedspread up to my chin, switched off the light, and closed the door behind her.

Twenty minutes later, as I was finally drifting off, someone gave three sharp knocks on my door. "Tim? Are you asleep?"

My father didn't bother turning on the light. He just pushed open the door and stumbled into the dark. He sat down on the edge of my bed. "Don't be afraid. I won't hurt you. I would never hurt you."

"You scared Mom."

"I know, and I'm sorry. There are a lot of scary people in the world." He looked down at his own hands, turning them over as if seeing them for the first time.

"I don't want you to hurt Mom. Or Liz."

"You don't have to worry about that. I promise." He leaned forward to give me a hug. "Remember, no matter how much right we do in this world, we always do a little bit of wrong. It's not fair, I know, but it's just the way we're programmed."

I nodded, my head drooping as I struggled to keep my eyes open.

"I've made a lot of mistakes," he said. "Big ones and small ones, enough to bury a man alive." He swallowed hard, the lump in his throat as big as a walnut. "I want you to write down all the stories I've been telling you. As soon as you can. Promise me."

"I promise."

"Good." His voice sounded low and far away. "You'll need them when I'm gone."

"Where are you going?" I asked him.

"To fix things."

"Can I help? I'm a good fixer. I helped you change that tire, remember?"

He kissed me on the cheek. "I'm sorry, Tim. For everything. My brain goes a little haywire sometimes."

"From now on I'll be a great ninja." I told him. "Just like you taught me. I won't let you down."

He stood up and walked over to my bedroom door. "Take care of your mother and sister. You're the man of the house now." He saluted me and stepped out into the hallway, forgetting to shut the door behind him.

I realized I'd forgotten to say "I love you," and sat up to call him back, but he was already walking into the bathroom. I heard the fan whirr as the light clicked on, and when I jumped out of bed and looked down the hall I saw him lean against the sink, reach into his pocket, and pull out something shiny. Then he closed the door.

I lay back down and stared up at the ceiling. I wondered how many people in the world were fighting at that very moment. I wondered how many children were terrified of their parents and wishing for a different life. But most of all, I wondered what it would take for me to knuckle down and assume my legacy as a ninja. Could I become the glorious protector he'd always imagined? The one he needed now more than anything else in the world.

I held one of the pillows against my chest and closed my eyes. I listened to the house creak and groan, finally settling down after a long day of screaming and yelling and constant craziness.

A few minutes later, I rolled over and fell asleep.

And then the gun went off.

15.
Leg Foo Young

Lately, I can't seem to sit still. I'm always fidgeting at school and chewing on my fingernails, or taking long walks around the neighborhood with a stress ball in each hand. I'm afraid that if I stop moving I'll just collapse in a heap of sighs, victimized by the same depression that handed my father a loaded gun and steered him into the upstairs bathroom. Plus, the leaves are turning green and the flowers are starting to bloom, which means I'm constantly sneezing from all the ragweed that's blowing around Marblehead. I'm sure I look like a one-man rest home, and that's pretty much how I feel.

The only thing I have going for me right now is my date with Mellisa. We're driving into Boston on Saturday, which means I have less than forty-eight hours to convince Mom to let me borrow her BMW. I can't wait to open the car door like a proper gentleman, or brush against her shoulder while we're walking down the street, or pull out my bulging wallet when the waiter lays the check next to my crumpled up napkin. But the more I think about it, the more nervous I get. I want to hide in my bedroom until Monday morning, or run into the bathroom and throw up. I'm practically on the verge of dry heaving, so I pick up the phone and call Wynn, hoping he might enlighten me on proper dating etiquette.

"I'm working on *Fetus Dreams*," he says, his mouth full of whatever he's chewing. "But luckily for you I'm at a good stopping point." He swallows, burps, and shuffles around some papers. "Okay, so what's her name?"

"Mellisa. Remember? The girl I talked with in the library."

"Vaguely. Is she hot?"

"Oh, yeah. In fact, she's already made a few guest appearances in my nightly fantasies." I sit down at my desk. "Why? Is that important?"

"Duh," he says. "It changes your whole strategy."

"Why?"

"Because it ups the ante. It means you need to bring your 'A' game."

"You lost me," I tell him.

"If you're dating a plain Jane, you don't need to worry about which pick-up lines to use, or whether you should kiss her at the end of the night. Or if you should skip dessert because you think she might be watching her weight. That's one of the perks of dating a girl who's not as attractive as you are. She's grateful for all the attention, which means you're doing *her* a favor."

I grab a pencil. "Should I be writing this down?"

"You need to take Mellisa on an adventure date. And it doesn't matter if you hang out at Faneuil Hall, or take her to a show, or visit Plymouth Rock. Do something that's fun and hip, but cultural at the same time. Just don't sit somewhere for six hours and drink crappy lattes and talk about the weather.

I write that down.

"At the end of the night you want her to thank you for a wonderful time. You want her to think you're this super fun guy who's creative and likes to try new things. You don't want her dousing you with Holy water and saying, 'Demons be gone.'"

"What's your point?"

He groans. "Don't be super lame. Be Ryan Gosling in *The Notebook*."

"Okay. Now I get it."

"Good. Remember, you want her to be tickled pink from the moment she steps into your car until the moment she waves goodbye while you're pulling out of her driveway with a hard on."

"This sounds like a lot of work."

"And make sure you compliment her," he tells me. "Nice hair, nice shoes, nice necklace, whatever. Keep it simple, and don't overdo it, but let her know that you're paying attention to her, and that you think she's completely gorgeous. And don't compliment her fucking toes, alright? Otherwise she'll think you're some creepy foot fetishist who skulks around Payless."

"How am I supposed to remember all this stuff?"

"You're not obsessing about this, are you?"

"Now I am."

"Jokes can help break the ice," he says. "But not a dirty joke. And no sex jokes either. Not unless she's wearing a thong, or she's not wearing a bra. And don't tell the joke right away. Tell it after the pheromones have been simmering for a while. Maybe during dessert."

"Actually, I have a pretty funny clown joke she might like."

"Comedy will almost always get you to first base, Tim. Maybe second base depending on how hard she laughs. Girls love a good joke because it shows you have a sense of humor, which translates to you being a caring and sensitive guy. Which will help you get laid a lot quicker than if you're just a dumb asshole who only wants to park at the beach so you can fingerblast her for an hour. Oh, and mention that you really love animals. Especially dogs."

"Did you read this in a book, or are you speaking from experience?"

"Dude, never doubt me. One time, I made a girl laugh so hard that beer shot out of her nose. And I got a handjob that very same night. So step off and respect my skills."

"What else you got?"

"Ask her lots of questions. But spread them out over the course of the evening. Not hard core questions like 'Would you ever have an abortion' or 'Have you ever wanted to kill someone,' but fun stuff like 'Which celebrity do you fantasize about' or 'What's your favorite midnight snack?'"

"Should I go the clean-shaven route?" I ask him. "Or should I saddle up for the rugged macho look? I read somewhere that designer stubble is the newest rage."

"Nix the lumberjack routine," he says. "It's overrated. And flannel doesn't look good on you. Besides, you don't want her getting rug burn when you make out. No chick looks hot with a Band-Aid on her chin."

"Should I bring fresh flowers when I pick her up? Or write her romantic haikus?"

Wynn doesn't say anything for a minute. Then he gives a long, drawn-out sigh that sounds tired and painful. "Come on, Tim. Seriously? You're going on a date with this girl. You're not taking her to a fucking poetry slam."

Up until yesterday I'd been excited about my date with Mellisa. I'd been whistling love songs and imagining myself as James Bond with a license to woo. But Wynn's pep talk has beaten me up like one of SPECTRE's vile henchmen, and now I'm worried that Mellisa will cancel our date at the last minute, or that she'll excuse herself during the appetizer to ditch me for some muscle-bound jerk she met at the coat check.

I'm pacing the house with a yellow legal pad, trying to organize the entire date so it'll be perfect. I've been jotting down possible conversation topics, like health care and the newest celebrity hook-ups, or maybe the approaching World Cup. I've also been rifling through Mom's collection of Linda Lael Miller books, trying to learn some sexy one-liners that I can toss out during our walk to the restaurant. I have so many questions about dating protocol, like how often should I compliment her purse, or is there a basic rule regarding personal space I'm supposed to observe?

I don't want to call Wynn again, and I don't feel comfortable talking with Mom about girls and fashion accessories. I could ask Liz, but I know she'll just roll her eyes and mock my naivety, bitching under her breath because she doesn't want anyone else to be happy while she's still miserable.

I have less than twenty-four hours to pull myself together, and this includes shaving and finding a clean pair of boxer shorts. I've been carrying around a checklist in my back pocket, jotting down adventurous ideas like playing laser tag and canoeing, but it's only when the three of us sit down to eat dinner on Friday night, which is chicken cutlets and spaghetti Milanese, that I suddenly remember my transportation dilemma.

"So, Mom." I twirl the pasta with my fork and spoon. "Is it cool with you if...uh...maybe I borrow the car tomorrow night?"

She's about to cut into her chicken, but now she puts down her knife and takes a sip of white Zinfandel. "That depends. No more joyriding in Swampscott, I hope?"

"I have a date," I tell her. "With a girl....An American girl....Who's my age."

Perhaps mentioning the opposite sex will weaken her defenses. Maybe the possibility of her only son finding unconditional love and supplying her with dozens of cute grandkids will override the deep love she has for her leather interior darling.

She smiles. "And does this girl have a name?"

"Mellisa. She's a friend. From school."

"Now remember," Liz says, "just be yourself, make her feel comfortable, and don't stare at other women. And make sure you impress her with your listening skills."

I give her a dirty look. "What are you blabbering about?"

"You tell me," she says, laughing. "You're the moron who has it written on his hand."

Mom picks up her knife and cuts the chicken into bite-size squares. "Where are you taking this lucky lady?"

"Into Boston." I wet a napkin and scrub away the ink on my palm. "To the aquarium."

"How long will you be gone?"

"I'm not sure. I'm supposed to pick her up at noon, so I guess we'll probably spend a few hours looking at fish, and then...uh...I don't know. Maybe go out to eat, take a walk in the park."

"Bring her to Magnolias. I'll tell Jack you're coming and maybe he can hook you up with some free food. That way you won't look like a cheap date."

I take a bite of chicken and chew slowly, waiting for her to continue. "So does that mean I can use the car?"

"Be home by midnight," she says. "And so help me God, if I get a call from any law enforcement agency, and I don't care if it's the goddamn Coast Guard, you'll be writing IOUs for the rest of your natural life. Are we crystal?"

"Yes, ma'am."

She takes another sip of Zinfandel. "Offer to pay for everything. And don't walk at your usual brisk pace. You need to be a gentleman, not a marathon runner. And make sure you kiss the poor girl goodnight, otherwise she might think there's something wrong with her."

I look down at my plate, blushing. "It's just a date, Mom. I'm not going on tour."

11:01 A.M.: I've decided that fashion is an addiction, like gambling, or snorting lines of coke. I've never really cared much about clothes, but I just spent the last two hours tearing apart my closet so I'll look somewhat presentable. In the end, I decide to stay away from anything black or brown because I don't want Mellisa thinking I enjoy dressing Goth and listening to punk rock, or that I'm trying to drag her to a Wicca meeting. And while anything red or green will cast me in a sexual light, I don't want it to seem like I'm trying to seduce her with my entire wardrobe, especially when I could just as easily feed her raw oysters or chocolate-covered strawberries.

To be honest, I'm really not expecting to let my little Godzilla terrorize the town between her legs, but I am holding out for a kiss goodnight, even if it's just a quick peck on the cheek. My love life has been a continuous letdown, and it sure would be nice to round first base tonight and nibble on some "leg foo young," as Uncle Jack likes to call it.

Swearing for hours, I rip apart numerous wire hangers before I finally decide on a pair of jeans, some blue flip flops, and a white golf shirt. White symbolizes purity and cleanliness, and I think women adore men who are generous and giving and don't smell bad. Flip flops suggest the beach and the ocean, which can signify unfaltering serenity and compassion. And blue jeans are a fixed staple of sexiness. Every guy who wears blue jeans in a TV commercial always has dozens of hot supermodels pawing away at his rock hard abs.

Satisfied with my attire, I shower, shave, and spray myself with

Drakkar. I'm trying to look sporty but casual, relaxed yet interested. I want Mellisa to find me sexually exciting and socially approachable, but as soon as I walk downstairs Liz tells me I look like a golf caddie. She suggests I buy an Irish tweed hat and toss a nine iron into the backseat. Mom says I look respectable, and that if I'm lucky Mellisa won't notice the grease stains on my collar or the numerous wrinkles that confess my inability to iron.

12:03 P.M.: I'm nervous about meeting Mellisa's parents, so my plan is to pull into her driveway, wait a few minutes, and then step out of the car just as she's leaving the house. I can't stand people who aren't punctual, and I don't want to sit in her living room for half an hour while her parents offer me cheese and crackers and pat my leg to ask, "What would you like to be when you grow up?"

I pull into her driveway going five miles an hour in case her parents are watching me from the front window with binoculars and a score sheet. I think about honking the horn, but I don't want them thinking I'm rude or impatient, so I open the window and hum along with the radio. When she doesn't come outside, I pretend to rifle through the glove compartment. Then I reprogram all the radio stations and hang a new air freshener from the rearview mirror. Just when I've given up hope and memorized an introductory speech, she steps outside.

She's wearing a pair of jeans. The knees are scuffed and worn down. She's also sporting a green T-shirt and a white flannel vest with bits of red lint all over it. She looks rugged and athletic, like a mountaineer about to embark on a thrilling adventure. I notice she's put on some makeup, too. Not enough to look slutty, but just enough to accent her features.

Mellisa gets in the car and smiles. "What are you, a chauffeur? My parents wanted to meet you."

Her silver hoop earrings shine in the sunlight, dangling through curls of strawberry blonde hair that fall past her shoulders like a waterfall. When I see that she's wearing sandals, and that her toes are painted bright purple, I have to slink down in my seat and take a deep breath.

"I had an eyelash," I tell her. "And my leg cramped up."

"Don't sweat it," she says, fastening her seat belt. "I told them we were in a hurry because of the traffic."

"Traffic is a completely legitimate excuse," I say. "You know Boston. There's two seasons. Winter and construction."

She takes off her vest and drapes it over the back of her seat. I watch the seat belt dig into her chest. Her breasts stand out, pressed tight against her T-shirt, and her nipples poke through the fabric like miniature lifesavers.

I'm trying not to stare because I know it's bad first-date etiquette, but whenever I turn to look at her, my eyes wander south. Like most girls, she probably knows I'm admiring her chest, but if she accuses me of being rude, I can always tell her I'm interested in being a cardiologist.

12:56 P.M.: The aquarium is only fifteen miles away, but it takes us an hour to get there and park. Usually, I hate driving into Boston, what with all the rusty bulldozers and sweaty construction workers lounging on the side of the road, but the ride is definitely much smoother when there's a beautiful woman sitting next to me. Mellisa just sings along with the radio and props her small feet on the dashboard, which disturbs my concentration. I count at least five times when I almost swerve into oncoming traffic.

Because we're stopping every twenty feet, I know conversation is crucial, although I'm not sure what to talk about. Liz told me not to talk about ex-girlfriends, which shouldn't be a problem, or personal issues, which could be a total mood killer. So we talk about college, the topic of choice for graduating seniors. Mellisa decided on James Madison University; I chose Northwestern. Apparently, the Business department thought my application essay was a practical joke, so they sent it to the English department, which sent me a formal letter offering me admission into their Creative Writing program. I was pretty stoked when I opened the envelope. I've always enjoyed reading and writing, but I never thought my wacky life would provide such fascinating entertainment.

We talk for five minutes about leaving Marblehead in August, about saying goodbye to the beach-bum life and missing the smell of the Atlantic Ocean. Mellisa is excited about Southern culture, says she wants to eat grits for breakfast and audition for the Shenandoah Shakespeare Express. Me, I can't wait to catch a Cub's game at Wrigley Field and see a show at Second City, to gorge on deep dish pizza and spend an entire afternoon wandering through the Art Institute.

Eventually, the conversation falls apart. We don't want to talk about comp classes and ten-page essays and cramped dorm rooms the size of my closet. We have three months of freedom left, and Mellisa says that's plenty of time to fool around in the sandbox and make sloppy mud pies.

As I turn left onto Broad Street, I decide to take Wynn's advice and tell a joke. "Why don't cannibals eat clowns?"

"No idea," she says. "Why?"

"Because they taste funny."

She smiles, which isn't what I'd hoped for, but it's still better than a frown or a blank stare, or even a slap across the face. I'm about to suggest a game of "I Spy," when she says, "I like your taste," and holds up *Journey's Greatest Hits*. She slides it into the CD player and cranks up the volume. We roll down the windows and wave our hands high in the air, bobbing our heads as we pump our fists in victory. Setting the CD player on repeat, we sing "Don't Stop Believin'" all the way into the city, coasting on that familiar rock and roll rhythm until our voices are cracked and hoarse.

1:35 P.M.: Mellisa and I spend four hours in the aquarium. First, we head to the Giant Ocean tank where sand tiger and nurse sharks cruise around inside a four-story coral reef exhibit, swimming past barracuda and sea turtles and moray eels, darting around rocks and seaweed in their never-ending quest for a blood slick. We watch them glide past us, silent, their beady eyes unblinking as workers toss pieces of chum into the murky water. The tank becomes a feeding frenzy, and it reminds me of an all-you-can-eat buffet at a Chinese restaurant. Pointing and laughing, we press our noses up against the glass and dare the sharks to attack us.

She says, "Some sharks never stop swimming their entire lives. If they do, they just sink to the bottom and die, so they keep on swimming, every hour of every day, even when they're eating and sleeping. Isn't that crazy?"

I've never given much thought to a shark's lifestyle, but the idea of perpetual motion is pretty depressing.

Mellisa watches a nurse shark glide past us. "It must be nice to have all that power. To rule as King Jaws at the top of the food chain. To take down anything you want, whenever you want it, with one huge bite."

I stare into the shadowy depths of the tank. "But sharks swim in the dark. And that's one place where nobody wants to stay because you never have any control. You just spin around in confused circles, scared and alone, trying to find all the exits."

She smiles and leans into me. "It's one hell of a ride, though, isn't it? And you can't deny how good it feels once you've finally seen some light."

2:43 P.M.: A crowd has gathered to watch the sea lions feed. A pimply intern tosses them handfuls of rockfish and herring, which they devour for the next fifteen minutes. They roll over each other and clap their flippers. They swim around the pool with their whiskers twitching. They seem so cool and laidback, like they're the Fonzies of the ocean, and it makes me sad to see them put on display, munching all those fish while people angle for shots like they're Steven Spielberg, turning captivity into something meaningful.

We sit on a bench and watch two pups toss a yellow Nerf ball back and forth. The older sea lions laze in the sun and swat flies with their flippers. Unlike the sharks, the sea lions look like they're having a regular old block party. They bark and nuzzle their neighbors. They somersault in the water and scoff leftover fish guts. It's like *Beach Blanket Bingo*, but with a wet dog smell.

I hope Mellisa is having a good time. I'm pretty sure she is, but I'm afraid to ask because I'm not in the mood for criticism. Still, I wonder if she really likes me, and if she's already thinking about our second date. I even start to wonder what our lives might be like if the two of us ever got married. Would we move to another state? Would we start to look like each other? I wonder where we'd go on summer vacations, or how we'd deal with money problems and nagging in-laws.

I consider asking Mellisa if she'd like to get married someday and have kids and go to PTA meetings and all that domestic crap, but I chicken out and stare at her toes. I realize that such a question, as innocent as it might seem, is a definite social faux pas. Long-term commitment is just not a suitable topic to discuss when you're trying to woo a potential girlfriend in a sea lion exhibit. True, there are lots of questions I'd like to ask her, but they need to be spread out over the coming months. They need to be dropped into her lap with precision and care, like savvy fashion tips.

3:59 P.M.: Our last stop is at the Pacific Reef Community, a gorgeous blue maze full of tropical fish. Schools of them dart through the water in zigzag patterns, swooshing through the exhibit in Technicolor clouds. They seem completely careless of the world around them. Plus, they have a memory span of only eight seconds, which some people might consider a blessing.

Mellisa taps my arm and points to a puffer. "Ever have a pet fish when you were a kid?"

"Yeah, for about two days. It was a goldfish. The kind you carry home in a big plastic bag?"

She nods.

"I won it at the Barnstable County Fair one summer. But my father flushed it down the toilet a few days later."

"Bummer," she says. "Was it sick?"

"Not really. It was more of a..." I look down at my shoes and kick away a piece of popcorn that someone spilled on the floor. "My father convinced me it was a radioactive fish smuggled into the country from a secret military base in North Korea."

She laughs. "You thought the cute, little goldfish you won at the county fair was an aquatic terrorist shipped to Marblehead on a top secret mission?"

"I was seven-years-old," I tell her. "It's not that big of a stretch when you consider I also believed in Santa Claus, the Tooth Fairy, and the Easter Bunny."

"I don't think you're weird or in desperate need of shock therapy," she says, smiling. "When I was six-years-old I thought there were lawn gnomes living in my attic." She pats me on the back. "I'm famished. Let's get something to eat."

6:29 P.M.: We have dinner at Magnolias in Cambridge. I manage to keep my elbows off the table, and I don't spill any food in my lap. We both drink sparkling water with a lemon wedge, and I even sip from the glass without using a straw. For appetizers we order Maryland crab cakes with a tangy Chipotle tartar sauce.

Uncle Jack comes to the table after we order the main course. I'm afraid he might embarrass me by telling one of his Ethiopian jokes, but he acts like a true diplomat. He shakes Mellisa's hand and gives me a giant bear hug. He tells us dessert is on the house because he can't remember the last time he saw me smile.

"Waiting for this guy to crack a grin is like waiting for Haley's comet," he says to her, "so you must be doing something right, sweetheart."

This makes me blush, which makes Mellisa blush, and pretty soon our faces look like two stop lights.

My dinner is sautéed veal with artichokes and wild mushrooms, and topped with fresh crab meat. Mellisa orders blackened shrimp and scallops with a rum and molasses glaze. The conversation takes a quick hiatus while we shovel the rich food into our mouths. At one point she asks if I'd like to try a piece of her shrimp. I politely say no, claiming I'm full.

I'm not trying to be rude, but I hate eating food off other people's plates. Who knows what germs I might snag on someone else's fork? Still, if I intend to develop a relationship with this girl, I might as well get used to swapping bodily fluids, and what better way to start than by sharing a bit of flavored saliva?

"Sure," I say. "Let me try a small bite."

186

She stabs a shrimp and rolls it around in the rum and molasses glaze. Leaning across the table, she holds up her fork while I scoot closer and open my mouth as wide as I can, my elbows sliding on the tablecloth as I try not to get poked in the eye. As soon as the fork is in my mouth, I clamp down with my teeth and pull away, dripping molasses into the bread basket and almost knocking over my glass of water.

But now I feel obligated to ask Mellisa if she'd like to try my veal. If I don't, I'll feel like a cheap date. As well as a selfish asshole who doesn't know how to share. So I motion toward my plate and say something stupid like, "I can't eat all of this. Do you want any?"

She grabs her fork, leans across the table, and snags a huge piece of veal and a couple of wild mushrooms.

While she's mopping up some sauce, I move to the left so I can stare down her shirt. I know it's immature, but how can I be expected to look away when her breasts are being shoved right in my face like white frosted cupcakes in a bakery window?

When she's finished chewing she says, "What kind of music do you listen to? Old stuff? New stuff? Rock? Alternative?"

"I'm all about Prince," I tell her. "The man is funky. He's not afraid to try new jams, to experiment with different grooves. He'll play twenty different instruments and then order a pizza like it's no big deal."

"Example?"

"His entire catalogue is a lesson in confidence," I tell her. "Like *Little Red Corvette*. It's not just about a pimped out car. It's about this guy who's making love to this really experienced woman, and he's feeling insecure because he knows she's been around the block more than a few times. But he's really digging her, so he wants to measure up. He wants to make sure that he has enough gas to go the distance. And the corvette in the song is actually...well, it's her..." I blush and look down, pointing a finger between my legs.

"Her vagina?"

I nod. "He has to find the courage to hop into the front seat, rev up the engine, and tame her little red love machine. Which he totally pulls off because after they finish making love he tells her how smooth the ride was. So the song ends on a hopeful note cause you get the feeling that he can offer this woman a love that will truly last." I lean forward and smile. "Which is what everybody wants, right?"

Mellisa listens with her elbows on the table, her chin resting in her hands. She doesn't interrupt me or excuse herself to use the bathroom. She just nods as if she understands exactly what I'm talking about. She looks so gorgeous in the dim light that I reach over and take her hand, squeezing it gently as I imagine her warm body vibrating like a pager.

7:38 P.M.: Dessert is southern pecan pie with homemade vanilla ice cream. Since we've both eaten way too much, and since we've already swapped millions of bacteria, we decide to share. The waiter brings two silver spoons that clink together when he lays them on the table, and for a second it feels like we're celebrating our twentieth wedding anniversary. We take turns cutting into the pie and scooping out ice cream, and the entire plate is clean in less than five minutes.

We push back our chairs and groan, rubbing our bellies because I tell Mellisa that massaging your stomach is supposed to aid in digestion. I don't know if it's true or not, but it makes me sound smart and sexy, which, according to *Vogue*, are two of the top qualities a woman looks for in a man.

While we're waiting for the bill, Mellisa says, "What pisses you off most, Tim?"

I push away the dessert plate and drop my napkin on the table. "Probably wasted time."

"Why?"

"Cause I just spent the last few years thinking I was someone else. And now I have to take a giant step back and reconsider everything I thought I already knew."

She reaches across the table and pats my hand. "Don't waste time obsessing over the past. If you do that, nostalgia will make you its bitch."

The waiter walks past and I motion for the check. "I always feel like I'm stuck inside a choose-your-own-adventure book," I tell her. "I get so engrossed in what's happening around me, and I feel totally in control, and I agonize over which decisions to make, and then I end up sitting around with my thumb up my ass, hoping for a really great ending, but knowing all along that I'll probably have to flip back to the beginning and give it another go-round."

"Speak for yourself, but I think you made some great decisions today. I had an awesome time at the aquarium, you held open every door for me, and dinner was absolutely fantastic." She smiles. "At the very least, you've impressed me."

"I do have my moments," I tell her. "I make amazing French toast. I can eat my weight in chocolate. And I always remember to put the cap back on the toothpaste."

She bats her eyelashes. "My hero."

"It's an obsession, really. I can't stand that crusty, white ring that forms around the opening."

"Well, I'm sold," she says, laughing. "Where do I sign up?"

I thump my chest. "Right here. And the line's not that long. So you get first dibs."

The waiter finally arrives with the check and lays it next to the dessert plate. "Thank you, sir," he says with a slight bow. "It was a pleasure serving you. Have a wonderful evening."

I straighten up and tilt my head, trying to look worldly and sophisticated. "Everything was absolutely superb. My compliments to the chef."

I grab the check, run through the numbers, and calculate the tip on my iPhone. Mellisa offers to split the bill, but I wave her away as if it's not even an option. I pull out my wallet and pay cash, making sure to use crisp, clean bills and not wrinkled ones that look tired and beat up. Leaving the restaurant, I hold the door open and guide her outside, my hand pressing against the small of her back.

8:14 P.M.: Feeling the need to exercise, we decide to take a walk along the Charles. In the darkness the river spreads out before us, shining like polished onyx. The air is balmy and quiet, the moonlight rippling across the water, and in the distance, just beyond the trees, there's a soft steady hum from the downtown traffic.

I want to take Mellisa's hand, but I'm not sure if it's appropriate. What if she's not ready to take our relationship to the next level? What if she's offended by public displays of affection? I'm worried I might squeeze her hand too hard and break one of her nails. Or that I'll miss her hand entirely and grope her thigh. And what if my hand is hot and sweaty? She might be grossed out and never want to touch me again. On any part of my body.

Plus, I have to consider technique. Is Mellisa the kind of girl who prefers to wrap her hand in mine, or is she a fan of interlocking fingers? Should I give her advance warning, like a few casual brushes, or should I be spontaneous?

Turns out I don't have to worry. A few minutes later, while I'm debating which hand to use, Mellisa reaches out, takes my hand, and wraps it in hers like it's no big deal.

So here we are, walking along the river, holding hands like a real couple, and me feeling like a complete asshole because *I* should have been the one to take *her* hand.

We sit on a park bench and gaze out at the river. Mellisa puts her hand on my leg and leans into me. We look at each other and smile, neither of us speaking. Our faces are inches apart, and in the space of those next ten seconds I contemplate dozens of possibilities and hundreds of consequences. I know I've botched the hand-holding stage, but there is no way in hell I'm going to screw up our first kiss.

I move my hand onto her leg and Mellisa tilts her head back, letting me know all systems are go and we are ready for launch. I prime my lips by moistening them with a quick flick of my tongue, and then I lean in, praying to God we won't bang teeth. I kiss her, not fast and sloppy, but so slow that I count each revolution as my tongue circles the inside of her mouth. I slide my other hand all the way up her back, feeling each knuckle of her spine, my eyes shut tight as I scoot forward and draw her closer.

Trying to mix up my moves, I pull away so I can take in a breath and nibble her lower lip, which is soft and smooth and tastes like peppermint. I lay my hand across the nape of her neck, feeling her foot tap against my ankle as I run my fingers through her hair. I want to kiss her all night long, but finally, when I'm dizzy and short of breath, and my tongue is beginning to cramp up, we pull apart and wipe our mouths, hearts racing as we gulp down the crisp night air.

10:37 P.M.: I drive Mellisa home and tell her I had a wonderful time, which sounds totally cliché, but I really mean it. I park the car at the end of her driveway and shut off the engine, pretending to stretch so I can put my arm around her. I'm trying to think of cute ways to say goodnight, like "Sweet dreams" or "Ciao, Bella." I don't want to sound mushy, but I also don't want to ram my tongue down her throat, say, "I'll call you sometime," and kick her out of my car like some chauvinist pig.

"You look really beautiful," I say. "I meant to tell you earlier, but I forgot."

She kisses my cheek and puts her head on my shoulder. We sit in her driveway for the next ten minutes, listening to some shitty rock station while we make out like the crazy kids that we are.

"I wish we had done this sooner," I say when we finally pull apart.

"Me, too. We'll have to plan the sequel. Maybe next time we can go cosmic bowling. Or hang out here and watch a movie."

And right then, as I'm staring into her face and thinking about blockbuster movies and buttered popcorn, as I'm thinking about laser lights and glow in the dark bowling balls, I suddenly remember a socially awkward moment from last summer.

"Whoa, wait a second." My mouth hangs open. "It was you, wasn't

190

it? You were the one at the video store. The one who wanted to rent *The Big Lebowski*?"

"Bravo." She claps her hands. "It's about time, Mister Attentive. Only took you eight months. I was beginning to think you'd never remember."

Right now I want to punch the steering wheel and scream out loud. I want to crawl inside the glove compartment and hide there until morning. "So, why didn't you...I mean...why didn't you say anything?"

"Because it doesn't matter," she says, shrugging. "It was just a moment that got left behind. No sense dwelling on it."

I switch off the radio. "I can't believe I did it again."

"Did what?"

I look up, embarrassed. "I chose the wrong adventure."

"Who cares? If you had, maybe we wouldn't be here right now. Maybe we'd both be sitting at home alone, watching dumb horror movies and eating junk food. Or looking at skeezy dating sites on the Internet." She puts her hand on my arm. "Besides, I like the way this adventure is turning out."

I brush a strand of hair from her eyes. "I'll make it up to you. I promise."

"I know you will," she says. "And I'll let you, too."

I take her hand and kiss it, staring into her light green eyes as I deliver a really long smooch that builds up suction and makes a faint popping sound when I pull my lips away. I saw a gangster do it once in a French film, and the lead actress started crying and collapsed in his arms.

Mellisa leans over to kiss me goodnight. "You know something?" she says, smiling. "You're one of the most interesting people I know, Tim Dimmick."

She gets out of the car and shuts the door. I watch her walk up the driveway, her sandals scraping against the asphalt, and as I count each step I wonder if she'll dance around her bedroom later and replay the entire evening in her head. I wonder if she'll feel so giddy that she won't be able to fall asleep until her clock ticks its way past three o'clock in the morning. And when she does, I hope she falls asleep thinking of me, wondering if maybe, somewhere on the other side of town, I'm lying awake, too, dizzy with thoughts of her.

I wait until she's safely inside the house, and then I back out of her driveway without even looking behind me. Glancing up at the sky, I notice the stars look brighter, winking at me in the darkness as if they're sending good wishes. The entire ride home I listen to *Journey*, already planning our next date. I'm not sure when it will be, but for some reason I don't mind having to hold my breath and wait. A light breeze blows through the window, and I shiver in the night air. It's a good shiver, though, like one that shocks your body when you suddenly realize the world still has some hope left inside of it.

16.
Monsters under my Bed

Our annual visit to Waterside Cemetery is always the Sunday nearest to Dad's birthday, July 8th. Mom usually meets us in the foyer around nine o'clock, holding a single yellow lily as she cries into one of his frayed silk handkerchiefs. She wears her green sundress with brown sandals, and Liz wears her favorite tan skirt with a red button-up blouse. Although I'm not a classy dresser, I'll typically wear khakis and a white dress shirt, and my black loafers will gleam in the sunlight, buffed with a banana peel because that's the only fashion-savvy trick Dad ever taught me. The three of us will drive over to the cemetery and lay flowers on his grave, saying a few prayers before driving over to IHOP for all-you-can-eat pancakes. It's the one day during the entire year when we feel most like a real family, although this temporary closeness only reminds us that we're anything but.

This year, I've decided to visit Dad's grave alone. I tell Mom I need private time, and she agrees. She gives me a longer than usual hug, hands me the car keys, and says, "Keep it under ninety." She doesn't push me to give me a reason, mostly because Dr. Wayne thought it was a pretty good idea when I suggested it last week during our monthly session.

Before leaving the house, I take two Hostess cupcakes from the kitchen cabinet and put them in my jacket pocket. They were Dad's favorite snack, and whenever the two of us watched a Red Sox game, he would open up a double pack and share it with me. He taught me to eat the frosting first, then the outer edge of the cake, and finally that huge glob of whipped cream, which I've always loved to lick off my fingers. It might seem silly to leave a Hostess cupcake in front of someone's grave, but I've seen people leave China dolls, Hawaiian shirts, and bottles of booze, so no one should slam me for leaving processed junk food.

I leave home early and arrive at the cemetery sometime after eight o'clock. The place is empty, at least above ground, and the trees are motionless, as though even the wind feels impolite to weave through all these chipped granite headstones that are lined up like ornate dominos. The sky is dark and cloudy, and the few people I pass wear nothing but black—black shirts, black pants, black shoes, black blouses, and black purses. The whole countryside is bleak and dreary, like some industrial city in one of Dickens' novels, but at least the flowers are bright and colorful. In every direction, their petals shine red and orange and yellow and blue, as visible in this stark landscape as a distress flare at sea.

I park the car on the side of the road and get out, checking to make sure the doors are locked, and careful not to tread on the newly-mown grass. It's quiet, and there's nobody else around. The only sounds come from a flock of birds flying overhead and a few sprinklers trying to rescue some crab grass. The air is beginning to warm up, even though the sky is still overcast.

I head up the hill toward his grave, wondering what I want to say, and how I want to say it. Usually, I'll close my eyes and picture him sitting there on the edge of my bed, drops of foamy white spit flying from his mouth while his hands slice through the air in search of some mystical truth. Standing in front of his grave, my head bowed, I'll usually hold that picture in my mind until Mom and Liz have said their prayers and returned to the car. Then, once I'm alone, I'll kneel down in front of his marker and retell some of the same stories he once told me.

But this year I don't want to retell those stories. I don't want to dream about future kingdoms and butterfly swords. I'm now seeing the world from an entirely new vantage point, and that glorious path my father once touted has now vanished. I'm angry at him for telling me all those demented secrets, and I'm angry at Mom for not telling me enough. I know parents are supposed to share stories with their children, but only to entertain, not to justify their own delusions. Most of all, though, I'm sorry that the one story my father never told me was the one I needed to hear the most.

I reach the top of the hill and turn left, following a path of daisies. Looking all around me, I can't help but visualize the hundreds of bodies lying beneath me in various stages of decay, all of them shoved into expensive coffins and dressed in Sunday's best. Maybe that's why cemeteries are so dismal. There's nothing to think about except the certainty of death and the uncertainty that follows.

Walking through the cemetery, I remember that two summers ago a young woman vanished, and her car was found next to Black Joe's Pond. A teacher at the local elementary school, it was widely rumored she had thrown herself into the water. Police dredged the pond, but all they found were empty beer bottles and a cache of flintlock muskets from the Revolutionary War. Her parents set up a vigil by the pond, and every night friends and family would encircle the shore with novena candles.

Rumors continued to circulate, as they always do. One day she was suicidal and suffering from depression, the next she was bipolar and forgot to take her medication. Months later, I read in the newspaper that the woman had indeed drowned in the pond. Playing in the woods, two young boys found her body near the shore. They thought it was a scarecrow until they poked at it with some branches and the body broke apart like a rotten melon. They ran away when the branches got caught in her ribs.

I didn't know the woman, but her death reminded me that one's life can end suddenly, like a car stalling in the middle of an intersection. I read her obituary dozens of times, scared at the certainty that someday my body will rot away and I'll be nothing more than a pile of ashes at a gravesite overrun with weeds.

For months afterwards I was consumed with one question: What made this woman hate her life so much that she felt compelled to drown herself in a pond full of floating algae and duckweed? Now, years later, I realize she probably just lost hope, her mind corroded by an onslaught of negative thoughts. She probably spiraled down into a full blown depression, and there was no one on hand to siphon off her constant fears and doubts.

I finally arrive at Dad's grave, still out of breath from the walk up-hill. I clear oak leaves from the base and wipe away streaks of dirt from the top edges. After saying a quick prayer, I take a cupcake out of each jacket pocket and remove the plastic wrappers. I place one cupcake on the dewy grass, right in front of Dad's headstone and below the date he died: May 29th, 2004.

The other cupcake I eat, partly out of nostalgia, but also because I'm starving. I cram it into my mouth all at once, chewing slowly as bits of cake and cream and frosting spill out of my mouth and fall onto consecrated ground. I lick the extra frosting off my fingers and stare down at the second cupcake. I'm still hungry, and it looks really good, but I don't want to be selfish. Especially at a cemetery.

Now is the time during my visit when I'll usually retell those old stories. I'll talk about his tour of duty in Iraq, or those nights sitting on the front porch when we stared up at the sky and wondered if there were ninjas on other planets. I'll ask him if he remembers the time we sparred in the backyard and then drank green tea with lemon and honey. I'll tell him how alone I feel, and that his stories are a warm blanket I can pull over my shoulders whenever I'm feeling scared and vulnerable.

But lately the air has grown stuffy under that blanket, and I need some time to breathe on my own. Having survived this past year, I feel embarrassed that I didn't perceive the goofiness in all my crazy antics. I'm mortified that I constantly acted like a raging thunderstorm when I was nothing more than an afternoon shower with a few scattered clouds. I just couldn't admit that Dad's constant outbursts were more devastating than profound. I spent so much time running around inside his stories that I never bothered to stop and look around. Instead, I took every one of them at face value, so entranced by prophecies and exotic locales that I tried to live a life that was never even mine to begin with.

My father got drunk on ninjutsu, and I ended up with the hangover. Now, though, after so many years, everything has finally come back into focus, and it seems there's just not that much to say. Mom pretty much said it all, or tried to anyway, but I never respected her opinion.

I sit down on the cold grass, wipe away a thick glob of frosting from the corner of my mouth, and pull a folded piece of paper from my back pocket. It's a long list of Dad's stories, creased and yellow and torn in one corner. I scribbled them down the day after he died, while Uncle Jack was downstairs making funeral arrangements and Mom was sobbing in her king-size bed, doped up on tranquilizers.

I flatten out the paper as a drop of water hits my forehead. It's beginning to rain, but the drops are light and sporadic. Somehow, rain feels natural in a cemetery, as if it's meant to wash away all the bad feelings that people drag through here like so many bouquets of lilies and roses. But today I don't want to feel all sad and mopey. I don't want to dredge up the past by reciting old ninja stories.

I have a new story I'd like to tell, and I think it's one that Dad will appreciate.

***

Since the beginning of June, Mom's been spending every weekend on the Cape, sprucing up grandma and grandpa's house with fresh coats of paint and a team of interior designers she hired from Boston. She walks through their house with a glass of Merlot and tells people where to hang pictures and how to peel wallpaper. She talks about crown molding and stainless steel sinks, and she's constantly watching all those decorating shows on HGTV.

A few weeks after graduation, Wynn drove up for the weekend to help me clean out the pool. We shoveled out all the soggy leaves and pine cones, cramming them into fourteen heavy duty trash bags that we carted away to the dump in a neighbor's pick-up truck. Mom had the lining replaced and the diving board fixed, and then a specialist came to the house. He fixed the pump, installed a salt water chlorinator, and tested the pH levels. Despite the exorbitant cost, the entire project was completed in only three days. I told Mom it wasn't as difficult to repair as I'd originally thought, and she agreed.

For the 4th of July, she decided to throw a barbeque, so Liz and I cleaned up the backyard, which means I mowed while Liz set out lawn chairs and dusted off the bocce balls. We pulled rusted badminton rackets from the garage, and scavenged old board games from the hall closet. Excited about her patriotic soirée, Mom bought hamburgers and hot dogs, veggie kabobs and sauerkraut. She took extensive notes while watching the food network and even planned a three-course meal and baked her signature chocolate-fudge brownies. I thought it was a bit extreme to line the driveway with fifty miniature flags, but Mom was in such high spirits, talking and laughing and dancing around the house, that I was more than happy to put up with an overdose of red, white, and blue.

I invited Mellisa, whom Mom refers to as "that cute thespian with a good head on her shoulders." Mom likes Mellisa because she uses dental floss, cleans the table without being asked, and eats cottage cheese right out of the container, which I find absolutely disgusting. Plus, Mellisa likes seltzer water, especially lime-flavored, and Mom is a firm believer that seltzer water can be mixed with any kind of alcohol to create a lazy afternoon cocktail, preferably one that involves Smirnoff or coconut-flavored rum.

"That girl is a bona fide knockout," Mom keeps telling me, "and she's patient, too. If you say something stupid, she doesn't look at you like you're an idiot. Make sure you hold onto her, Tim. Girls like Mellisa aren't just falling off trees like crab apples."

The entire day was hot and sunny, and the temperature peaked in the mid eighties. We sat around in tropical Adirondack chairs, catching whiffs of a salty sea breeze that blew in from Old Silver Beach. The four of us drank margaritas and swapped dirty jokes. We ate nachos and played badminton. We hooked up the stereo and listened to Bruce Springsteen and John Mellencamp. Later, we dove into the pool and paddled around in the deep end, singing *Born in the U.S.A.* as loud as we could, our faces streaked with suntan lotion.

Mellisa laughed the whole time, chatting with Mom and Liz while she draped her arm over my shoulder and snacked on a bag of Doritos. She helped Liz make a tomato and cucumber salad, and she complimented Mom on her fake tan. I was really nervous about having her spend the entire day with my family, but Mellisa seemed to humor every single topic that erupted poolside. Not once did she chew off her leg to escape Mom's discussion of Tiffany jewelry, nor did she fall asleep during Liz's detailed analysis of why clowns shouldn't be allowed in department stores. I kept apologizing for what I perceived as ridiculously silly banter, but Mellisa just smiled and said, "No worries, Tim. Sometimes the conversation has to fit the mood."

I love my girlfriend because she doesn't judge me like every other person in my life. She doesn't demand that I practice Yoga or learn how to change a tire. She doesn't insist that I pay for dinner all the time, or that I constantly gaze into her eyes and spin silken words like an Oxford scholar. She's just happy that I exist, and she doesn't burden me with unreasonable expectations.

I've seen this happen in other people's lives, and now it's happening in mine.

***

My stomach rumbles, so I grab the other cupcake and take a quick bite, placing it back on the ground with the chewed side facing away in case anyone happens to stroll by. I stand up to stretch, listening to my knees pop as I brush dirt off the bottom of my pants. I'm thirsty, too, and wishing I'd brought something cold to drink. I wonder why cemeteries don't have big-ass water coolers set up all over the place like golf courses, maybe by the side of the road or in the shade of an oak tree. Being young, I can handle a bit of strenuous exercise, but some of these old people must have a hell of a time traipsing around in this humidity. Plus, it must be difficult to pray when you're sweaty and cranky and suffering from heat stroke.

Sitting back down, I realize that telling stories is super exhausting. I'm always stopping mid-sentence to reflect on certain moments, always replaying a particular conversation in my head, or recalling a specific emotion that rises up suddenly from deep down in my chest, forcing me to find some hidden meaning that will make everything all better.

I guess what's great about telling stories is the freedom to exaggerate. Years from now I could be the best customer that Stormy ever serviced; I could receive thousands of e-mails from mail-order brides searching for a better life; or Katrina could seduce me at the video store and then beg me to love her unconditionally when I put my hand on her shoulder and let her down easy.

Right now, with Mellisa, I'm creating my own private gallery of special moments. I can replay select scenes whenever I want, like that day at Lynn Heritage State Park when we sat on the grass and stared up at the sky, pointing out all the clouds that looked like animals. Or I can take all these great memories and store them away in their entirety, preserved for some time later when I can thaw them out and soak in their nostalgia, peeling away different layers depending on my mood.

I'm also learning to appreciate the fact that just telling a story, just sitting down and starting at the beginning, is sometimes enough to make you smile or laugh, and that it doesn't always matter whether or not the story is true, but how the story is told. Sometimes, all that really matters is how the story makes you feel. And that's where Dad stumbled most of the time. He didn't understand that stories can have a happy ending. That, or he didn't know how to tell one. His stories were just constant reminders that the world is full of ugliness and evil, and that mankind should never be trusted. His life lessons weren't poignant revelations, but angry outbursts at how bad things can sometimes happen to good people. Plus, he kept repeating the same stories, night after night, week after week, until I became accustomed to their familiarity, grasping at their words like a child who needs to play with the same toy over and over again.

Dad meant well, but that's probably how most disasters start in the first place.

***

Wynn arrived just before dinner. We were grilling burgers when he swung his Yugo into the driveway, clogging the air with sooty exhaust. He hugged Liz and Mellisa, then kissed Mom on the cheek and handed her a bag of Fritos, a box of doughnuts, and a huge carton of potato salad he'd bought at Stop & Shop.

After stuffing himself with three cheeseburgers, he changed into his swim trunks and joined me for a dip in the pool. The girls disappeared down the street for one of those scenic walks around the neighborhood where they admire fences and flower beds, and perform imaginary makeovers on dilapidated houses.

I drank my strawberry margarita and nibbled on potato chips, loafing in a corner of the deep end where I could spread out my arms and tread water.

Wynn swam over and splashed me in the face. "Tell me, smooth operator. How's the love life treating you?"

"Awesome. Like eating chocolate cake every day for breakfast, lunch, and dinner."

He looked generally impressed. "Wow. What makes this girl so special?"

I thought back to our long conversation on the church steps during that wintry night at Christmas Eve mass, how she kept asking me all those questions because she took a genuine interest in my half-baked ideas about people and religion. I remembered our talk in the school library, how she sat across from me, listening as I opened up about Mom and Dad and my personal views on love and relationships. And the morning I got home from jail, how she paid attention to my falling confidence, and then picked me back up with sensible advice.

"She's seen all the monsters under my bed," I told him. "And she's still here."

"True story," he said, smiling. "She's a keeper, all right." He swam over to the ladder and set his margarita down on the concrete. Then he climbed out of the pool, walked over to the diving board, and flexed his muscles. "Now check out the greatest cannonball you're likely to ever see."

He got a good running start from fifteen feet back, and jumped as high as he could into the air, but he forgot to tuck in his legs. His back hit the water like plywood on concrete. His skin was red and pruned, and he had tears in his eyes, so I spent the next ten minutes laughing and making fun of him until he swam over and tweaked my nipple.

It was right then, while bitching about his sore back, that Wynn announced he was moving to Los Angeles. "I've finally finished *Fetus Dreams*," he said, "and I think it's a script that Michael Bay or Brett Ratner might want to direct, so I figure I might as well establish base camp in Hollywood and see if I can score some lucrative deals. Besides, ever since your stupid ass got shitcanned, the video store has been about as exciting as a bachelor party without any strippers."

"I started working at the Barnacle last weekend. You should stop by for dinner one night. I might be able to hook you up with some free food. The fried scallops are terrific."

"You're a busboy," he said, laughing. "The only thing you can do is wipe down my table and give me a free glass of water."

"It's a summer job," I said, flipping him off. "Besides, I need money for Chicago."

"You need to save up for a plane ticket, so we can gatecrash all those juicy L.A. nightclubs and do some East Coast pimpin'."

"Where will you live?" I asked him. "Where will you work? Have you actually mapped out a sensible plan of action?"

"Sort of. Maybe I'll become a bohemian and impress people with my extensive vocabulary. I could live in some crappy studio apartment with five other roommates who don't do the dishes and constantly bitch about never getting laid. Or I could work nights at a video store, and during the day I could wear a beret and polish *Fetus Dreams*. Maybe I'll buy a bean-bag chair."

"Why don't you just keep working here at the video store until you get an offer from some big shot agent? What happens if you move out to California and become homeless? What if you starve to death under an expressway? Do you really want to become some smelly schlep who drinks forties from a tatty paper bag and oils the wheels on his rusted shopping cart?"

"Don't worry," he says, "I won't start sifting through dumpsters. And I'm selling my car, so I won't even be near an expressway. Besides, if you can finally get a girlfriend, Master Spank Monkey, then I'm confident that I can storm Cali and sell my script to some high-level executive." He raised his margarita and saluted me. "Tim, you're living proof that fate shows no favoritism."

The girls returned home an hour later, chatting about color schemes and bedding ensembles, and at eight o'clock we drove to the Heights to watch the fireworks. The beach was jam-packed, but we managed to find a primo spot down by the shore. Mom had brought one of Grandma's wool blankets, and after weighing it down with shoes and purses, the five of us sat down on our own private island.

Wynn kept commenting on all the lovely ladies, jumping up every ten seconds to snap dozens of pictures with his digital camera. I snacked on a bag of peanut butter M&Ms, and the girls discussed the possibility of redecorating the downstairs bathroom in a floral theme with Georgia O'Keefe pictures. Liz ran off to gather seashells while Mom drew sketches on the back of a Wal-Mart receipt.

Mellisa was cold, so I put my arm around her. We stared out at the barge in the middle of Vineyard Sound, waiting for that initial burst of light to explode in the sky. I felt so relaxed and peaceful, not minding the roar of the crowd or the bits of sand that flew in my face when screaming kids ran past. I watched two boys write their names in the air with sparklers, swishing them back and forth like miniature swords until they grew tired of the fizzing light and started a game of freeze tag, kicking up even more sand as they snaked their way through the tangled mess of chairs and blankets.

Mellisa shivered, and I felt goose bumps dotting her arm. I took off my windbreaker and handed it to her.

"Such a gentleman," she said.

"Really? You're not just saying that because I might catch a cold?"

She kissed me. "You don't give yourself enough credit, Tim."

Before I could say anything, the first firecracker burst apart in a shower of sparks, a rainstorm of red and blue and green that echoed across the ocean like cannon fire. The crowd clapped and cheered, and then it oohed and aahed, and when the last dribble of color finally faded away, everyone stopped talking, even the kids, and we all just sat there, mesmerized.

For the next hour we watched hundreds of fireworks paint the sky in a glorious parade of light and sound. Some died when they left the barge, popping like party favors as their whitewashed colors trickled into the clear, black sky. Others shot high into the smoky air, almost touching the moon as they exploded above us in vibrant jolts, their bright colors suspended beneath the stars like an opened umbrella.

As the finale shook the ground, filling the sky with every color imaginable, Mellisa turned to me and said, "Do you realize that we've been dating for three months?"

We'd actually been dating for seventy-five days, but I didn't think she was interested in that kind of accuracy.

"Do you know what that means?" she asked me.

I had no idea, but the way she phrased the question was intimidating, as though this was an easy question that any man should be able to answer. I thought about guessing, but I didn't want to anger her by shaming the integrity of the moment. I've learned it's a lot easier to shrug and say, "I don't know" than it is to fabricate a story that you think will carry you from point A to point B, but, instead, drops you off in some remote wasteland with no possibility of rescue.

"I don't know," I said. "Give me a hint."

She took my hand and squeezed it three times.

One.

Two.

Three.

"It means you make me so incredibly happy," she said.

I damn near cried. For some reason, the idea that I could make another person happy had seemed as distant to me as life on another planet.

I took her hand and kissed it. "I'm happy, too." Then, feeling the need to be über-romantic, I stared into her eyes and said, "You know what else? I love the way your chin fits right in my shoulder whenever I hold you close."

Smiling, she snuggled into me and turned her face upwards, watching colors stream down from the sky in long, beautiful ribbons.

***

The rain is falling harder now, turning all the gravestones an ashy gray. I stand up and yawn, shaking drops of water from my hair. It feels good to tell my father a story, but it feels even better to know it's one he's never heard before.

I look down at the wrinkled piece of paper still clutched in the palm of my hand. These poorly-scribbled, one-line sentences are all that's left of Dad's legacy, and it makes me sad to think that such a loving and flawed man is only remembered for screwing up royally, and that everything he did do, no matter how violent or stupid or crazy, arose from a genuine concern for his family that simply shifted out of place and never had the chance to reposition itself.

Dad's headstone doesn't even display any inspiring quotations, or brilliant words of wisdom. Just letters and numbers scratched into granite. Kneeling down, I promise myself that I won't die with a blank epitaph. I want to succeed, to make some sense out of my bizarre, jumbled life. It's hard to believe, but next month I'll move to Chicago to begin my freshman year of college. I'll be living far away from home in a huge city, and I'll need to be smart and responsible, which means I can't depend on silly ninja adventures to help me fit in and make new friends.

Wherever my father is, I hope he understands why I'm ready to pack away his stories and start telling some of my own. I hope he knows that I don't blame him for what happened to our family.

I place the piece of paper in front of his grave, weighing it down with sticks and stones. It flutters in the wind, a hard cracking sound like fingers snapping, as if demanding that I bend down and pick it up again. Mom tells me there are some things in life that need to be cut loose, and she's right. But it's not the cutting that hurts. It's watching everything float away and fade off into the distance, out of reach and never to be seen again.

Taking in a breath, I run my hand along the top of his gravestone. "Don't worry about me, Dad. I know I've had a rough couple of years, but for the first time in my life I feel pretty good about where I'm headed. If I can survive all this crazy drama, I can probably scrape my way through any mess. I might not be a highly-trained warrior, or even some covert spy that's hell bent on saving the world, but I think I finally understand what it means to be a fair-weather ninja."

I reach out and touch his name, running a finger over the polished grooves. "I'll do my best to make you proud," I tell him, "and I'll try really hard to become the man I know you should have become. You deserved better. You just had lousy luck." I glance down at the wrinkled list, my eyes watering as I remember the last time we ever spoke. "I love you."

I begin the long walk back to the car. I see lightning off to my left, and a few seconds later a clap of thunder shakes the sky. My shoes sink into the mud, but I lower my head and brave forward. My socks are damp, and normally I'd stop to remove them, but today I just want to drive home, collapse on the couch, and eat some of Mom's homemade chicken noodle soup. So I slog my way through the forming puddles, wiping the tears from my eyes as I try not to slip on the grass. When I look back, I can see raindrops soaking into the paper and pasting it to the wet ground, washing all the words away in tiny blue rivers that I can finally wade across.

www.ingramcontent.com/pod-product-compliance
Lightning Source LLC
Chambersburg PA
CBHW032117020726
47494CB00007BA/2110